An Alabaster Box

Mary Eleanor Wilkins Freeman and Florence Morse Kingsley

Copyright © 2017 Okitoks Press

ISBN: 1981432264

ISBN-13: 978-1981432264

Table of Contents

Chapter I

"We," said Mrs. Solomon Black with weighty emphasis, "are going to get up a church fair and raise that money, and we are going to pay your salary. We can't stand it another minute. We had better run in debt to the butcher and baker than to the Lord."

Wesley Elliot regarded her gloomily. "I never liked the idea of church fairs very well," he returned hesitatingly. "It has always seemed to me like sheer beggary."

"Then," said Mrs. Solomon Black, "we will beg."

Mrs. Solomon Black was a woman who had always had her way. There was not one line which denoted yielding in her large, still handsome face, set about with very elaborate water-waves which she had arranged so many years that her black hair needed scarcely any attention. It would almost seem as if Mrs. Solomon Black had been born with water waves.

She spoke firmly but she smiled, as his mother might have done, at the young man, who had preached his innocent best in Brookville for months without any emolument.

"Now don't you worry one mite about it," said she. "Church fairs may be begging, but they belong to the history of the United States of America, and I miss my guess if there would have been much preaching of the gospel in a good many places without them. I guess it ain't any worse to hold church fairs in this country than it is to have the outrageous goings on in the old country. I guess we can cheat a little with mats and cakes and things and not stand any more danger of hell-fire than all those men putting each other's eyes out and killing everybody they can hit, and spending the money for guns and awful exploding stuff that ought to go for the good of the world. I ain't worried one mite about church fairs when the world is where it is now. You just run right into your study, Mr. Elliot, and finish your sermon; and there's a pan of hot doughnuts on the kitchen table. You go through the kitchen and get some doughnuts. We had breakfast early and you hadn't ought to work too hard on an empty stomach. You run along. Don't you worry. All this is up to me and Maria Dodge and Abby Daggett and a few others. You haven't got one blessed thing to do with it. All you've got to do is to preach as well as you can, and keep us from a free fight. Almost always there is a fuss when women get up a fair. If you can preach the gospel so we are all on speaking terms when it is finished, you will earn your money twice over. Run along."

Wesley Elliot obeyed. He always obeyed, at least in the literal sense, when Mrs. Solomon Black ordered him. There was about her a fairly masterly maternity. She loved the young minister as firmly for his own good as if he had been her son. She chuckled happily when she heard him open the kitchen door. "He'll light into those hot doughnuts," she thought. She loved to pet the boy in the man.

Wesley Elliot in his study upstairs—a makeshift of a study—sat munching hot doughnuts and reflecting. He had only about one-third of his sermon written and it was Saturday, but that did not disturb him. He had a quick-moving mind. He sometimes wondered whether it did not move too quickly. Wesley was not a conceited man in one sense. He never had doubt of his power, but he had grave doubts of the merits of his productions. However, today he was glad of the high rate of speed of which he was capable, and did not worry as much as he sometimes did about his landing at the exact goal. He knew very well that he could finish his sermon, easily, eat his doughnuts, and sit reflecting as long as he chose. He chose to do so for a long time, although his reflections were not particularly happy ones. When he had left the theological seminary a year ago, he had had his life planned out so exactly that it did not seem possible to him that the plans could fail. He had graduated at the head of his class. He had had no doubt of a city church. One of the professors, a rich man with much influence, had practically promised him one. Wesley went home to his doting mother, and told her the news. Wesley's mother believed in much more than the city church. She believed her son to be capable of anything. "I shall have a large salary, mother," boasted Wesley, "and you shall have the best clothes money can buy, and the parsonage is sure to be beautiful."

"How will your old mother look in fine feathers, in such a beautiful home?" asked Wesley's mother, but she asked as a lovely, much-petted woman asks such a question. She had her little conscious smile all ready for the rejoinder which she knew her son would not fail to give. He was very proud of his mother.

"Why, mother," he said, "as far as that goes, I wouldn't balk at a throne for you as queen dowager."

"You are a silly boy," said Mrs. Elliot, but she stole a glance at herself in an opposite mirror, and smiled complacently. She did not look old enough to be the mother of her son. She was tall and slender, and fair-haired, and she knew how to dress well on her very small income. She was rosy, and carried herself with a sweet serenity. People said Wesley would not need a wife as long as he had such a mother. But he did not have her long. Only a month later she died, and while the boy was still striving to play the rôle of hero in that calamity, there came news of another. His professor friend had a son in the trenches. The son had been wounded, and the father had obeyed a hurried call, found his son dead, and himself died of the shock on the return voyage. Wesley, mourning the man who had been his stanch friend, was guiltily conscious of his thwarted ambition. "There goes my city church," he thought, and flung the thought back at himself in anger at his own self-seeking. He was forced into accepting the first opportunity which offered. His mother had an annuity, which he himself had insisted upon for her greater comfort. When she died, the son was nearly penniless, except for the house, which was old and in need of repair.

He rented that as soon as he received his call to Brookville, after preaching a humiliating number of trial sermons in other places. Wesley was of the lowly in mind, with no expectation of inheriting the earth, when he came to rest in the little village and began boarding at Mrs. Solomon Black's. But even then he did not know how bad the situation really was. He had rented his house, and the rent kept him in decent clothes, but not enough books. He had only a little shelf filled with the absolutely necessary volumes, most of them relics of his college course. He did not know that there was small chance of even his meager salary being paid until June, and he had been ordained in February. He had wondered why nobody said anything about his reimbursement. He had refrained from mentioning it, to even his deacons.

Mrs. Solomon Black had revealed the state of affairs, that morning. "You may as well know," said she. "There ain't a cent to pay you, and I said when you came that if we couldn't pay for gospel privileges we should all take to our closets and pray like Sam Hill, and no charge; but they wouldn't listen to me, though I spoke right out in conference meeting and it's seldom a woman does that, you know. Folks in this place have been hanging onto the ragged edge of nothing so long they don't seem to sense it. They thought the money for your salary was going to be brought down from heaven by a dove or something, when all the time, those wicked flying things are going round on the other side of the earth, and there don't seem as if there could be a dove left. Well, now that the time's come when you ought to be paid, if there's any decency left in the place, they comes to me and says, 'Oh, Mrs. Black, what shall we do?' I said, 'Why didn't you listen when I spoke out in meeting about our not being able to afford luxuries like gospel preaching?' and they said they thought matters would have improved by this time. Improved! How, I'd like to know? The whole world is sliding down hill faster and faster every minute, and folks in Brookville think matters are going to improve, when they are sliding right along with the Emperor of Germany and the King of England, and all the rest of the big bugs. I can't figure it out, but in some queer, outlandish way that war over there has made it so folks in Brookville can't pay their minister's salary. They didn't have much before, but such a one got a little for selling eggs and chickens that has had to eat them, and the street railway failed, and the chair factory, that was the only industry left here, failed, and folks that had a little to pay had to eat their payings. And here you are, and it's got to be the fair. Seems queer the war in Europe should be the means of getting up a fair in Brookville, but I guess it'll get up more'n that before they're through fighting."

All this had been the preliminary to the speech which sent Wesley forth for doughnuts, then to his study, ostensibly to finish his lovely sermon, but in reality to think thoughts which made his young forehead, of almost boyhood, frown, and his pleasant mouth droop, then inexplicably smooth and smile. It was a day which no man in the flush of youth could resist. That June day fairly rioted in through the open windows. Mrs. Black's muslin curtains danced in the June breeze like filmy-skirted nymphs. Wesley, whose imagination was active, seemed to see forced upon his eager, yet reluctant, eyes, radiant maidens, flinging their white draperies about, dancing a dance of the innocence which preludes the knowledge of love. Sweet scents came in through the windows, almond scents, honey scents, rose scents, all mingled into an ineffable bouquet of youth and the quest of youth.

Wesley rose stealthily; he got his hat; he tiptoed across the room. Heavens! how thankful he was for access to the back stairs. Mrs. Black was sweeping the parlor, and the rear of the house was deserted. Down the precipitous back stairs crept the young minister, listening to the sound of the broom on Mrs. Black's parlor carpet. As long as that regular swish continued he was safe. Through the kitchen he passed, feeling guilty as he smelled new peas cooking for his delectation on Mrs. Black's stove. Out of the kitchen door, under the green hood of the back porch, and he was afield, and the day had him fast. He did not belong any more to his aspirations, to his high and noble ambitions, to his steadfast purpose in life. He belonged to the spring of the planet from which his animal life had sprung. Young Wesley Elliot became one with June, with eternal youth, with joy which escapes care, with the present which has nothing to do with the past or the future, with that day sufficient unto itself, that day dangerous for those whose feet are held fast by the toils of the years.

Wesley sped across a field which was like a field of green glory. He saw a hollow like a nest, blue with violets, and all his thoughts leaped with irresponsive joy. He crossed a brook on rocky stones, as if he were crossing a song. A bird sang in perfect tune with his mood. He was bound for a place which had a romantic interest for him: the unoccupied parsonage, which he could occupy were he supplied with a salary and had a wife. He loved to sit on the back veranda and dream. Sometimes he had company. Brookville was a hot little village, with a long line of hills cutting off the south wind, but on that back veranda of the old parsonage there was always a breeze. Sometimes it seemed mysterious to Wesley, that breeze. It never failed in the hottest days.

Now that the parsonage was vacant, women often came there with their needlework of an afternoon, and sat and sewed and chatted. Wesley knew of the custom, and had made them welcome. But sometimes of a morning a girl came. Wesley wondered if she would be there that morning. After he had left the field, he plunged knee-deep through the weedage of his predecessor's garden, and heart-deep into luxuriant ranks of dewy vegetables which he, in the intervals of his mental labors, should raise for his own table. Wesley had an inherent love of gardening which he had never been in a position to gratify. Wesley was, in fancy, eating his own green peas and squashes and things when he came in sight of the back veranda. It was vacant, and his fancy sank in his mind like a plummet of lead. However, he approached, and the breeze of blessing greeted him like a presence.

The parsonage was a gray old shadow of a building. Its walls were stained with past rains, the roof showed depressions, the veranda steps were unsteady, in fact one was gone. Wesley mounted and seated himself in one of the gnarled old rustic chairs which defied weather. From where he sat he could see a pink and white plumage of blossoms over an orchard; even the weedy garden showed lovely lights under the triumphant June sun. Butterflies skimmed over it, always in pairs, now and then a dew-light like a jewel gleamed out, and gave a delectable thrill of mystery. Wesley wished the girl were there. Then she came. He saw a flutter of blue in the garden, then a face like a rose overtopped the weeds. The sunlight glanced from a dark head, giving it high-lights of gold.

The girl approached. When she saw the minister, she started, but not as if with surprise; rather as if she had made ready to start. She stood at the foot of the steps, glowing with blushes, but still not confused. She smiled with friendly confidence. She was very pretty and she wore a delicious gown, if one were not a woman, to observe the lack of fashion and the faded streaks, and she carried a little silk work-bag.

Wesley rose. He also blushed, and looked more confused than the girl. "Good morning, Miss Dodge," he said. His hands twitched a little.

Fanny Dodge noted his confusion quite calmly. "Are you busy?" said she.

"You are laughing at me, Miss Dodge. What on earth am I busy about?"

"Oh," said the girl. "Of course I have eyes, and I can see that you are not writing; but I can't see your mind, or your thoughts. For all I know, they may be simply grinding out a sermon, and today is Saturday. I don't want to break up the meeting." She laughed.

"Come on up here," said Wesley with camaraderie. "You know I am not doing a blessed thing. I can finish my sermon in an hour after dinner. Come on up. The breeze is heavenly. What have you got in that bag?"

"I," stated Fanny Dodge, mounting the steps, "have my work in my bag. I am embroidering a center-piece which is to be sold for at least twice its value—for I can't embroider worth a cent—at the fair." She sat down beside him, and fished out of the bag a square of white linen and some colored silks.

"Mrs. Black has just told me about that fair," said Wesley. "Say, do you know, I loathe the idea of it?"

"Why? A fair is no end of fun. We always have them."

"Beggary."

"Nonsense!"

"Yes, it is. I might just as well put on some black glasses, get a little dog with a string, and a basket, and done with it."

The girl giggled. "I know what you mean," said she, "but your salary has to be paid, and folks have to be cajoled into handing out the money." Suddenly she looked troubled. "If there is any to hand," she added.

"I want you to tell me something and be quite frank about it."

Fanny shot a glance at him. Her lashes were long, and she could look through them with liquid fire of dark eyes.

"Well?" said she. She threaded a needle with pink silk.

"Is Brookville a very poor village?"

Fanny inserted her pink-threaded needle into the square of linen.

"What," she inquired with gravity, "is the past tense of bust?"

"I am in earnest."

"So am I. But I know a minister is never supposed to know about such a word as bust, even if he is bust two-thirds of is life. I'll tell you. First Brookville was bust, now it's busted."

Wesley stared at her.

"Fact," said Fanny, calmly, starting a rose on the linen in a career of bloom. "First, years ago, when I was nothing but a kid, Andrew Bolton—you have heard of Andrew Bolton?"

"I have heard him mentioned. I have never understood why everybody was so down on him, though he is serving a term in prison, I believe. Nobody seems to like to explain."

"The reason for that is plain enough," stated Fanny. "Nobody likes to admit he's been made a fool of. The man who takes the gold brick always tries to hide it if he can't blame it off on his wife or sister or aunt. Andrew Bolton must have made perfectly awful fools of everybody in Brookville. They must have thought of him as a little tin god on wheels till he wrecked the bank and the silk factory, and ran off with a lot of money belonging to his disciples, and got caught by the hand of the law, and landed in State's Prison. That's why they don't tell. Reckon my poor father, if he were alive, wouldn't tell. I didn't have anything to do with it, so I am telling. When Andrew Bolton embezzled the town went bust. Now the war in Europe, through the grinding of wheels which I can't comprehend, has bankrupted the street railway and the chair factory, and the town is busted."

"But, as you say, if there is no money, why a fair?" Wesley had paled a little.

"Oh," replied the girl, "there is always the hoarding instinct to be taken into account. There are still a lot of stockings and feather beds and teapots in Brookville. We still have faith that a fair can mine a little gold out of them for you. Of course we don't know, but this is a Yankee village, and Yankees never do spend the last cent. I admit you may get somebody's funeral expenses out of the teapot."

"Good Lord!" groaned Wesley.

"That," remarked the girl, "is almost swearing. I am surprised, and you a minister."

"But it is an awful state of things."

"Well," said Fanny, "Mrs. B. H. Slocum may come over from Grenoble. She used to live here, and has never lost her interest in Brookville. She is rich. She can buy a lot, and she is very good-natured about being cheated for the gospel's sake. Then, too, Brookville has never lost its guardian angels."

"What on earth do you mean?"

"What I say. The faith of the people here in guardian angels is a wonderful thing. Sometimes it seems to me as if all Brookville considered itself under special guardianship, sort of a hen-and-chicken arrangement, you know. Anyhow, they do go ahead and undertake the craziest things, and come out somehow."

"I think," said Wesley Elliot soberly, "that I ought to resign."

Then the girl paled, and bent closer over her work. "Resign!" she gasped.

"Yes, resign. I admit I haven't enough money to live without a salary, though I would like to stay here forever." Wesley spoke with fervor, his eyes on the girl.

"Oh, no, you wouldn't."

"I most certainly would, but I can't run in debt, and—I want to marry some day—like other young men—and I must earn."

The girl bent her head lower. "Why don't you resign and go away, and get—married, if you want to?"

"Fanny!"

He bent over her. His lips touched her hair. "You know," he began—then came a voice like the legendary sword which divides lovers for their best temporal and spiritual good.

"Dinner is ready and the peas are getting cold," said Mrs. Solomon Black.

Then it happened that Wesley Elliot, although a man and a clergyman, followed like a little boy the large woman with the water-waves through the weedage of the pastoral garden, and the girl sat weeping awhile from mixed emotions of anger and grief. Then she took a little puff from her bag, powdered her nose, straightened her hair and, also, went home, bag in hand, to her own noon dinner.

Chapter II

A church fair is one of the purely feminine functions which will be the last to disappear when the balance between the sexes is more evenly adjusted. It is almost a pity to assume that it will finally, in the nature of things, disappear, for it is charming; it is innocent with the innocence of very good, simple women; it is at the same time subtle with that inimitable subtlety which only such women can achieve. It is petty finance on such a moral height that even the sufferers by its code must look up to it. Before even woman, showing anything except a timid face of discovery at the sights of New York under male escort, invaded Wall Street, the church fair was in full tide, and the managers thereof might have put financiers to shame by the cunning, if not magnitude, of their operations. Good Christian women, mothers of families, would sell a tidy of no use except to wear to a frayed edge the masculine nerves, and hand-painted plates of such bad art that it verged on immorality, for prices so above all reason, that a broker would have been taken aback. And it was all for worthy objects, these pretty functions graced by girls and matrons in their best attire, with the products of their little hands offered, or even forced, upon the outsider who was held up for the ticket. They gambled shamelessly to buy a new carpet for the church. There was plain and brazen raffling for dreadful lamps and patent rockers and dolls which did not look fit to be owned by nice little girl-mothers, and all for the church organ, the minister's salary and such like. Of this description was the church fair held in Brookville to raise money to pay the Reverend Wesley Elliot. He came early, and haunted the place like a morbid spirit. He was both angry and shamed that such means must be employed to pay his just dues, but since it had to be he could not absent himself.

There was no parlor in the church, and not long after the infamous exit of Andrew Bolton the town hall had been destroyed by fire. Therefore all such functions were held in a place which otherwise was a source of sad humiliation to its owner: Mrs. Amos Whittle, the deacon's wife's unfurnished best parlor. It was a very large room, and poor Mrs. Whittle had always dreamed of a fine tapestry carpet, furniture upholstered with plush, a piano, and lace curtains.

Her dreams had never been realized. The old tragedy of the little village had cropped dreams, like a species of celestial foliage, close to their roots. Poor Mrs. Whittle, although she did not realize it, missed her dreams more than she would have missed the furniture of that best parlor, had she ever possessed and lost it. She had come to think of it as a room in one of the "many mansions," although she would have been horrified had she known that she did so. She was one who kept her religion and her daily life chemically differentiated. She endeavored to maintain her soul on a high level of orthodoxy, while her large, flat feet trod her round of household tasks. It was only when her best parlor, great empty room, was in demand for some social function like the church fair, that she felt her old dreams return and stimulate her as with some wine of youth.

The room was very prettily decorated with blossoming boughs, and Japanese lanterns, and set about with long tables covered with white, which contained the articles for sale. In the center of the room was the flower-booth, and that was lovely. It was a circle of green, with oval openings to frame young girl-faces, and on the circular shelf were heaped flowers in brilliant masses. At seven o'clock the fair was in full swing, as far as the wares and saleswomen were concerned. At the flower-booth were four pretty girls: Fanny Dodge, Ellen Dix, Joyce Fulsom and Ethel Mixter. Each stood looking out of her frame of green, and beamed with happiness in her own youth and beauty. They did not, could not share the anxiety of the older women. The more anxious gathered about the cake table. Four pathetically bedizened middle-aged creatures, three too stout, one too thin, put their heads together in conference. One woman was Mrs. Maria Dodge, Fanny's mother, one was Mrs. Amos Dix, one was Mrs. Deacon Whittle, and one was unmarried.

She was the stoutest of the four, tightly laced in an ancient silk, with frizzed hair standing erect from bulging temples. She was Lois Daggett, and a tragedy. She loved the young minister, Wesley Elliot, with all her heart and soul and strength. She had fastened, to attract his admiration, a little bunch of rose geranium leaves and heliotrope in her tightly frizzed hair. That little posy had, all unrecognized, a touching pathos. It was as the aigrette, the splendid curves of waving plumage which birds adopt in the desire for love. Lois had never had a lover. She had never been pretty, or attractive, but always in her heart had been the hunger for love. The young minister seemed the ideal of all the dreams of her life. He was as a god to her. She trembled under his occasional glances, his casual address caused vibrations in every nerve. She cherished no illusions. She knew he was not for her, but she loved and worshipped, and she tucked on an absurd little bow of ribbon, and she frizzed tightly her thin hair, and she wore little posies, following out the primitive instinct of her sex, even while her reason lagged behind. If once Wesley should look at that pitiful little floral ornament, should think it pretty, it would have meant as much to that starved virgin soul as a kiss—to do her justice, as a spiritual kiss. There was in reality only pathos and tragedy in her adoration. It was not in the least earthy, or ridiculous, but it needed a saint to understand that. Even while she conferred with her friends, she never lost sight of the young man, always hoped for that one fleeting glance of approbation.

When her sister-in-law, Mrs. Daggett, appeared, she restrained her wandering eyes. All four women conferred anxiously. They, with Mrs. Solomon Black, had engineered the fair. Mrs. Black had not yet appeared and they all wondered why. Abby Daggett, who had the expression of a saint—a fleshy saint, in old purple muslin— gazed about her with admiration.

"Don't it look perfectly lovely!" she exclaimed.

Mrs. Whittle fairly snapped at her, like an angry old dog. "Lovely!" said she with a fine edge of sarcasm in her tone, "perfectly lovely! Yes it does. But I think we are a set of fools, the whole of us. Here we've got a fair all ready, and worked our fingers to the bone (I don't know but I'll have a felon on account of that drawn-in rug there) and we've used up all our butter and eggs, and I don't see, for one, who is going to buy anything. I ain't got any money t' spend. I don't believe Mrs. Slocum will come over from Grenoble, and if she does, she can't buy everything."

7

"Well, what made us get up the fair?" asked Mrs. Dodge.

"I suppose we all thought somebody might have some money," ventured Abby Daggett.

"I'd like to know who? Not one of us four has, and I don't believe Mrs. Solomon Black has, unless she turns in her egg-money, and if she does I don't see how she is going to feed the minister. Where is Phoebe Black?"

"She is awfully late," said Lois. She looked at the door, and, so doing, got a chance to observe the minister, who was standing beside the flower-table talking to Ellen Dix. Fanny Dodge was busily arranging some flowers, with her face averted. Ellen Dix was very pretty, with an odd prettiness for a New England girl. Her pale olive skin was flawless and fine of texture. Her mouth was intensely red, and her eyes very dark and heavily shaded by long lashes. She wore at the throat of her white dress a beautiful coral brooch. It had been one of her mother's girlhood treasures. The Dix family had been really almost opulent once, before the Andrew Bolton cataclysm had involved the village, and there were still left in the family little reminiscences of former splendor. Mrs. Dix wore a superb old lace scarf over her ancient black silk, and a diamond sparkled at her throat. The other women considered the lace much too old and yellow to be worn, but Mrs. Dix was proud both of the lace and her own superior sense of values. If the lace had been admired she would not have cared so much for it.

Suddenly a little woman came hurrying up, her face sharp with news. "What do you think?" she said to the others. "What do you think?"

They stared at her. "What do you mean, Mrs. Fulsom?" asked Mrs. Whittle acidly.

The little woman tossed her head importantly. "Oh, nothing much," said she, "only I thought the rest of you might not know. Mrs. Solomon Black has got another boarder. That's what's making her late. She had to get something for her to eat."

"Another boarder!" said Mrs. Whittle.

"Yes," said the little woman, "a young lady, and Mrs. Solomon Black is on her way here now."

"With *her*?" gasped the others.

"Yes, she's coming, and she looks to me as if she might have money."

"Who is she?" asked Mrs. Whittle.

"How do I know? Mrs. Mixter's Tommy told my Sam, and he told me, and I saw Mrs. Black and the boarder coming out of her yard, when I went out of mine, and I hurried so's to get here first. Hush! Here they come now."

While the women were conferring many people had entered the room, although none had purchased the wares. Now there was stark silence and a concentrated fire of attention as Mrs. Black entered with a strange young woman. Mrs. Black looked doubtfully important. She, as a matter of fact, was far from sure of her wisdom in the course she was taking. She was even a little pale, and her lips moved nervously as she introduced the girl to one and another. "Miss Orr," she said; sometimes "Miss Lydia Orr."

As for the girl, she looked timid, yet determined. She was pretty, perhaps a beauty, had she made the most of her personal advantages instead of apparently ignoring them. Her beautiful fair hair, which had red-gold lights, should have shaded her forehead, which was too high. Instead it was drawn smoothly back, and fastened in a mat of compact flat braids at the back of her head. She was dressed very simply, in black, and her costume was not of the latest mode.

"I don't see anything about her to have made Mrs. Fulsom think she was rich," Mrs. Whittle whispered to Mrs. Daggett, who made an unexpectedly shrewd retort: "I can see. She don't look as if she cared what anybody thought of her clothes; as if she had so much she's never minded."

Mrs. Whittle failed to understand. She grunted non-assent. "I don't see," said she. "Her sleeves are way out of date."

For awhile there was a loud buzz of conversation all over the room. Then it ceased, for things were happening, amazing things. The strange young lady was buying and she was paying cash down. Some of the women examined the bank notes suspiciously and handed them to their husbands to verify. The girl saw, and flushed, but she continued. She went from table to table, and she bought everything, from quilts and hideous drawn-in rugs to frosted cakes. She bought in the midst of that ominous hush of suspicion. Once she even heard a woman hiss to another, "She's crazy. She got out of an insane asylum."

However nobody of all the stunned throng refused to sell. Her first failure came in the case of a young man. He was Jim Dodge, Fanny's brother. Jim Dodge was a sort of Ishmael in the village estimation, and yet he was liked. He was a handsome young fellow with a wild freedom of carriage. He had worked in the chair factory to support his mother and sister, before it closed. He haunted the woods, and made a little by selling skins. He had

8

brought as his contribution to the fair a beautiful fox skin, and when the young woman essayed to buy that he strode forward. "That is not for sale," said he. "I beg you to accept that as a gift, Miss Orr."

The young fellow blushed a little before the girl's blue eyes, although he held himself proudly. "I won't have this sold to a young lady who is buying as much as you are," he continued.

The girl hesitated. Then she took the skin. "Thank you, it is beautiful," she said.

Jim's mother sidled close to him. "You did just right, Jim," she whispered. "I don't know who she is, but I feel ashamed of my life. She can't really want all that truck. She's buying to help. I feel as if we were a parcel of beggars."

"Well, she won't buy that fox skin to help!" Jim whispered back fiercely.

The whole did not take very long. Finally the girl talked in a low voice to Mrs. Black who then became her spokeswoman. Mrs. Black now looked confident, even triumphant. "Miss Orr says of course she can't possibly use all the cake and pies and jelly," she said, "and she wants you to take away all you care for. And she wants to know if Mrs. Whittle will let the other things stay here till she's got a place to put them in. I tell her there's no room in my house."

"I s'pose so," said Mrs. Whittle in a thick voice. She and many others looked fairly pale and shocked.

Mrs. Solomon Black, the girl and the minister went out.

The hush continued for a few seconds. Then Mrs. Whittle spoke. "There's something wrong about that girl," said she. Other women echoed her. The room seemed full of feminine snarls.

Jim Dodge turned on them, and his voice rang out. "You are a lot of cats," said he. "Come on home, mother and Fanny, I am mortal shamed for the whole of it. That girl's buying to help, when she can't want the things, and all you women turning on her for it!"

After the Dodges had gone there was another hush. Then it was broken by a man's voice, an old man's voice with a cackle of derision and shrewd amusement in it. "By gosh!" said this voice, resounding through the whole room, "that strange young woman has bought the whole church fair!"

"There's something wrong," said Mrs. Whittle again.

"Ain't you got the money?" queried the man's voice.

"Yes, but—"

"Then for God's sake hang onto it!"

Chapter III

After Jim Dodge had taken his mother and sister home, he stole off by himself for a solitary walk. The night was wonderful, and the young man, who was in a whirl of undefined emotion, unconsciously felt the need of a lesson of eternal peace. The advent of the strange girl, and her unprecedented conduct had caused in him a sort of masculine vertigo over the whole situation. Why in the name of common sense was that girl in Brookville, and why should she have done such a thing? He admired her; he was angry with her; he was puzzled by her.

He did not like the minister. He did not wonder that Elliot should wish for emolument enough to pay his way, but he had a little contempt for him, for his assumption of such superior wisdom that he could teach his fellow men spiritual knowledge and claim from them financial reward. Aside from keeping those he loved in comfort, Jim had no wish for money. He had all the beauty of nature for the taking. He listened, as he strolled along, to the mysterious high notes of insects and night-birds; he saw the lovely shadows of the trees, and he honestly wondered within himself why Brookville people considered themselves so wronged by an occurrence of years ago, for which the perpetrator had paid so dearly. At the same time he experienced a sense of angry humiliation at the poverty of the place which had caused such an occurrence as that church fair.

When he reached Mrs. Solomon Black's house, he stared up at its glossy whiteness, reflecting the moonlight like something infinitely more precious than paint, and he seemed to perceive again a delicate, elusive fragrance which he had noticed about the girl's raiment when she thanked him for his fox skin.

"She smelled like a new kind of flower," Jim told himself as he swung down the road. The expression was not elegant, but it was sincere. He thought of the girl as he might have thought of an entirely new species of blossom, with a strictly individual fragrance which he had encountered in an expedition afield.

After he had left the Black house, there was only a half mile before he reached the old Andrew Bolton place. The house had been very pretentious in an ugly architectural period. There were truncated towers, a mansard roof, hideous dormers, and a reckless outbreak of perfectly useless bay windows. The house, which was large, stood aloof from the road, with a small plantation of evergreen trees before it. It had not been painted for years, and loomed up like the vaguest shadow of a dwelling even in the brilliant moonlight. Suddenly Jim caught sight of a tiny swinging gleam of light. It bobbed along at the height of a man's knee. It was a lantern, which seemed rather an odd article to be used on such a night. Then Jim came face to face with the man who carried the lantern, and saw who he was—Deacon Amos Whittle. To Jim's mind, the man resembled a fox, skulking along the road, although Deacon Amos Whittle was not predatory. He was a small, thin, wiry man with a queer swirl of white whisker, and hopping gait.

He seemed somewhat blinded by his lantern, for he ran full tilt into Jim, who stood the shock with such firmness that the older man staggered back, and danced uncertainly to recover his balance. Deacon Amos Whittle stuttered uncertain remarks, as was his wont when startled. "It is only Jim Dodge," said Jim. "Guess your lantern sort of blinded you, Deacon."

Then the lantern almost blinded Jim, for Whittle swung it higher until it came on a level with Jim's eyes. Over it peered Whittle's little keen ones, spectacled under a gray shag of eyebrows. "Oh it is you!" said the man with a somewhat contemptuous accent. He held Jim in slight esteem.

Jim laughed lightly. Unless he cared for people, their opinion of him always seemed a perfectly negligible matter, and he did not care at all for Amos Whittle.

Suddenly, to his amazement, Amos took hold of his coat. "Look a' here, Jim," said he.

"Well?"

"Do you know anything about that strange woman that's boardin' to Mis' Solomon Black's?"

"How in creation should I know anything about her?"

"Hev you seen her?"

"I saw her at the fair tonight."

"The fair at my house?"

"Don't know of any other fair."

"Well, what do you think of her?"

"Don't think of her."

Jim tried to pass, but the old man danced before him with his swinging lantern.

"I must be going along," said Jim.

"Wait a minute. Do you know she bought the whole fair?"

"Yes, I do. You are blinding me with that lantern, Deacon Whittle."

"And she paid good money down. I seen it."

"All right. I've got to get past you."

"Wait a minute. Do you s'pose that young woman is all right?"

"I don't see why not. Nothing against the law of the land for her to buy out a church fair, that I know of."

"Don't you think it looks sort of suspicious?"

"It's none of my business. I confess I don't see why it's suspicious, unless somebody wants to make her out a fool. I don't understand what any sane person wants with all that truck; but I don't pretend to understand women."

Whittle shook his head slowly. "I dunno," he said.

"Well, I don't know who does, or cares either. They've got the money. I suppose that was what they were after." Jim again tried to pass.

"Wait just a minute. Say, Jim, I'm going to tell you something. Don't you speak of it till it gets out."

"Fire away. I'm in a hurry."

"She wants to buy this old Bolton place here."

Jim whistled.

"You know the assignees of the Bolton estate had to take the house, and it's been running down all these years, and a lot of money has got to be spent on it or it'll tumble down. Now, this young woman has offered to pay a good round sum for it, and take it just as it is. S'pose it's all right?"

"How in creation should I know? If I held it, and wanted to sell it, I'd know darn well whether it was all right or not. I wouldn't go around asking other folks."

"But you see it don't seem natural. Folks don't do things like that. She's offering to pay more than the place is worth. She'll have to spend thousands on it to make it fit to live in. She says she'll pay cash, too."

"Well, I suppose you'll know cash when you see it. I've got to go."

"But cash! Lord A'mighty! We dunno what to do."

"I suppose you know whether you want to sell or not."

"Want to sell! If we didn't want to sell this old shebang we'd be dumb idiots."

"Then, why in the name of common sense don't you sell?"

"Because, somehow it don't look natural to me."

"Well, I must confess that to throw away much money on an old shell like that doesn't look any too natural to me."

"Come now, Jim, that was a real nice house when it was built."

Jim laughed sarcastically. "Running up your wares now, are you?"

"That house cost Andrew Bolton a pile of money. And now, if it's fixed up, it'll be the best house in Brookville."

"That isn't saying much. See here, you've got to let me pass. If you want to sell—I should think you would—I don't see what you are worrying about. I don't suppose you are worrying for fear you may cheat the girl."

"We ain't goin' to cheat the girl, but—I dunno." Whittle stood aside, shaking his head, and Jim passed on. He loitered along the shaggy hedge which bordered the old Bolton estate, and a little farther, then turned back. He had reached the house again when he started. In front of the gate stood a shadowy figure, a woman, by the outlines of the dress. Jim continued hesitatingly. He feared to startle her. But he did not. When he came abreast of her, she turned and looked full in his face, and he recognized Miss Orr. He took off his hat, but was so astonished he could scarcely utter a greeting. The girl was so shy that she stammered a little, but she laughed too, like a child caught in some mischief.

"Oh, I am so glad it is you!" she said.

"Well, taking all things into consideration, so am I," said Jim.

"You mean—?"

"I mean it is pretty late for you to be out alone, and I'm as good as a Sunday School picnic, with the superintendent and the minister thrown in, for you to meet. I'll see you home."

"Goodness! There's nothing to be afraid of in this little place," said the girl. "I have lived in New York."

"Where there are policemen."

"Oh, yes, but one never counts on that. One never counts on anything in New York. You can't, you know. Its mathematics are as high as its buildings, too high to take chances. But here—why, I saw pretty near the whole village at that funny fair, didn't I?"

"Well, yes, but Brookville is not a walled town. People not so desirable as those you saw at the fair have free entrance and egress. It is pretty late."

"I am not in the least afraid," said the girl.

"You have no reason to be, now."

"You mean because you have happened along. Well, I am glad you did. I begun to think it was rather late myself for me to be prowling around, but you will simply have to leave me before I get to my boarding house. That Mrs. Black is as kind as can be, but she doesn't know what to make of me, and on the whole I think I would rather take my chances stealing in alone than to have her spy you."

"If you wanted to come out, why didn't you ask the minister to come with you?" Jim asked bluntly.

"The minister! Oh, I don't like ministers when they are young. They are much better when all the doctrines they have learned at their theological seminaries have settled in their minds, and have stopped bubbling. However, this minister here seems rather nice, very young, but he doesn't give the impression of taking himself so seriously that he is a nervous wreck on account of his convictions. I wouldn't have asked him for the world. In the first place, Mrs. Black would have thought it very queer, and in the second place he was so hopping mad about that fair, and having me buy it, that he wouldn't have been agreeable. I don't blame him. I would feel just so in his place. It must be frightful to be a poor minister."

"None too pleasant, anyway."

"You are right, it certainly is not. I have been poor myself, and I know. I went to my room, and looked out of the window, and it was so perfectly beautiful outdoors, and I did want to see how this place looked by moonlight, so I just went down the back stairs and came alone. I hope nobody will break in while I am gone. I left the door unlocked."

"No burglars live in Brookville," said Jim. "Mighty good reasons for none to come in, too."

"What reasons?"

"Not a blessed thing to burgle. Never has been for years."

There was a silence. The girl spoke in a hushed voice. "I—understand," said she, "that the people here hold the man who used to live in this house responsible for that."

"Why, yes, I suppose he was. Brookville never would have been a Tuxedo under any circumstances, but I reckon it would have fared a little better if Mr. Bolton hadn't failed to see the difference between mine and thine. I was nothing but a kid, but I have heard a good deal about it. Some of the older people are pretty bitter, and some of the younger ones have it in their veins. I suppose the poor man did start us down hill."

"You say 'poor man'; why?" asked the girl and her voice trembled.

"Lord, yes. I'm like a hound sneaking round back doors for bones, on account of Mr. Bolton, myself. My father lost more than 'most anybody, but I wouldn't change places with the man. Say, do you know he has been in State's Prison for years?"

"Yes."

"Of course any man who does wrong is a poor man, even if he doesn't get caught. I'm mighty glad I wasn't born bitter as some of the people here were. My sister Fanny isn't either. She doesn't have much, poor girl, but I've never heard her say one word, and mother never blames it on Mr. Bolton, either. Mother says he is getting his punishment, and it isn't for any of us to add to it."

"Your sister was that pretty girl at the flower table?"

"Yes—I suppose you would call her pretty. I don't really know. A fellow never does know, when the girl is his sister. She may look the best of the bunch to him, but he's never sure."

"She is lovely," said Lydia Orr. She pointed to the shadowy house. "That must have been a nice place once."

"Best in the village; show place. Say, what in the name of common sense do you want to buy it for?"

"Who told you?"

"Oh, I met old Whittle just before I met you. He told me. The place must be terribly run down. It will cost a mint of money to get it in shape."

"I have considerable money," stated the girl quite simply.

"Well, it's none of my business, but you will have to sink considerable in that place, and perhaps when you are through it won't be satisfactory."

"I have taken a notion to it," said the girl. She spoke very shyly. Her curiously timid, almost apologetic manner returned suddenly. "I suppose it does look strange," she added.

"Nobody's business how it looks," said Jim, "but I think you ought to know the truth about it, and I think I am more likely to give you information than Whittle. Of course he has an ax to grind. Perhaps if I had an ax to grind, you couldn't trust me."

"Yes, I could," returned the girl with conviction. "I knew that the minute I looked at you. I always know the people I can trust. I know I could not trust Deacon Whittle. I made allowances, the way one does for a clock that runs too fast or too slow. I think one always has to be doing addition or subtraction with people, to understand them."

"Well, you had better try a little subtraction with me."

"I don't have to. I didn't mean with everybody. Of course there are exceptions. That was a beautiful skin you gave me. I didn't half thank you."

"Nonsense. I was glad to give it."

"Do you hunt much?"

"About all I am good for except to run our little farm and do odd jobs. I used to work in the chair factory."

"I shouldn't think you would have liked that."

"Didn't; had to do what I could."

"What would you like to do?"

"Oh, I don't know. I never had any choice, so I never gave it any thought. Something that would keep me out of doors, I reckon."

"Do you know much about plants and trees?"

"I don't know whether I know much; I love them, that's all."

"You could do some landscape gardening for a place like this, I should think."

Jim stared at her, and drew himself up haughtily. "It really is late, Miss Orr," he said. "I think, if you will allow me, I will take you home."

"What are you angry about?"

12

"I am not angry."

"Yes, you are. You are angry because I said that about landscape gardening."

"I am not a beggar or a man who undertakes a job he is not competent to perform, if I am poor."

"Will you undertake setting those grounds to rights, if I buy the place?"

"Why don't you hire a regular landscape man if you have so much money?" asked Jim rudely.

"I would rather have you. I want somebody I can work with. I have my own ideas. I want to hire you to work with me. Will you?"

"Time enough to settle that when you've bought the place. You must go home now. Here, take my arm. This sidewalk is an apology for one."

Lydia took the young man's arm obediently, and they began walking.

"What on earth are you going to do with all that truck you bought?" asked Jim.

Lydia laughed. "To tell you the truth, I haven't the slightest idea," said she. "Pretty awful, most of it, isn't it?"

"I wouldn't give it house room."

"I won't either. I bought it, but I won't have it."

"You must take us for a pretty set of paupers, to throw away money like that."

"Now, don't you get mad again. I did want to buy it. I never wanted to buy things so much in my life."

"I never saw such a queer girl."

"You will know I am not queer some time, and I would tell you why now, but—"

"Don't you tell me a thing you don't want to."

"I think I had better wait just a little. But I don't know about all those things."

"Say, why don't you send them to missionaries out West?"

"Oh, could I?"

"Of course you can. What's to hinder?"

"When I buy that place will you help me?"

"Of course I will. Now you are talking! I'm glad to do anything like that. I think I'd be nutty if I had to live in the same house as that fair."

The girl burst into a lovely peal of laughter. "Exactly what I thought all the time," said she. "I wanted to buy them; you don't know how much; but it was like buying rabbits, and white elephants, and—oh, I don't know! a perfect menagerie of things I couldn't bear to live with, and I didn't see how I could give them away, and I couldn't think of a place to throw them away." She laughed again.

Jim stopped suddenly. "Say."

"What?"

"Why, it will be an awful piece of work to pack off all those contraptions, and it strikes me it is pretty hard on the missionaries. There's a gravel pit down back of the Bolton place, and if you buy it—"

"What?"

"Well, bury the fair there."

Lydia stopped short, and laughed till she cried. "You don't suppose they would ever find out?"

"Trust me. You just have the whole lot moved into the house, and we'll fix it up."

"Oh, I can't tell you how thankful I am to you," said Lydia fervently. "I felt like a nightmare with all those things. Some of them can be used of course, but some—oh, those picture throws, and those postage stamp plates!"

"They are funny, but sort of pitiful, too," said Jim. "Women are sort of pitiful, lots of them. I'm glad I am a man."

"I should think you would be," said the girl. She looked up in his face with an expression which he did not see. He was regarding women in the abstract; she was suddenly regarding men in the individual.

Chapter IV

Elliot slept later than usual the morning after the fair. Generally he slept the beautiful, undisturbed sleep of the young and healthy; that night, for some reason, he did not. Possibly the strange break which the buying of the fair had made in the course of his everyday life caused one also between his conscious and unconscious state, which his brain refused to bridge readily. Wesley had not been brought face to face, many times in his life, with the unprecedented. He had been brought before it, although in a limited fashion, at the church fair. The unprecedented is more or less shattering, partaking of the nature of a spiritual bomb. Lydia Orr's mad purchase of that collection of things called a fair disturbed his sense of values. He asked himself over and over who was this girl? More earnestly he asked himself what her motives could be.

But the question which most agitated him was his relations with the girl, Fanny Dodge. He realized that recently he had approached the verge of an emotional crisis. If Mrs. Black whom he had at the time fairly cursed in his heart, in spite of his profession, had not appeared with her notice of dinner, he would be in a most unpleasant predicament. Only the girl's innate good sense could have served as a refuge, and he reflected with the utmost tenderness that he might confidently rely upon that. He was almost sure that the poor girl loved him. He was quite sure that he loved her. But he was also sure, with a strong sense of pride in her, that she would have refused him, not on mercenary grounds, for Fanny he knew would have shared a crust and hovel with the man she loved; but Fanny would love the man too well to consent to the crust and the hovel, on his own account. She would not have said in so many words, "What! marry you, a minister so poor that a begging fair has to be held to pay his salary?" She would have not refused him her love and sympathy, but she would have let him down so gently from the high prospect of matrimony that he would have suffered no jolt.

Elliot was a good fellow. It was on the girl's account that he suffered. He suffered, as a matter of course. He wanted Fanny badly, but he realized himself something of a cad. He discounted his own suffering; perhaps, as he told himself with sudden suspicion of self-conceit, he overestimated hers. Still, he was sure that the girl would suffer more than he wished. He blamed himself immeasurably. He tried to construct air castles which would not fall, even before the impact of his own thoughts, in which he could marry this girl and live with her happily ever after, but the man had too much common sense. He did not for a moment now consider the possibility of stepping, without influence, into a fat pastorate. He was sure that he could count confidently upon nothing better than this.

The next morning he looked about his room wearily, and a plan which he had often considered grew upon him. He got the keys of the unoccupied parsonage next door, from Mrs. Black, and went over the house after breakfast. It was rather a spacious house, old, but in tolerable preservation. There was a southeast room of one story in height, obviously an architectural afterthought, which immediately appealed to him. It was practically empty except for charming possibilities, but it contained a few essentials, and probably the former incumbent had used it as a study. There was a wood stove, a standing desk fixed to the wall, some shelves, an old table, and a couple of armchairs. Wesley at once resolved to carry out his plan. He would move his small store of books from his bedroom at Mrs. Black's, arrange them on the shelves, and set up his study there. He was reasonably sure of obtaining wood enough for a fire to heat the room when the weather was cold.

He returned and told Mrs. Black, who agreed with him that the plan was a good one. "A minister ought to have his study," said she, "and of course the parsonage is at your disposal. The parish can't rent it. That room used to be the study, and you will have offers of all the wood you want to heat it. There's plenty of cut wood that folks are glad to donate. They've always sent loads of wood to heat the minister's study. Maybe they thought they'd stand less chance of hell fire if they heated up the gospel in this life."

"Then I'll move my books and writing materials right over there," said Elliot with a most boyish glee.

Mrs. Black nodded approvingly. "So I would." She hesitated a moment, then she spoke again. "I was just a little bit doubtful about taking that young woman in yesterday," said she.

Elliot regarded her curiously. "Then you never had met her before?"

"No, she just landed here with her trunk. The garage man brought her, and she said he told her I took boarders, and she asked me to take her. I don't know but I was kind of weak to give in, but the poor little thing looked sort of nice, and her manners were pretty, so I took her. I thought I would ask you how you felt about it this morning, but there ain't any reason to, perhaps, for she ain't going to stay here very long, anyway. She says she's going to buy the old Bolton place and have it fixed up and settle down there as soon as she can. She told me after you had gone out. She's gone now to look at it. Mr. Whittle was going to meet her there. Queer, ain't it?"

"It does look extraordinary, rather," agreed Elliot, "but Miss Orr may be older than she looks."

"Oh, she ain't old, but she's of age. She told me that, and I guess she's got plenty of money."

"Well," said Elliot, "that is rather a fine old place. She may be connected with the Bolton family."

"That's exactly what I think, and if she was she wouldn't mention it, of course. I think she's getting the house in some sort of a business way. Andrew Bolton may have died in prison by this time, and she may be an heir. I think she is going to be married and have the house fixed up to live in."

"That sounds very probable."

"Yes, it does; but what gets me is her buying that fair. I own I felt a little scared, and wondered if she had all her buttons, but when she told me about the house I knew of course she could use the things for furnishing, all except the cake and candy, and I suppose if she's got a lot of money she thought she'd like to buy to help. I feel glad she's coming. She may be a real help in the church. Now don't color up. Ministers have to take help. It's part of their discipline."

Sometimes Mrs. Solomon Black said a wise and consoling thing. Elliot, moving his effects to the old parsonage, considered that she had done so then. "She is right. I have no business to be proud in the profession calling for the lowly-hearted of the whole world," he told himself.

After he had his books arranged he sat down in an armchair beside a front window, and felt rather happy and at home. He reproached himself for his content when he read the morning paper, and considered the horrors going on in Europe. Why should he, an able-bodied man, sit securely in a room and gaze out at a peaceful village street? he asked himself as he had scores of times before. Then the imperial individual, which obtrudes even when conscience cries out against it, occupied his mind. Pretty Fanny Dodge in her blue linen was passing. She never once glanced at the parsonage. Forgetting his own scruples and resolves, he thought unreasonably that she might at least glance up, if she had the day before at all in her mind. Suddenly the unwelcome reflection that he might not be as desirable as he had thought himself came over him.

He got up, put on his hat, and walked rapidly in the direction of the old Bolton house. Satisfying his curiosity might serve as a palliative to his sudden depression with regard to his love affair. It is very much more comfortable to consider oneself a cad, and acknowledge to oneself love for a girl, and be sure of her unfortunate love for you, than to consider oneself the dupe of the girl. Fanny had a keen sense of humor. Suppose she had been making fun of him. Suppose she had her own aspirations in other quarters. He walked on until he reached the old Bolton house. The door stood open, askew upon rusty hinges. Wesley Elliot entered and glanced about him with growing curiosity. The room was obviously a kitchen, one side being occupied by a huge brick chimney inclosing a built-in range half devoured with rust; wall cupboards, a sink and a decrepit table showed gray and ugly in the greenish light of two tall windows, completely blocked on the outside with over-grown shrubs. An indescribable odor of decaying plaster, chimney-soot and mildew hung in the heavy air.

A door to the right, also half open, led the investigator further. Here the floor shook ominously under foot, suggesting rotten beams and unsteady sills. The minister walked cautiously, noting in passing a portrait defaced with cobwebs over the marble mantelpiece and the great circular window opening upon an expanse of tangled grass and weeds, through which the sun streamed hot and yellow. Voices came from an adjoining room; he could hear Deacon Whittle's nasal tones upraised in fervid assertion.

"Yes, ma'am!" he was saying, "this house is a little out of repair, you can see that fer yourself; but it's well built; couldn't be better. A few hundred dollars expended here an' there'll make it as good as new; in fact, I'll say better'n new! They don't put no such material in houses nowadays. Why, this woodwork—doors, windows, floors and all—is clear, white pine. You can't buy it today for no price. Costs as much as m'hogany, come to figure it out. Yes, ma'am! the woodwork alone in this house is worth the price of one of them little new shacks a builder'll run up in a couple of months. And look at them mantelpieces, pure tombstone marble; and all carved like you see. Yes, ma'am! there's as many as seven of 'em in the house. Where'll you find anything like that, I'd like to know!"

"I—think the house might be made to look very pleasant, Mr. Whittle," Lydia replied, in a hesitating voice.

Wesley Elliot fancied he could detect a slight tremor in its even flow. He pushed open the door and walked boldly in.

"Good-morning, Miss Orr," he exclaimed, advancing with outstretched hand. "Good-morning, Deacon! ...Well, well! what a melancholy old ruin this is, to be sure. I never chanced to see the interior before."

Deacon Whittle regarded his pastor sourly from under puckered brows.

"Some s'prised to see you, dominie," said he. "Thought you was generally occupied at your desk of a Friday morning."

The minister included Lydia Orr in the genial warmth of his smile as he replied:

"I had a special call into the country this morning, and seeing your conveyance hitched to the trees outside, Deacon, I thought I'd step in. I'm not sure it's altogether safe for all of us to be standing in the middle of this big room, though. Sills pretty well rotted out—eh, Deacon?"

"Sound as an oak," snarled the Deacon. "As I was telling th' young lady, there ain't no better built house anywheres 'round than this one. Andrew Bolton didn't spare other folks' money when he built it—no, sir! It's good for a hundred years yet, with trifling repairs."

"Who owns the house now?" asked Lydia unexpectedly. She had walked over to one of the long windows opening on a rickety balcony and stood looking out.

15

"Who owns it?" echoed Deacon Whittle. "Well, now, we can give you a clear title, ma'am, when it comes to that; sound an' clear. You don't have to worry none about that. You see it was this way; dunno as anybody's mentioned it in your hearing since you come to Brookville; but we use to have a bank here in Brookville, about eighteen years ago, and—"

"Yes, Ellen Dix told me," interrupted Lydia Orr, without turning her head. "Has nobody lived here since?"

Deacon Whittle cast an impatient glance at Wesley Elliot, who stood with his eyes fixed broodingly on the dusty floor.

"Wal," said he. "There'd have been plenty of folks glad enough to live here; but the house wa'n't really suited to our kind o' folks. It wa'n't a farm—there being only twenty acres going with it. And you see the house is different to what folks in moderate circumstances could handle. Nobody had the cash to buy it, an' ain't had, all these years. It's a pity to see a fine old property like this a-going down, all for the lack of a few hundreds. But if you was to buy it, ma'am, I could put it in shape fer you, equal to the best, and at a figure— Wall; I tell ye, it won't cost ye what some folks'd think."

"Didn't that man—the banker who stole—everybody's money, I mean—didn't he have any family?" asked Lydia, still without turning her head. "I suppose he—he died a long time ago?"

"I see the matter of th' title's worrying you, ma'am," said Deacon Whittle briskly. "I like to see a female cautious in a business way: I do, indeed. And 'tain't often you see it, neither. Now, I'll tell *you*—"

"Wouldn't it be well to show Miss Orr some more desirable property, Deacon?" interposed Wesley Elliot. "It seems to me—"

"Oh, I shall buy the house," said the girl at the window, quickly.

She turned and faced the two men, her delicate head thrown back, a clear color staining her pale cheeks.

"I shall buy it," she repeated. "I—I like it very much. It is just what I wanted—in—in every way."

Deacon Whittle gave vent to a snort of astonishment.

"There was another party looking at the place a spell back," he said, rubbing his dry old hands. "I dunno's I exac'ly give him an option on it; but I was sort of looking for him to turn up 'most any day. Course I'd have to give him the first chance, if it comes to a—"

"What is an option?" asked Lydia.

"An option is a—now, let me see if I can make a legal term plain to the female mind: An option, my dear young lady, is—"

The minister crossed the floor to where the girl was standing, a slight, delicate figure in her black dress, her small face under the shadowy brim of her wide had looking unnaturally pale in the greenish light from without.

"An option," he interposed hurriedly, "must be bought with money; should you change your mind later you lose whatever you have paid. Let me advise you—"

Deacon Whittle cleared his throat with an angry, rasping sound.

"Me an' this young lady came here this morning for the purpose of transacting a little business, mutually advantageous," he snarled. "If it was anybody but the dominie, I should say he was butting in without cause."

"Oh, don't, please!" begged the girl. "Mr. Elliot meant it kindly, I'm sure. I—I want an option, if you please. You'll let me have it, won't you? I want it—now."

Deacon Whittle blinked and drew back a pace or two, as if her eagerness actually frightened him.

"I—I guess I can accommodate ye," he stuttered; "but—there'll be some preliminaries—I wa'n't exactly prepared— There's the price of the property and the terms— S'pose likely you'll want a mortgage—eh?"

He rubbed his bristly chin dubiously.

"I want to buy the house," Lydia said. "I want to be sure—"

"Have you seen the rooms upstairs?" asked the minister, turning his back upon his senior deacon.

She shook her head.

"Well, then, why not—"

Wesley Elliot took a step or two toward the winding stair, dimly seen through the gloom of the hall.

"Hold on, dominie, them stairs ain't safe!" warned the Deacon. "They'll mebbe want a little shoring up, before— Say, I wish—"

"I don't care to go up now, really," protested the girl. "It—it's the location I like and—"

She glanced about the desolate place with a shiver. The air of the long-closed rooms was chilly, despite the warmth of the June day outside.

"I'll tell you what," said the deacon briskly. "You come right along down to the village with me, Miss Orr. It's kind of close in here; the house is built so tight, there can't no air git in. I tell you, them walls—"

He smote the one nearest him with a jocular palm. There followed the hollow sound of dropping plaster from behind the lath.

"Guess we'd better fix things up between us, so you won't be noways disappointed in case that other party—" he added, with a crafty glance at the minister. "You see, he might turn up 'most any day."

"Oh, yes!" exclaimed the girl, walking hurriedly to the door. "I—I should like to go at once."

She turned and held out her hand to the minister with a smile.

"Thank you for coming," she said. "I wanted you to see the house as it is now."

He looked down into her upturned face with its almost childish appeal of utter candor, frowning slightly.

"Have you no one—that is, no near relative to advise you in the matter?" he asked. "The purchase of a large property, such as this, ought to be carefully considered, I should say."

Deacon Whittle coughed in an exasperated manner.

"I guess we'd better be gitting along," said he, "if we want to catch Jedge Fulsom in his office before he goes to dinner."

Lydia turned obediently.

"I'm coming," she said.

Then to Elliot: "No; there is no one to—to advise me. I am obliged to decide for myself."

Wesley Elliot returned to Brookville and his unfinished sermon by a long detour which led him over the shoulder of a hill overlooking the valley. He did not choose to examine his motive for avoiding the road along which Fanny Dodge would presently return. But as the path, increasingly rough and stony as it climbed the steep ascent, led him at length to a point from whence he could look down upon a toy village, arranged in stiff rows about a toy church, with its tiny pointing steeple piercing the vivid green of many trees, he sat down with a sigh of relief and something very like gratitude.

As far back as he could remember Wesley Elliot had cherished a firm, though somewhat undefined, belief in a quasi-omnipotent power to be reckoned as either hostile or friendly to the purposes of man, showing now a smiling, now a frowning face. In short, that unquestioned, wholly uncontrollable influence outside of a man's life, which appears to rule his destiny. In this rôle "Providence," as he had been taught to call it, had heretofore smiled rather evasively upon Wesley Elliot. He had been permitted to make sure his sacred calling; but he had not secured the earnestly coveted city pulpit. On the other hand, he had just been saved—or so he told himself, as the fragrant June breeze fanned his heated forehead—by a distinct intervention of "Providence" from making a fool of himself. His subsequent musings, interrupted at length by the shrieking whistle of the noon train as it came to a standstill at the toy railway station, might be termed important, since they were to influence the immediate future of a number of persons, thus affording a fresh illustration of the mysterious workings of "Providence," sometimes called "Divine."

Chapter V

There existed in Brookville two separate and distinct forums for the discussion of topics of public and private interest. These were the barroom of the village tavern, known as the Brookville House, and Henry Daggett's General Store, located on the corner opposite the old Bolton Bank Building. Mr. Daggett, besides being Brookville's leading merchant, was also postmaster, and twice each day withdrew to the official privacy of the office for the transaction of United States business. The post office was conveniently located in one corner of Mr. Daggett's store and presented to the inquiring eye a small glass window, which could be raised and lowered at will by the person behind the partition, a few numbered boxes and a slit, marked "Letters."

In the evening of the day on which Miss Lydia Orr had visited the old Bolton house in company with Deacon Whittle, both forums were in full blast. The wagon-shed behind the Brookville House sheltered an unusual number of "rigs," whose owners, after partaking of liquid refreshment dispensed by the oily young man behind the bar, by common consent strolled out to the veranda where a row of battered wooden armchairs invited to reposeful consideration of the surprising events of the past few days.

The central chair supported the large presence of "Judge" Fulsom, who was dispensing both information and tobacco juice.

"The practice of the legal profession," said the Judge, after a brief period devoted to the ruminative processes, "is full of surprises."

17

Having spoken, Judge Fulsom folded his fat hands across the somewhat soiled expanse of his white waistcoat and relapsed into a weighty silence.

"They was sayin' over to the post office this evening that the young woman that cleaned up the church fair has bought the old Bolton place. How about it, Jedge?"

Judge Fulsom grunted, as he leveled a displeased stare upon the speaker, a young farmer with a bibulous eye and slight swagger of defiance. At the proper moment, with the right audience, the Judge was willing to impart information with lavish generosity. But any attempt to force his hand was looked upon as a distinct infringement of his privilege.

"You want to keep your face shut, Lute, till th' Jedge gets ready to talk," counseled a middle-aged man who sat tilted back in the next chair. "Set down, son, and cool off."

"Well, you see I got to hurry along," objected the young farmer impatiently, "and I wanted to know if there was anything in it. Our folks had money in the old bank, an' we'd give up getting anything more out the smash years ago. But if the Bolton place has actually been sold—"

He finished with a prolonged whistle.

The greatness in the middle chair emitted a grunt.

"Humph!" he muttered, and again, "Hr-m-m-ph!"

"It would be surprising," conceded the middle-aged man, "after all these years."

"Considerable many of th' creditors has died since," piped up a lean youth who was smoking a very large cigar. "I s'pose th' children of all such would come in for their share—eh, Judge?"

Judge Fulsom frowned and pursed his lips thoughtfully.

"The proceedings has not yet reached the point you mention, Henry," he said. "You're going a little too fast."

Nobody spoke, but the growing excitement took the form of a shuffling of feet. The Judge deliberately lighted his pipe, a token of mental relaxation. Then from out the haze of blue smoke, like the voice of an oracle from the seclusion of a shrine, issued the familiar recitative tone for which everybody had been waiting.

"Well, boys, I'll tell you how 'twas: Along about ten minutes of twelve I had my hat on my head, and was just drawing on my linen duster with the idea of going home to dinner, when I happened to look out of my office window, and there was Deacon Whittle—and the girl, just coming up th' steps. In five minutes more I'd have been gone, most likely for the day."

"Gosh!" breathed the excitable young farmer.

The middle-aged man sternly motioned him to keep silence.

"I s'pose most of you boys saw her at the fair last night," proceeded the Judge, ignoring the interruption. "She's a nice appearing young female; but nobody'd think to look at her—"

He paused to ram down the tobacco in the glowing bowl of his pipe.

"Well, as I was saying, she'd been over to the Bolton house with the Deacon. Guess we'll have to set the Deacon down for a right smart real-estate boomer. We didn't none of us give him credit for it. He'd got the girl all worked up to th' point of bein' afraid another party'd be right along to buy the place. She wanted an option on it."

"Shucks!" again interrupted the young farmer disgustedly. "Them options ain't no good. I had one once on five acres of timber, and—"

"Shut up, Lute!" came in low chorus from the spell-bound audience.

"Wanted an option," repeated Judge Fulsom loudly, "just till I could fix up the paper. 'And, if you please,' said she, 'I'd like t' pay five thousand dollars for the option, then I'd feel more sure.' And before I had a chance to open my mouth, she whips out a check-book."

"Gr-reat jumping Judas!" cried the irrepressible Lute, whose other name was Parsons. "Five thousand dollars! Why, the old place ain't worth no five thousand dollars!"

Judge Fulsom removed his pipe from his mouth, knocked out the half-burned tobacco, blew through the stem, then proceeded to fill and light it again. From the resultant haze issued his voice once more, bland, authoritative, reminiscent.

"Well, now, son, that depends on how you look at it. Time was when Andrew Bolton wouldn't have parted with the place for three times that amount. It was rated, I remember, at eighteen thousand, including live stock, conveyances an' furniture, when it was deeded over to the assignees. We sold out the furniture and stock at auction for about half what they were worth. But there weren't any bidders worth mentioning for the house and land. So it was held by the assignees—Cephas Dix, Deacon Whittle and myself—for private sale. We could

18

have sold it on easy terms the next year for six thousand; but in process of trying to jack up our customer to seven, we lost out on the deal. But now—"

Judge Fulsom arose, brushed the tobacco from his waistcoat front and cleared his throat.

"Guess I'll have to be getting along," said he; "important papers to look over, and—"

"A female woman, like her, is likely to change her mind before tomorrow morning," said the middle-aged man dubiously. "And I heard Mrs. Solomon Black had offered to sell her place to the young woman for twenty-nine hundred—all in good repair and neat as wax. She might take it into her head to buy it."

"Right in the village, too," growled Lute Parsons. "Say, Jedge, did you give her that option she was looking for? Because if you did she can't get out of it so easy."

Judge Fulsom twinkled pleasantly over his bulging cheeks.

"I sure did accommodate the young lady with the option, as aforesaid," he vouchsafed. "And what's more, I telephoned to the Grenoble Bank to see if her check for five thousand dollars was O. K.... Well; so long, boys!"

He stepped ponderously down from the piazza and turned his broad back on the row of excited faces.

"Hold on, Jedge!" the middle-aged man called after him. "Was her check any good? You didn't tell us!"

The Judge did not reply. He merely waved his hand.

"He's going over to the post office," surmised the lean youth, shifting the stub of his cigar to the corner of his mouth in a knowing manner.

He lowered his heels to the floor with a thud and prepared to follow. Five minutes later the bartender, not hearing the familiar hum of voices from the piazza, thrust his head out of the door.

"Say!" he called out to the hatchet-faced woman who was writing down sundry items in a ledger at a high desk. "The boys has all cleared out. What's up, I wonder?"

"They'll be back," said the woman imperturbably, "an' more with 'em. You want t' git your glasses all washed up, Gus; an' you may as well fetch up another demijohn out the cellar."

Was it foreknowledge, or merely coincidence which at this same hour led Mrs. Solomon Black, frugally inspecting her supplies for tomorrow morning's breakfast, to discover that her baking-powder can was empty?

"I'll have to roll out a few biscuits for their breakfast," she decided, "or else I'll run short of bread for dinner."

Her two boarders, Lydia Orr and the minister, were sitting on the piazza, engaged in what appeared to be a most interesting conversation, when Mrs. Black unlatched the front gate and emerged upon the street, her second-best hat carefully disposed upon her water-waves.

"I won't be gone a minute," she paused to assure them; "I just got to step down to the grocery."

A sudden hush fell upon a loud and excited conversation when Mrs. Solomon Black, very erect as to her spinal column and noticeably composed and dignified in her manner, entered Henry Daggett's store. She walked straight past the group of men who stood about the door to the counter, where Mr. Daggett was wrapping in brown paper two large dill pickles dripping sourness for a small girl with straw-colored pig-tails.

Mr. Daggett beamed cordially upon Mrs. Black, as he dropped two copper pennies in his cash-drawer.

"Good evening, ma'am," said he. "What can I do for you?"

"A ten-cent can of baking-powder, if you please," replied the lady primly.

"Must take a lot of victuals to feed them two boarders o' yourn," hazarded Mr. Daggett, still cordially, and with a dash of confidential sympathy in his voice.

Mr. Daggett had, by virtue of long association with his wife, acquired something of her spontaneous warm-heartedness. He had found it useful in his business.

"Oh, they ain't neither of 'em so hearty," said Mrs. Black, searching in her pocket-book with the air of one who is in haste.

"We was just speakin' about the young woman that's stopping at your house," murmured Mr. Daggett. "Let me see; I disremember which kind of bakin'-powder you use, Mis' Black."

"The Golden Rule brand, if you please, Mr. Daggett."

"H'm; let me see if I've got one of them Golden Rules left," mused Mr. Daggett.... "I told the boys I guessed she was some relation of th' Grenoble Orrs, an' mebbe—"

"Well; she ain't," denied Mrs. Black crisply.

"M-m-m?" interrogated Mr. Daggett, intent upon a careful search among the various canned products on his shelf. "How'd she happen to come to Brookville?"

Mrs. Black tossed her head.

"Of course it ain't for me to say," she returned, with a dignity which made her appear taller than she really was. "But folks has heard of the table I set, 'way to Boston."

"You don't say!" exclaimed Mr. Daggett. "So she come from Boston, did she? I thought she seemed kind of—"

"I don't know as there's any secret about where she *come* from," returned Mrs. Black aggressively. "I never s'posed there was. Folks ain't had time to git acquainted with her yit."

"That's so," agreed Mr. Daggett, as if the idea was a new and valuable one. "Yes, ma'am; you're right! we ain't none of us had time to git acquainted."

He beamed cordially upon Mrs. Black over the tops of his spectacles. "Looks like we're going to git a chance to know her," he went on. "It seems the young woman has made up her mind to settle amongst us. Yes, ma'am; we've been hearing she's on the point of buying property and settling right down here in Brookville."

An excited buzz of comment in the front of the store broke in upon this confidential conversation. Mrs. Black appeared to become aware for the first time of the score of masculine eyes fixed upon her.

"Ain't you got any of the Golden Rule?" she demanded sharply. "That looks like it to me—over in behind them cans of tomatoes. It's got a blue label."

"Why, yes; here 'tis, sure enough," admitted Mr. Daggett. "I guess I must be losing my eyesight.... It's going to be quite a chore to fix up the old Bolton house," he added, as he inserted the blue labeled can of reputation in a red and yellow striped paper bag.

"That ain't decided," snapped Mrs. Black. "She could do better than to buy that tumble-down old shack."

"So she could; so she could," soothed the postmaster. "But it's going to be a good thing for the creditors, if she can swing it. Let me see, you wa'n't a loser in the Bolton Bank; was you, Mis' Black?"

"No; I wa'n't; my late departed husband had too much horse-sense."

And having thus impugned less fortunate persons, Mrs. Solomon Black departed, a little stiffer as to her back-bone than when she entered. She had imparted information; she had also acquired it. When she had returned rather later than usual from selling her strawberries in Grenoble she had hurried her vegetables on to boil and set the table for dinner. She could hear the minister pacing up and down his room in the restless way which Mrs. Black secretly resented, since it would necessitate changing the side breadths of matting to the middle of the floor long before this should be done. But of Lydia Orr there was no sign. The minister came promptly down stairs at sound of the belated dinner-bell. But to Mrs. Black's voluble explanations for the unwonted hour he returned the briefest of perfunctory replies. He seemed hungry and ate heartily of the cold boiled beef and vegetables.

"Did you see anything of *her* this morning?" asked Mrs. Black pointedly, as she cut the dried-apple pie. "I can't think what's become of her."

Wesley Elliot glanced up from an absent-minded contemplation of an egg spot on the tablecloth.

"If you refer to Miss Orr," said he, "I did see her—in a carriage with Deacon Whittle."

He was instantly ashamed of the innocent prevarication. But he told himself he did not choose to discuss Miss Orr's affairs with Mrs. Black.

Just then Lydia came in, her eyes shining, her cheeks very pink; but like the minister she seemed disposed to silence, and Mrs. Black was forced to restrain her curiosity.

"How'd you make out this morning?" she inquired, as Lydia, having hurried through her dinner, rose to leave the table.

"Very well, thank you, Mrs. Black," said the girl brightly. Then she went at once to her room and closed the door.

At supper time it was just the same; neither the minister nor the girl who sat opposite him had anything to say. But no sooner had Mrs. Black begun to clear away the dishes than the two withdrew to the vine-shaded porch, as if by common consent.

"She ought to know right off about Fanny Dodge and the minister," Mrs. Black told herself.

She was still revolving this in her mind as she walked sedately along the street, the red and yellow striped bag clasped tightly in both hands. Of course everybody in the village would suppose she knew all about Lydia Orr. But the fact was she knew very little. The week before, one of her customers in Grenoble, in the course of a business transaction which involved a pair of chickens, a dozen eggs and two boxes of strawberries, had asked, in a casual way, if Mrs. Black knew any one in Brookville who kept boarders.

"The minister of our church boards with me," she told the Grenoble woman, with pardonable pride. "I don't know of anybody else that takes boarders in Brookville." She added that she had an extra room.

"Well, one of my boarders—a real nice young lady from Boston—has taken a queer notion to board in Brookville," said the woman. "She was out autoing the other day and went through there. I guess the country 'round Brookville must be real pretty this time of year."

"Yes; it is, real pretty," she had told the Grenoble woman.

And this had been the simple prelude to Lydia Orr's appearance in Brookville.

Wooded hills did not interest Mrs. Black, nor did the meandering of the silver river through its narrow valley. But she took an honest pride in her own freshly painted white house with its vividly green blinds, and in her front yard with its prim rows of annuals and thrifty young dahlias. As for Miss Lydia Orr's girlish rapture over the view from her bedroom window, so long as it was productive of honestly earned dollars, Mrs. Black was disposed to view it with indulgence. There was nothing about the girl or her possessions to indicate wealth or social importance, beyond the fact that she arrived in a hired automobile from Grenoble instead of riding over in Mrs. Solomon Black's spring wagon. Miss Orr brought with her to Brookville one trunk, the contents of which she had arranged at once in the bureau drawers and wardrobe of Mrs. Black's second-best bedroom. It was evident from a private inspection of their contents that Miss Orr was in mourning.

At this point in her meditations Mrs. Black became aware of an insistent voice hailing her from the other side of the picket fence.

It was Mrs. Daggett, her large fair face flushed with the exertion of hurrying down the walk leading from Mrs. Whittle's house.

"Some of us ladies has been clearing up after the fair," she explained, as she joined Mrs. Solomon Black. "It didn't seem no more than right; for even if Ann Whittle doesn't use her parlor, on account of not having it furnished up, she wants it broom-clean. My! You'd ought to have seen the muss we swept out."

"I'd have been glad to help," said Mrs. Black stiffly; "but what with it being my day to go over to Grenoble, and my boarders t' cook for and all—"

"Oh, we didn't expect you," said Abby Daggett tranquilly. "There was enough of us to do everything."

She beamed warmly upon Mrs. Black.

"Us ladies was saying we'd all better give you a rising vote of thanks for bringing that sweet Miss Orr to the fair. Why, 'twas a real success after all; we took in two hundred and forty-seven dollars and twenty-nine cents. Ain't that splendid?"

Mrs. Black nodded. She felt suddenly proud of her share in this success.

"I guess she wouldn't have come to the fair if I hadn't told her about it," she admitted. "She only come to my house yesterd'y morning."

"In an auto?" inquired Abby Daggett eagerly.

"Yes," nodded Mrs. Black. "I told her I could bring her over in the wagon just as well as not; but she said she had the man all engaged. I told her we was going to have a fair, and she said right off she wanted to come."

Abby Daggett laid her warm plump hand on Mrs. Black's arm.

"I dunno when I've took such a fancy to anybody at first sight," she said musingly. "She's what I call a real sweet girl. I'm just going to love her, I know."

She gazed beseechingly at Mrs. Solomon Black.

"Mebbe you'll think it's just gossipy curiosity; but I *would* like to know where that girl come from, and who her folks was, and how she happened to come to Brookville. I s'pose you know all about her; don't you?"

Mrs. Solomon Black coughed slightly. She was aware of the distinction she had already acquired in the eyes of Brookville from the mere fact of Lydia Orr's presence in her house.

"If I do," she began cautiously, "I don't know as it's for me to say."

"Don't fer pity's sake think I'm nosey," besought Abby Daggett almost tearfully. "You know I ain't that kind; but I don't see how folks is going to help being interested in a sweet pretty girl like Miss Orr, and her coming so unexpected. And you know there's them that'll invent things that ain't true, if they don't hear the facts."

"She's from Boston," said Mrs. Solomon Black grudgingly. "You can tell Lois Daggett that much, if she's getting anxious."

Mrs. Daggett's large face crimsoned. She was one of those soft, easily hurt persons whose blushes bring tears. She sniffed a little and raised her handkerchief to her eyes.

"I was afraid you'd—"

"Well, of course I ain't scared of you, Abby," relented Mrs. Black. "But I says to myself, 'I'm goin' to let Lydia Orr stand on her two own feet in this town,' I says. She can say what she likes about herself, an' there won't be no lies coming home to roost at *my* house. I guess you'd feel the very same way if you was in my place, Abby."

Mrs. Daggett glanced with childish admiration at the other woman's magenta-tinted face under its jetty water-waves. Even Mrs. Black's everyday hat was handsomer than her own Sunday-best.

"You always was so smart an' sensible, Phoebe," she said mildly. "I remember 'way back in school, when we was both girls, you always could see through arithmetic problems right off, when I couldn't for the life of me. I guess you're right about letting her speak for herself."

"Course I am!" agreed Mrs. Black triumphantly.

She had extricated herself from a difficulty with flying colors. She would still preserve her reputation for being a close-mouthed woman who knew a lot more about everything than she chose to tell.

"Anybody can see she's wearing mournin'," she added benevolently.

"Oh, I thought mebbe she had a black dress on because they're stylish. She did look awful pretty in it, with her arms and neck showing through. I like black myself; but mourning—that's different. Poor young thing, I wonder who it was. Her father, mebbe, or her mother. You didn't happen to hear her say, did you, Phoebe?"

Mrs. Solomon Black compressed her lips tightly. She paused at her own gate with majestic dignity.

"I guess I'll have to hurry right in, Abby," said she. "I have my bread to set."

Mrs. Solomon Black had closed her gate behind her, noticing as she did so that Wesley Elliot and Lydia Orr had disappeared from the piazza where she had left them. She glanced at Mrs. Daggett, lingering wistfully before the gate.

"Goodnight, Abby," said she firmly.

Chapter VI

Mrs. Maria Dodge sifted flour over her molding board preparatory to transferring the sticky mass of newly made dough from the big yellow mixing bowl to the board. More flour and a skillful twirl or two of the lump and the process of kneading was begun. It continued monotonously for the space of two minutes; then the motions became gradually slower, finally coming to a full stop.

"My patience!" murmured Mrs. Dodge, slapping her dough smartly. "Fanny ought to be ready by now. They'll be late—both of 'em."

She hurriedly crossed the kitchen to where, through a partly open door, an uncarpeted stair could be seen winding upward.

"Fanny!" she called sharply. "Fanny! ain't you ready yet?"

A quick step in the passage above, a subdued whistle, and her son Jim came clattering down the stair. He glanced at his mother, a slight pucker between his handsome brows. She returned the look with one of fond maternal admiration.

"How nice you do look, Jim," said she, and smiled up at her tall son. "I always did like you in red, and that necktie—"

Jim Dodge shrugged his shoulders with a laugh.

"Don't know about that tie," he said. "Kind of crude and flashy, ain't it, mother?"

"Flashy? No, of course it ain't. It looks real stylish with the brown suit."

"Stylish," repeated the young man. "Yes, I'm a regular swell—everything up to date, latest Broadway cut."

He looked down with some bitterness at his stalwart young person clad in clothes somewhat shabby, despite a recent pressing.

Mrs. Dodge had returned to her bread which had spread in a mass of stickiness all over the board.

"Where's Fanny?" she asked, glancing up at the noisy little clock on the shelf above her head. "Tell her to hurry, Jim. You're late, now."

Jim passed his hand thoughtfully over his clean-shaven chin.

"You might as well know, mother; Fan isn't going."

"Not going?" echoed Mrs. Dodge, sharp dismay in voice and eyes. "Why, I did up her white dress a-purpose, and she's been making up ribbon bows."

She extricated her fingers from the bread and again hurried across the floor.

Her son intercepted her with a single long stride.

"No use, mother," he said quietly. "Better let her alone."

"You think it's—?"

The young man slammed the door leading to the stairway with a fierce gesture.

"If you weren't blinder than a bat, mother, you'd know by this time what ailed Fan," he said angrily.

Mrs. Dodge sank into a chair by the table.

"Oh, I ain't blind," she denied weakly; "but I thought mebbe Fannie—I hoped—"

"Did you think she'd refused him?" demanded Jim roughly. "Did you suppose—? Huh! makes me mad clean through to think of it."

Mrs. Dodge began picking the dough off her fingers and rolling it into little balls which she laid in a row on the edge of the table.

"I've been awful worried about Fanny—ever since the night of the fair," she confessed. "He was here all that afternoon and stayed to tea; don't you remember? And they were just as happy together—I guess I can tell! But he ain't been near her since."

She paused to wipe her eyes on a corner of her gingham apron.

"Fanny thought—at least I sort of imagined Mr. Elliot didn't like the way you treated him that night," she went on piteously. "You're kind of short in your ways, Jim, if you don't like anybody; don't you know you are?"

The young man had thrust his hands deep in his trousers' pockets and was glowering at the dough on the molding board.

"That's rotten nonsense, mother," he burst out. "Do you suppose, if a man's really in love with a girl, he's going to care a cotton hat about the way her brother treats him? You don't know much about men if you think so. No; you're on the wrong track. It wasn't my fault."

His mother's tragic dark eyes entreated him timidly.

"I'm awfully afraid Fanny's let herself get all wrapped up in the minister," she half whispered. "And if he—"

"I'd like to thrash him!" interrupted her son in a low tense voice. "He's a white-livered, cowardly hypocrite, that's my name for Wesley Elliot!"

"But, Jim, that ain't goin' to help Fanny—what you think of Mr. Elliot. And anyway, it ain't so. It's something else. Do you—suppose, you could—You wouldn't like to—to speak to him, Jim—would you?"

"What! speak to that fellow about my sister? Why, mother, you must be crazy! What could I say?—'My sister Fanny is in love with you; and I don't think you're treating her right.' Is that your idea?"

"Hush, Jim! Don't talk so loud. She might hear you."

"No danger of that, mother; she was lying on her bed, her face in the pillow, when I looked in her room ten minutes ago. Said she had a headache and wasn't going."

Mrs. Dodge drew a deep, dispirited sigh.

"If there was only something a body could do," she began. "You might get into conversation with him, kind of careless, couldn't you, Jim? And then you might mention that he hadn't been to see us for two weeks— 'course you'd put it real cautious, then perhaps he—"

A light hurried step on the stair warned them to silence; the door was pushed open and Fanny Dodge entered the kitchen. She was wearing the freshly ironed white dress, garnished with crisp pink ribbons; her cheeks were brilliant with color, her pretty head poised high.

"I changed my mind," said she, in a hard, sweet voice. "I decided I'd go, after all. My—my head feels better."

Mother and son exchanged stealthy glances behind the girl's back as she leaned toward the cracked mirror between the windows, apparently intent upon capturing an airy tendril of hair which had escaped confinement.

"That's real sensible, Fanny," approved Mrs. Dodge with perfunctory cheerfulness. "I want you should go out all you can, whilst you're young, an' have a good time."

Jim Dodge was silent; but the scowl between his eyes deepened.

Mrs. Dodge formed three words with her lips, as she shook her head at him warningly.

Fanny burst into a sudden ringing laugh.

"Oh, I can see you in the glass, mother," she cried. "I don't care what Jim says to me; he can say anything he likes."

"Oh, I can see you in the glass, mother," she cried

Her beautiful face, half turned over her shoulder, quivered slightly.

"If you knew how I—" she began, then stopped short.

"That's just what I was saying to Jim," put in her mother eagerly.

The girl flung up both hands in a gesture of angry protest.

"Please don't talk about me, mother—to Jim, or anybody. Do you hear?"

Her voice shrilled suddenly loud and harsh, like an untuned string under the bow.

Jim Dodge flung his hat on his head with an impatient exclamation.

"Come on, Fan," he said roughly. "Nobody's going to bother you. Don't you worry."

Mrs. Dodge had gone back to her kneading board and was thumping the dough with regular slapping motions of her capable hands, but her thin dark face was drawn into a myriad folds and puckers of anxiety.

Fanny stooped and brushed the lined forehead with her fresh young lips.

"Goodnight, mother," said she. "I wish you were going."

She drew back a little and looked down at her mother, smiling brilliantly.

"And don't you worry another minute about me, mother," she said resolutely. "I'm all right."

"Oh, I do hope so, child," returned her mother, sniffing back her ready tears. "I'd hate to feel that you—"

The girl hurried to the door, where her brother stood watching her.

"Come on, Jim," she said. "We have to stop for Ellen."

She followed him down the narrow path to the gate, holding her crisp white skirts well away from the dew-drenched border. As the two emerged upon the road, lying white before them under the brilliant moonlight, Fanny glanced up timidly at her brother's dimly seen profile under the downward sweep of his hat-brim.

"It's real dusty, isn't it?" said she, by way of breaking a silence she found unbearable. "It'll make my shoes look horrid."

"Walk over on the side more," advised Jim laconically.

"Then I'll get in with all those weeds; they're covered with dust and wet, besides," objected Fanny.... "Say, Jim!"

"Well?"

"Wouldn't it be nice if we had an auto, then I could step in, right in front of the house, and keep as clean as—"

The young man laughed.

"Wouldn't you like an aëroplane better, Fan? I believe I would."

"You could keep it in the barn; couldn't you, Jim?"

"No," derided Jim, "the barn isn't what you'd call up-to-date. I require a hangar—or whatever you call 'em."

The girl smothered a sigh.

"If we weren't so poor—" she began.

"Well?"

"Oh—lots of things.... They say that Orr girl has heaps of money."

"Who says so?" demanded her brother roughly.

"Why, everybody. Joyce Fulsom told me her father said so; and he ought to know. Do you suppose—?"

"Do I suppose what?"

Jim's tone was almost savage.

"What's the matter with you, Jim?"

Fanny's sweet voice conveyed impatience, almost reproach. It was as if she had said to her brother, "You know how I must feel, and yet you are cross with me."

Jim glanced down at her, sudden relenting in his heart.

"I was just thinking it's pretty hard lines for both of us," said he. "If we were rich and could come speeding into town in a snappy auto, our clothes in the latest style, I guess things would be different. There's no use talking, Fan; there's mighty little chance for our sort. And if there's one thing I hate more than another it's what folks call sympathy."

"So do I!" cried Fanny. "I simply can't bear it to know that people are saying behind my back, 'There's *poor* Fanny Dodge; I wonder—' Then they squeeze your hand, and gaze at you and sigh. Even mother—I want you to tell mother I'm not—that it isn't true—I can't talk to her, Jim."

"I'll put her wise," said Jim gruffly.

After a pause, during which both walked faster than before, he said hurriedly, as if the words broke loose:

"Don't you give that fellow another thought, Fan. He isn't worth it!"

The girl started like a blooded horse under the whip. She did not pretend to misunderstand.

"I know you never liked him, Jim," she said after a short silence.

"You bet I didn't! Forget him, Fan. That's all I have to say."

"But—if I only knew what it was—I must have done something—said something— I keep wondering and wondering. I can't help it, Jim."

There was an irrepressible sob in the girl's voice.

"Come, Fan, pull yourself together," he urged. "Here's Ellen waiting for us by the gate. Don't for heaven's sake give yourself away. Keep a stiff upper lip, old girl!"

"Well, I thought you two were never coming!" Ellen's full rich voice floated out to them, as they came abreast of the Dix homestead nestled back among tall locust trees.

The girl herself daintily picked her way toward them among the weeds by the roadside. She uttered a little cry of dismay as a stray branch caught in her muslin skirts.

"That's the sign of a beau, Ellen," laughed Fanny, with extravagant gayety. "The bigger the stick the handsomer and richer the beau."

"What made you so late?" inquired Ellen, as all three proceeded on their way, the two girls linked affectionately arm in arm; Jim Dodge striding in the middle of the road a little apart from his companions.

"Oh, I don't know," fibbed Fanny. "I guess I was slow starting to dress. The days are so long now I didn't realize how late it was getting."

Ellen glanced sympathizingly at her friend.

"I was afraid you wouldn't want to come, Fanny," she murmured, "Seeing the social is at Mrs. Solomon Black's house."

"Why shouldn't I want to come?" demanded Fanny aggressively.

"Well, I didn't know," replied Ellen.

After a pause she said:

"That Orr girl has really bought the Bolton house; I suppose you heard? It's all settled; and she's going to begin fixing up the place right off. Don't you think it's funny for a girl like her to want a house all to herself. I should think she'd rather board, as long as she's single."

"Oh, I don't know about that," said Jim Dodge coolly.

"You folks'll get money out of it; so shall we," Ellen went on. "Everybody's so excited! I went down for the mail this afternoon and seemed to me 'most everybody was out in the street talking it over. My! I'd hate to be her tonight."

"Why?" asked Fanny shortly.

"Oh, I don't know. Everybody will be crowding around, asking questions and saying things.... Do you think she's pretty, Jim?"

"Pretty?" echoed the young man.

He shot a keen glance at Ellen Dix from under half-closed lids. The girl's big, black eyes were fixed full upon him; she was leaning forward, a suggestion of timid defiance in the poise of her head.

"Well, that depends," he said slowly. "No, I don't think she's *pretty*."

Ellen burst into a sudden trill of laughter.

"Well, I never!" she exclaimed. "I supposed all the men—"

"But I do think she's beautiful," he finished calmly. "There's a difference, you know."

Ellen Dix tossed her head.

"Oh, is there?" she said airily. "Well, I don't even think she's pretty; do you, Fan?—with all that light hair, drawn back plain from her forehead, and those big, solemn eyes. But I guess she *thinks* she's pretty, all right."

"She doesn't think anything about herself," said Jim doggedly. "She isn't that kind of a girl."

Ellen Dix bit a vexed exclamation short.

"I don't believe any of us know her very well," she said, after a pause. "You know what a gossip Lois Daggett is? Well, I met her and Mrs. Fulsom and Mrs. Whittle coming out of the Daggetts' house. They'd been talking it over; when they saw me they stopped me to ask if I'd been to see Miss Orr, and when I said no, not yet, but I was going, Lois Daggett said, 'Well, I do hope she won't be quite so close-mouthed with you girls. When I asked her, real sympathizing, who she was wearing black for, she said she had lost a dear friend and never even told who it was!'"

Jim Dodge threw back his head and burst into a laugh.

"Served her right," he said.

"You mean Lois?"

"You didn't suppose I meant Miss Orr; did you?"

Jim's voice held a disdainful note which brought the hot color to Ellen's cheeks.

"I'm not so stupid as you seem to think, Jim Dodge," she said, with spirit.

"I never thought you were stupid, Ellen," he returned quickly. "Don't make a mistake and be so now."

Ellen gazed at him in hurt silence. She guessed at his meaning and it humiliated her girlish pride.

It was Fanny who said somewhat impatiently: "I'm sure I can't think what you mean, Jim."

"Well, in my humble opinion, it would be downright stupid for you two girls to fool yourselves into disliking Lydia Orr. She'd like to be friends with everybody; why not give her a chance?"

Again Ellen did not reply; and again it was Fanny who spoke the words that rose to her friend's lips unuttered:

"I can't see how you should know so much about Miss Orr, Jim."

"I don't myself," he returned good-humoredly. "But sometimes a man can see through a woman better—or at least more fair-mindedly than another woman. You see," he added, "there's no sex jealousy in the way."

Both girls cried out in protest against this.

26

It wasn't so, they declared. He ought to be ashamed of himself! As for being *jealous* of any one—Fanny haughtily disclaimed the suggestion, with a bitterness which astonished her friend.

It was something of a relief to all three when the brilliantly illuminated house and grounds belonging to Mrs. Solomon Black came in view. Japanese lanterns in lavish abundance had been strung from tree to tree and outlined the piazza and the walk leading to the house.

"Doesn't it look lovely!" cried Ellen, scattering her vexation to the winds. "I never saw anything so pretty!"

Inside the house further surprises awaited them; the music of harp and violins stole pleasantly through the flower-scented rooms, which were softly lighted with shaded lamps the like of which Brookville had never seen before.

Mrs. Solomon Black, arrayed in a crisp blue taffeta, came bustling to meet them. But not before Fanny's swift gaze had penetrated the assembled guests. Yes! there was Wesley Elliot's tall figure. He was talking to Mrs. Henry Daggett at the far end of the double parlors.

"Go right up stairs and lay off your things," urged their hostess hospitably. "Ladies to the right; gents to the left. I'm so glad you came, Fanny. I'd begun to wonder—"

The girl's lip curled haughtily. The slight emphasis on the personal pronoun and the fervid squeeze of Mrs. Black's fat hand hurt her sore heart. But she smiled brilliantly.

"Thank you, Mrs. Black, I wouldn't have missed it for worlds!" she said coldly.

Chapter VII

"Does my hair look decent?" asked Ellen, as the two girls peered into the mirror together. "The dew does take the curl out so. It must be lovely to have naturally curly hair, like yours, Fanny. It looks all the prettier for being damp and ruffled up."

Fanny was pulling out the fluffy masses of curling brown hair about her forehead.

"Your hair looks all right, Ellen," she said absent-mindedly.

She was wondering if Wesley Elliot would speak to her.

"I saw that Orr girl," whispered Ellen; "she's got on a white dress, all lace, and a black sash. She does look pretty, Fanny; we'll have to acknowledge it."

"Ye-es," murmured Fanny who was drawing on a pair of fresh white gloves.

"You aren't going to wear those gloves down stairs, are you, Fan? I haven't got any."

"My hands are all stained up with currant jelly," explained Fanny hurriedly. "Your hands are real pretty, Ellen."

Ellen glanced down at her capable, brown hands, with their blunt finger-tips.

"Did you ever notice *her* hands, Fanny?"

Fanny shook her head.

"Her nails are cut kind of pointed, and all shined up. And her hands are so little and soft and white. I suppose a man—do you think Jim would notice that sort of thing, Fanny?"

Fanny snapped the fastenings of her gloves.

"Let's go down stairs," she suggested. "They'll be wondering what's become of us."

"Say, Fan!"

Ellen Dix caught at her friend's arm, her pretty face, with its full pouting lips and brilliant dark eyes upturned. "Well?"

"Do you suppose— You don't think Jim is mad at me for what I said about *her*, do you?"

"I don't remember you said anything to make anybody mad. Come, let's go down, Ellen."

"But, Fan, I was wondering if that girl— Do you know I—I kind of wish she hadn't come to Brookville. Everything seems—different, already. Don't you think so, Fanny?"

"Oh, I don't know. Why should you think about it? She's here and there's no use. I'm going down, Ellen."

Fanny moved toward the stairs, her fresh young beauty heightened by an air of dignified reserve which Ellen Dix had failed to penetrate.

Wesley Elliot, who had by now reached the wide opening into the hall in the course of his progress among the guests, glanced up as Fanny Dodge swept the last step of the stair with her unfashionable white gown.

"Why, good evening, Miss Dodge," he exclaimed, with commendable presence of mind, seeing the heart under his waistcoat had executed an uncomfortable *pas seul* at sight of her.

He held out his hand with every appearance of cordial welcome, and after an instant's hesitation Fanny laid her gloved fingers in it. She had meant to avoid his direct gaze, but somehow his glance had caught and held her own. What were his eyes saying to her? She blushed and trembled under the soft dark fire of them. In that instant she appeared so wholly adorable, so temptingly sweet that the young man felt his prudent resolves slipping away from him one by one. Had they been alone—...

But, no; Ellen Dix, her piquant, provokingly pretty face tip-tilted with ardent curiosity, was just behind. In another moment he was saying, in the easy, pleasant way everybody liked, that he was glad to see Ellen; and how was Mrs. Dix, this evening? And why wasn't she there?

Ellen replied demurely that it had been given out on Sunday as a young people's social; so her mother thought she wasn't included.

They entered the crowded room, where Deacon Whittle was presently heard declaring that he felt just as young as anybody, so he "picked up mother and came right along with Joe." And Mrs. Daggett, whose placid face had lighted with pleasure at sight of Fanny and Ellen, proclaimed that when the day came for *her* to stay at home from a young folks' social she hoped they'd bury her, right off.

So the instant—psychological or otherwise—passed. But Fanny Dodge's heavy heart was beating hopefully once more.

"If I could only see him alone," she was thinking. "He would explain everything."

Her thoughts flew onward to the moment when she would come down stairs once more, cloaked for departure. Perhaps Wesley—she ventured to call him Wesley in her joyously confused thoughts—perhaps Wesley would walk home with her as on other occasions not long past. Jim, she reflected, could go with Ellen.

Then all at once she came upon Lydia Orr, in her simple white dress, made with an elegant simplicity which convicted every girl in the room of dowdiness. She was talking with Judge Fulsom, who was slowly consuming a huge saucer of ice-cream, with every appearance of enjoyment.

"As I understand it, my dear young lady, you wish to employ Brookville talent exclusively in repairing your house," Fanny heard him saying, between smacking mouthfuls.

And Lydia Orr replied, "Yes, if you please, I do want everything to be done here. There are people who can, aren't there?"

When she saw that Fanny had paused and was gazing at her doubtfully, her hand went out with a smile, wistful and timid and sincere, all at once. There was something so appealing in the girl's upturned face, an honesty of purpose so crystal-clear in her lovely eyes, that Fanny, still confused and uncertain whether to be happy or not, was irresistibly drawn to her. She thought for a fleeting instant she would like to take Lydia Orr away to some dim secluded spot and there pour out her heart. The next minute she was ready to laugh at herself for entertaining so absurd an idea. She glanced down at Lydia's ungloved hands, which Ellen Dix had just described, and reflected soberly that Wesley Elliot sat at table with those dainty pink-tipped fingers three times each day. She had not answered Ellen's foolish little questions; but now she felt sure that any man, possessed of his normal faculties, could hardly fail to become aware of Lydia Orr's delicate beauty.

Fanny compelled herself to gaze with unprejudiced eyes at the fair transparent skin, with the warm color coming and going beneath it, at the masses of blond hair drawn softly back from the high round forehead, at the large blue eyes beneath the long sweep of darker lashes, at the exquisite curve of the lips and the firmly modeled chin. Yes; Jim had seen truly; the ordinary adjective "pretty"—applicable alike to a length of ribbon, a gown, or a girl of the commoner type—could not be applied to Lydia Orr. She was beautiful to the discerning eye, and Fanny unwillingly admitted it.

Lydia Orr, unabashed by the girl's frank inspection, returned her gaze with beaming friendliness.

"Did you know I'd bought a house?" she asked. "It's old and needs a lot of repairing; so I was just asking Judge Fulsom—"

"Deacon Amos Whittle is, so to say, a contractor," said the Judge ponderously, "and so, in a way, am I."

"A contractor?" puzzled Lydia. "Yes; but I—"

"If you'll just give over everything into our hands connected with putting the old place into A-number-one shape, I think you'll find you can dismiss the whole matter from your mind. In two months' time, my dear young lady, we'll guarantee to pass the house over to you in apple-pie order, good as new, if not better.... Yes, indeed; better!"

The Judge eyed his empty saucer regretfully.

"That's the best ice cream—" he added with total irrelevance. "Have some, won't you? I hear they're passing it out free and permiscuous in the back room."

"I think we should like some cream, if you please, Judge Fulsom," said Lydia, "if you'll keep us company."

"Oh, I'll keep company with you, as far as strawberry ice cream's concerned," chuckled the Judge, his big bulk shaking with humor. "But I see Mis' Fulsom over there; she's got her weather eye on us. Now, watch me skeedaddle for that cream! Pink, white or brown, Miss Orr; or, all three mixed? There's a young fellow out there in charge of the freezers that sure is a wonder. How about you, Fanny?"

The two girls looked at each other with a smile of understanding as the big figure of the Judge moved ponderously away.

"We never had ice cream before at a church sociable," said Fanny. "And I didn't know Mrs. Solomon Black had so many lanterns. Did you buy all this?"

Her gesture seemed to include the shaded lamps, the masses of flowers and trailing vines, the gay strains of music, and the plentiful refreshments which nearly every one was enjoying.

"It's just like a regular party," she added. "We're not used to such things in Brookville."

"Do you like it?" Lydia asked, doubtfully.

"Why, of course," returned Fanny, the color rising swiftly to her face.

She had caught a glimpse of Wesley Elliot edging his way past a group of the younger boys and girls, mad with the revelry of unlimited cake and ice cream. He was coming directly toward their corner; his eyes, alas! fixed upon the stranger in their midst. Unconsciously Fanny sighed deeply; the corners of her smiling lips drooped. She appeared all at once like a lovely rose which some one has worn for an hour and cast aside.

"It's such a little thing to do," murmured Lydia.

Then, before Fanny was aware of her intention, she had slipped away. At the same moment Judge Fulsom made his appearance, elbowing his smiling way through the crowd, a brimming saucer of vari-colored ice cream in each hand.

"Here we are!" he announced cheerfully. "Had to get a *habeas corpus* on this ice cream, though. Why, what's become of Miss Orr? Gone with a handsomer man—eh?"

He stared humorously at the minister.

"Twa'n't you, dominie; seen' you're here. Had any ice cream yet? No harm done, if you have. Seems to be a plenty. Take this, parson, and I'll replevin another plate for myself and one for Miss Orr. Won't be gone more'n another hour."

Fanny, piteously tongue-tied in the presence of the man she loved, glanced up at Wesley Elliot with a timidity she had never before felt in his company. His eyes under close-drawn brows were searching the crowd. Fanny divined that she was not in his thoughts.

"If you are looking for Miss Orr," she said distinctly, "I think she has gone out in the kitchen. I saw Mrs. Solomon Black beckon to her."

The minister glanced down at her; his rash impulse of an hour back was already forgotten.

"Don't you think it's awfully warm in here?" continued Fanny.

A sudden desperate desire had assailed her; she must—she would compel him to some sort of an explanation.

"It's a warm evening," commented the minister. "But why not eat your cream? You'll find it will cool you off."

"I—I don't care much for ice cream," said Fanny, in a low tremulous voice.

She gazed at him, her dark eyes brimming with eager questions.

"I was wondering if we couldn't—it's pleasant out in the yard—"

"If you'll excuse me for just a moment, Miss Dodge," Wesley Elliot's tone was blandly courteous—"I'll try and find you a chair. They appear to be scarce articles; I believe the ladies removed most of them to the rear of the house. Pardon me—"

He set down his plate of ice cream on the top shelf of Mrs. Solomon Black's what-not, thereby deranging a careful group of sea-shells and daguerreotypes, and walked quickly away.

Fanny's face flushed to a painful crimson; then as suddenly paled. She was a proud girl, accustomed to love and admiration since early childhood, when she had queened it over her playmates because her yellow curls were longer than theirs, her cheeks pinker, her eyes brighter and her slim, strong body taller. Fanny had never been compelled to stoop from her graceful height to secure masculine attention. It had been hers by a sort of divine right. She had not been at all surprised when the handsome young minister had looked at her twice, thrice, to every other girl's once, nor when he had singled her out from the others in the various social events of the country side.

Fanny had long ago resolved, in the secret of her own heart, that she would never, never become the hard-worked wife of a plodding farmer. Somewhere in the world—riding toward her on the steed of his passionate desire—was the fairy prince; her prince, coming to lift her out from the sordid commonplace of life in Brookville. Almost from the very first she had recognized Wesley Elliot as her deliverer.

Once he had said to her: "I have a strange feeling that I have known you always." She had cherished the saying in her heart, hoping—believing that it might, in some vague, mysterious way, be true. And not at all aware that this pretty sentiment is as old as the race and the merest banality on the masculine tongue, signifying: "At this moment I am drawn to you, as to no other woman; but an hour hence it may be otherwise." ... How else may man, as yet imperfectly monogamous, find the mate for whom he is ever ardently questing? In this woman he finds the trick of a lifted lash, or a shadowy dimple in the melting rose of her cheek. In another, the stately curve of neck and shoulder and the somber fire of dark eyes draws his roving gaze; in a third, there is a soft, adorable prettiness, like that of a baby. He has always known them—all. And thus it is, that love comes and goes unbidden, like the wind which blows where it listeth; and woman, hearing the sound thereof, cannot tell whence it cometh nor whither it goeth.

In this particular instance Wesley Elliot had not chosen to examine the secret movements of his own mind. Baldly speaking, he had cherished a fleeting fancy for Fanny Dodge, a sort of love in idleness, which comes to a man like the delicate, floating seeds of the parasite orchid, capable indeed of exquisite blossoming; but deadly to the tree upon which it fastens. He had resolved to free himself. It was a sensible resolve. He was glad he had made up his mind to it before it was too late. Upon the possible discomfiture of Fanny Dodge he bestowed but a single thought: She would get over it. "It" meaning a quite pardonable fancy—he refused to give it a more specific name—for himself. To the unvoiced opinions of Mrs. Solomon Black, Mrs. Deacon Whittle, Ellen Dix, Mrs. Abby Daggett and all the other women of his parish he was wholly indifferent. Men, he was glad to remember, never bothered their heads about another man's love affairs....

The chairs from the sitting room had been removed to the yard, where they were grouped about small tables adequately illuminated by the moon and numerous Japanese lanterns. Every second chair appeared to be filled by a giggling, pink-cheeked girl; the others being suitably occupied by youths of the opposite sex—all pleasantly occupied. The minister conscientiously searched for the chair he had promised to fetch to Fanny Dodge; but it never once occurred to him to bring Fanny out to the cool loveliness of mingled moon and lantern-light. There was no unoccupied chair, as he quickly discovered; but he came presently upon Lydia Orr, apparently doing nothing at all. She was standing near Mrs. Black's boundary picket fence, shielded from the observation of the joyous groups about the little tables by the down-dropping branches of an apple-tree.

"I was looking for you!" said Wesley Elliot.

It was the truth; but it surprised him nevertheless. He supposed he had been looking for a chair.

"Were you?" said Lydia, smiling.

She moved a little away from him.

"I must go in," she murmured.

"Why must you? It's delightful out here—so cool and—"

"Yes, I know. But the others— Why not bring Miss Dodge out of that hot room? I thought she looked tired."

"I didn't notice," he said.... "Just look at that flock of little white clouds up there with the moon shining through them!"

Lydia glided away over the soft grass.

"I've been looking at them for a long time," she said gently. "I must go now and help cut more cake."

He made a gesture of disgust.

"They're fairly stuffing," he complained. "And, anyway, there are plenty of women to attend to all that. I want to talk to you, Miss Orr."

His tone was authoritative.

She turned her head and looked at him.

"To talk to me?" she echoed.

"Yes; come back—for just a minute. I know what you're thinking: that it's my duty to be talking to parishioners. Well, I've been doing that all the evening. I think I'm entitled to a moment of relaxation; don't you?"

"I'm a parishioner," she reminded him.

30

"So you are," he agreed joyously. "And I haven't had a word with you this evening, so far; so you see it's my duty to talk to you; and it's your duty to listen."

"Well?" she murmured.

Her face upturned to his in the moonlight wore the austere loveliness of a saint's.

Her face, upturned to his in the moonlight, wore the austere loveliness of a saint's

"I wish you'd tell me something," he said, his fine dark eyes taking in every detail of delicate tint and outline. "Do you know it all seems very strange and unusual to me—your coming to Brookville the way you did, and doing so much to—to make the people here happy."

She drew a deep, sighing breath.

"I'm afraid it isn't going to be easy," she said slowly. "I thought it would be; but—"

"Then you came with that intention," he inferred quickly. "You meant to do it from the beginning. But just what was the beginning? What ever attracted your attention to this forlorn little place?"

She was silent for a moment, her eyes downcast. Then she smiled.

"I might ask you the same question," she said at last. "Why did you come to Brookville, Mr. Elliot?"

He made an impatient gesture.

"Oh, that is easily explained. I had a call to Brookville."

"So did I," she murmured. "Yes; I think that was the reason—if there must be a reason."

"There is always a reason for everything," he urged. "But you didn't understand me. Do you know I couldn't say this to another soul in Brookville; but I'm going to tell you: I wanted to live and work in a big city, and I tried to find a church—"

"Yes; I know," she said, unexpectedly. "One can't always go where one wishes to go, just at first. Things turn out that way, sometimes."

"They seemed to want me here in Brookville," he said, with some bitterness. "It was a last resort, for me. I might have taken a position in a school; but I couldn't bring myself to that. I'd dreamed of preaching—to big audiences."

She smiled at him, with a gentle sidewise motion of the head.

"God lets us do things, if we want to hard enough," she told him quite simply.

"Do you believe that?" he cried. "Perhaps you'll think it strange for me to ask; but do you?"

A great wave of emotion seemed to pass over her quiet face. He saw it alter strangely under his gaze. For an instant she stood transfigured; smiling, without word or movement. Then the inward light subsided. She was only an ordinary young woman, once more, upon whom one might bestow an indulgent smile—so simple, even childlike she was, in her unaffected modesty.

"I really must go in," she said apologetically, "and help them cut the cake."

Chapter VIII

Jim Dodge had been hoeing potatoes all day. It was hard, monotonous work, and he secretly detested it. But the hunting season was far away, and the growing potatoes were grievously beset by weeds; so he had cut and thrust with his sharp-bladed hoe from early morning till the sun burned the crest of the great high-shouldered hill which appeared to close in the valley like a rampart, off Grenoble way. As a matter of fact, the brawling stream which gave Brookville its name successfully skirted the hill by a narrow margin which likewise afforded space for the state road.

But the young man was not considering either the geographical contours of the country at large or the refreshed and renovated potato field, with its serried ranks of low-growing plants, as he tramped heavily crosslots toward the house. At noon, when he came in to dinner, in response to the wideflung summons of the tin horn which hung by the back door, he had found the two women of his household in a pleasurable state of excitement.

"We've got our share, Jim!" proclaimed Mrs. Dodge, a bright red spot glowing on either thin cheek. "See! here's the check; it came in the mail this morning."

And she spread a crackling bit of paper under her son's eyes.

"I was some surprised to get it so soon," she added. "Folks ain't generally in any great hurry to part with their money. But they do say Miss Orr paid right down for the place—never even asked 'em for any sort of terms; and th' land knows they'd have been glad to given them to her, or to anybody that had bought the place these dozen years back. Likely she didn't know that."

Jim scowled at the check.

"How much did she pay for the place?" he demanded. "It must have been a lot more than it was worth, judging from this."

"I don't know," Mrs. Dodge replied. "And I dunno as I care particularly, as long's we've got our share of it."

She was swaying back and forth in a squeaky old rocking-chair, the check clasped in both thin hands.

"Shall we bank it, children; or draw it all out in cash? Fanny needs new clothes; so do you, Jim. And I've got to have a new carpet, or something, for the parlor. Those skins of wild animals you brought in are all right, Jim, if one can't get anything better. I suppose we'd ought to be prudent and saving; but I declare we haven't had any money to speak of, for so long—"

Mrs. Dodge's faded eyes were glowing with joy; she spread the check upon her lap and gazed at it smilingly.

"I declare it's the biggest surprise I've had in all my life!"

"Let's spend every cent of it," proposed Fanny recklessly. "We didn't know we were going to have it. We can scrub along afterward the same as we always have. Let's divide it into four parts: one for the house—to fix it up—and one for each of us, to spend any way we like. What do you say, Jim?"

"I shouldn't wonder if Mrs. Deacon Whittle would furnish up her best parlor something elegant," surmised Mrs. Dodge. "She's always said she was goin' to have gilt paper and marble tops and electric blue plush upholstered furniture. I guess that'll be the last fair we'll ever have in that house. She wouldn't have everybody trampin' over her flowered Body-Brussels. I suppose *we* might buy some plush furniture; but I don't know as I'd care for electric blue. What do you think, son?"

Jim Dodge sat sprawled out in his chair before the half-set table. At this picture of magnificence, about to be realized in the abode of Deacon Amos Whittle, he gave vent to an inarticulate growl.

"What's the matter with you, Jim?" shrilled his mother, whose perpetually jangled nerves were capable of strange dissonances. "Anybody'd suppose you wasn't pleased at having the old Bolton place sold at last, and a little bit of all that's been owing to us since before your poor father died, paid off. My! If we was to have all that was coming to us by rights, with the interest money—"

"I'm hungry and tired, mother, and I want my dinner," said Jim brusquely. "That check won't hoe the potatoes; so I guess I'll have to do it, same as usual."

"For pity sake, Fanny!" cried his mother, "did you put the vegetables over to boil? I ain't thought of anything since this check came."

It appeared that Fanny had been less forgetful.

After his belated dinner, Jim had gone back to his potatoes, leaving his mother and sister deep in discussion over the comparative virtues of Nottingham lace and plain muslin, made up with ruffles, for parlor curtains.

"I really believe I'd rather spend more on the house than on clo'es at my age," he heard his mother saying, happily, as he strode away.

All during the afternoon, to the clink of myriad small stones against the busy blade of his hoe, Jim thought about Lydia Orr. He could not help seeing that it was to Lydia he owed the prospect of a much needed suit of clothes. It would be Lydia who hung curtains, of whatever sort, in their shabby best room. And no other than Lydia was to furnish Mrs. Whittle's empty parlor. She had already given the minister a new long-tailed coat, as Jim chose to characterize the ministerial black. His cheeks burned under the slanting rays of the afternoon sun with something deeper than an added coat of tan. Why should Lydia Orr—that slip of a girl, with the eyes of a baby, or a saint—do all this? Jim found himself unable to believe that she really wanted the Bolton place. Why, the house was an uninhabitable ruin! It would cost thousands of dollars to rebuild it.

He set his jaw savagely as he recalled his late conversation with Deacon Whittle. "The cheating old skinflint," as he mentally termed that worthy pillar of the church, had, he was sure, bamboozled the girl into buying a well-nigh worthless property, at a scandalous price. It was a shame! He, Jim Dodge, even now burned with the shame of it. He pondered briefly the possibilities of taking from his mother the check, which represented the *pro rata* share of the Dodge estate, and returning it to Lydia Orr. Reluctantly he abandoned this quixotic scheme. The swindle—for as such he chose to view it—had already been accomplished. Other people would not return their checks. On the contrary, there would be new and fertile schemes set on foot to part the unworldly stranger and her money.

He flung down his hoe in disgust and straightened his aching shoulders. The whole sordid transaction put him in mind of the greedy onslaught of a horde of hungry ants on a beautiful, defenseless flower, its torn corolla exuding sweetness.... And there must be some sort of reason behind it. Why had Lydia Orr come to Brookville?

And here, unwittingly, Jim's blind conjectures followed those of Wesley Elliot. He had told Lydia Orr he meant to call upon her. That he had not yet accomplished his purpose had been due to the watchfulness of Mrs. Solomon Black. On the two occasions when he had rung Mrs. Black's front door-bell, that lady herself had appeared in response to its summons. On both occasions she had informed Mr. Dodge tartly that Miss Orr wasn't at home.

On the occasion of his second disappointment he had offered to await the young lady's home-coming.

"There ain't no use of that, Jim," Mrs. Black had assured him. "Miss Orr's gone t' Boston to stay two days."

Then she had unlatched her close-shut lips to add: "She goes there frequent, on business."

Her eyes appeared to inform him further that Miss Orr's business, of whatever nature, was none of *his* business and never would be.

"That old girl is down on me for some reason or other," he told himself ruefully, as he walked away for the second time. But he was none the less resolved to pursue his hopefully nascent friendship with Lydia Orr.

He was thinking of her vaguely as he walked toward the house which had been his father's, and where he and Fanny had been born. It was little and low and old, as he viewed it indifferently in the fading light of the sunset sky. Its walls had needed painting so long, that for years nobody had even mentioned the subject. Its picturesquely mossy roof leaked. But a leaky roof was a commonplace in Brookville. It was customary to set rusty tin pans, their holes stopped with rags, under such spots as actually let in water; the emptying of the pans being a regular household "chore." Somehow, he found himself disliking to enter; his mother and Fanny would still be talking about the disposition of Lydia Orr's money. To his relief he found his sister alone in the kitchen, which served as a general living room. The small square table neatly spread for two stood against the wall; Fanny was standing by the window, her face close to the pane, and apparently intent upon the prospect without, which comprised a grassy stretch of yard flanked by a dull rampart of over-grown lilac bushes.

"Where's mother?" inquired Jim, as he hung his hat on the accustomed nail.

"She went down to the village," said Fanny, turning her back on the window with suspicious haste. "There was a meeting of the sewing society at Mrs. Daggett's."

"Good Lord!" exclaimed Jim. "What an opportunity!"

"Opportunity?" echoed Fanny vaguely.

"Yes; for talking it over. Can't you imagine the clack of tongues; the 'I says to *her*,' and 'she told *me*,' and 'what *do* you think!'"

"Don't be sarcastic and disagreeable, Jim," advised Fanny, with some heat. "When you think of it, it *is* a wonder—that girl coming here the way she did; buying out the fair, just as everybody was discouraged over it. And now—"

"How do you explain it, Fan?" asked her brother.

"Explain it? I can't explain it. Nobody seems to know anything about her, except that she's from Boston and seems to have heaps of money."

Jim was wiping his hands on the roller-towel behind the door.

"I had a chance to annex a little more of Miss Orr's money today," he observed grimly. "But I haven't made up my mind yet whether to do it, or not."

Fanny laughed and shrugged her shoulders.

"If you don't, somebody else will," she replied. "It was Deacon Whittle, wasn't it? He stopped at the house this afternoon and wanted to know where to find you."

"They're going right to work on the old place, and there's plenty to do for everybody, including yours truly, at four dollars a day."

"What sort of work?" inquired Fanny.

"All sorts: pulling down and building up; clearing away and replanting. The place is a jungle, you know. But four dollars a day! It's like taking candy from a baby."

"It sounds like a great deal," said the girl. "But why shouldn't you do it?"

Jim laughed.

"Why, indeed? I might earn enough to put a shingle or two on our own roof. It looks like honest money; but—"

Fanny was busy putting the finishing touches to the supper table.

"Mother's going to stop for tea at Mrs. Daggett's, and go to prayer meeting afterward," she said. "We may as well eat."

The two sat down, facing each other.

"What did you mean, Jim?" asked Fanny, as she passed the bread plate to her brother. "You said, 'It looks like honest money; but—'"

"I guess I'm a fool," he grumbled; "but there's something about the whole business I don't like.... Have some of this apple sauce, Fan?"

The girl passed her plate for a spoonful of the thick compound, and in return shoved the home-dried beef toward her brother.

"I don't see anything queer about it," she replied dully. "I suppose a person with money might come to Brookville and want to buy a house. The old Bolton place used to be beautiful, mother says. I suppose it can be again. And if she chooses to spend her money that way—"

"That's just the point I can't see: why on earth should she want to saddle herself with a proposition like that?"

Fanny's mute lips trembled. She was thinking she knew very well why Lydia Orr had chosen to come to Brookville: in some way unknown to Fanny, Miss Orr had chanced to meet the incomparable Wesley Elliot, and had straightway set her affections upon him. Fanny had been thinking it over, ever since the night of the social at Mrs. Solomon Black's. Up to the moment when Wesley—she couldn't help calling him Wesley still—had left her, on pretense of fetching a chair, she had instantly divined that it was a pretense, and of course he had not returned. Her cheeks tingled hotly as she recalled the way in which Joyce Fulsom had remarked the plate of melting ice cream on the top shelf of Mrs. Black's what-not:

"I guess Mr. Elliot forgot his cream," the girl had said, with a spark of malice. "I saw him out in the yard awhile ago talking to that Miss Orr."

Fanny had humiliated herself still further by pretending she didn't know it was the minister who had left his ice cream to dissolve in a pink and brown puddle of sweetness. Whereat Joyce Fulsom had giggled disagreeably.

"Better keep your eye on him, Fan," she had advised.

Of course she couldn't speak of this to Jim; but it was all plain enough to her.

"I'm going down to the village for awhile, Fan," her brother said, as he arose from the table. But he did not, as was his custom, invite her to accompany him.

After Jim had gone, Fanny washed the dishes with mechanical swiftness. Her mother had asked her if she would come to prayer meeting, and walk home with her afterwards. Not that Mrs. Dodge was timid; the neighborhood of Brookville had never been haunted after nightfall by anything more dangerous than whippoorwills and frogs. A plaintive chorus of night sounds greeted the girl, as she stepped out into the darkness. How sweet the honeysuckle and late roses smelled under the dew! Fanny walked slowly across the yard to the old summer-house, where the minister had asked her to call him Wesley, and sat down. It was very dark under the thick-growing vines, and after awhile tranquillity of a sort stole over the girl's spirit. She gazed out into the dim spaces beyond the summer-house and thought, with a curious detachment, of all that had happened. It was as if she had grown old and was looking back calmly to a girlhood long since past. She could almost smile at the recollection of herself stifling her sobs in her pillow, lest Jim should hear.

"Why should I care for him?" she asked herself wonderingly; and could not tell.

Then all at once she found herself weeping softly, her head on the rickety table.

Jim Dodge, too intently absorbed in his own confused thoughts to pay much attention to Fanny, had walked resolutely in the direction of Mrs. Solomon Black's house; from which, he reflected, the minister would be obliged to absent himself for at least an hour. He hoped Mrs. Black had not induced Lydia to go to the prayer meeting with her. Why any one should voluntarily go to a prayer meeting passed his comprehension. Jim had once attended what was known as a "protracted meeting," for the sole purpose of pleasing his mother, who all at once had appeared tearfully anxious about his "soul." He had not enjoyed the experience.

"Are you saved, my dear young brother?" Deacon Whittle had inquired of him, in his snuffling, whining, peculiarly objectionable tone.

"From what, Deacon?" Jim had blandly inquired. "You in for it, too?"

Whereat the Deacon had piously shaken his head and referred him to the "mourner's pew," with the hope that he might even yet be plucked as a brand from the burning.

Lydia had not gone to the prayer meeting. She was sitting on the piazza, quite alone. She arose when her determined visitor boldly walked up the steps.

"Oh, it is you!" said she.

An unreasonable feeling of elation arose in the young man's breast.

"Did you think I wasn't coming?" he inquired, with all the egotism of which he had been justly accused.

He did not wait for her reply; but proceeded with considerable humor to describe his previous unsuccessful attempts to see her.

"I suppose," he added, "Mrs. Solomon Black has kindly warned you against me?"

She could not deny it; so smiled instead.

"Well," said the young man, "I give you my word I'm not a villain: I neither drink, steal, nor gamble. But I'm not a saint, after the prescribed Brookville pattern."

He appeared rather proud of the fact, she thought. Aloud she said, with pardonable curiosity:

"What is the Brookville pattern? I ought to know, since I am to live here."

At this he dropped his bantering tone.

"I wanted to talk to you about that," he said gravely.

"You mean—?"

"About your buying the old Bolton place and paying such a preposterous price for it, and all the rest, including the minister's back-pay."

She remained silent, playing with the ribbon of her sash.

"I have a sort of inward conviction that you're not doing it because you think Brookville is such a pleasant place to live in," he went on, keenly observant of the sudden color fluttering in her cheeks, revealed by the light of Mrs. Solomon Black's parlor lamp which stood on a stand just inside the carefully screened window. "It looks," he finished, "as if you—well; it may be a queer thing for me to say; but I'll tell you frankly that when mother showed me the check she got today I felt that it was—charity."

She shook her head.

"Oh, no," she said quickly. "You are quite, quite in the wrong."

"But you can't make me believe that with all your money—pardon me for mentioning what everybody in the village is talking about— You'll have to convince me that the old Bolton place has oil under it, or coal or diamonds, before I—"

"Why should you need to be convinced of anything so unlikely?" she asked, with gentle coldness.

He reddened angrily.

"Of course it's none of my business," he conceded.

"I didn't mean that. But, naturally, I could have no idea of coal or oil—"

"Well; I won't work for you at any four dollars a day," he said loudly. "I thought I'd like to tell you."

"I don't want you to," she said. "Didn't Deacon Whittle give you my message?"

He got hurriedly to his feet with a muttered exclamation.

"Please sit down, Mr. Dodge," she bade him tranquilly. "I've been wanting to see you all day. But there are so few telephones in Brookville it is difficult to get word to people."

He eyed her with stubborn resentment.

"What I meant to say was that four dollars a day is too much! Don't you know anything about the value of money, Miss Orr? Somebody ought to have common honesty enough to inform you that there are plenty of men in Brookville who would be thankful to work for two dollars a day. I would, for one; and I won't take a cent more."

She was frowning a little over these statements. The stalwart young man in shabby clothes who sat facing her under the light of Mrs. Solomon Black's well-trimmed lamp appeared to puzzle her.

"But why shouldn't you want to earn all you can?" she propounded at last. "Isn't there anything you need to use money for?"

"Oh, just a few things," he admitted grudgingly. "I suppose you've noticed that I'm not exactly the glass of fashion and the mold of form."

He was instantly ashamed of himself for the crude personality.

"You must think I'm a fool!" burst from him, under the sting of his self-inflicted lash.

She smiled and shook her head.

"I'm not at all the sort of person you appear to think me," she said. Her grave blue eyes looked straight into his. "But don't let's waste time trying to be clever: I want to ask you if you are willing, for a fair salary, to take charge of the outdoor improvements at Bolton House."

She colored swiftly at sight of the quizzical lift of his brows.

"I've decided to call my place 'Bolton House' for several reasons," she went on rapidly: "for one thing, everybody has always called it the Bolton place, so it will be easier for the workmen and everybody to know what place is meant. Besides, I—"

"Yes; but the name of Bolton has an ill-omened sound in Brookville ears," he objected. "You've no idea how people here hate that man."

"It all happened so long ago, I should think they might forgive him by now," she offered, after a pause.

"I wouldn't call my house after a thief," he said strongly. "There are hundreds of prettier names. Why not— Pine Court, for example?"

"You haven't told me yet if you will accept the position I spoke of."

He passed his hand over his clean-shaven chin, a trick he had inherited from his father, and surveyed her steadily from under meditative brows.

"In the first place, I'm not a landscape gardener, Miss Orr," he stated. "That's the sort of man you want. You can get one in Boston, who'll group your evergreens, open vistas, build pergolas and all that sort of thing."

"You appear to know exactly what I want," she laughed.

"Perhaps I do," he defied her.

"But, seriously, I don't want and won't have a landscape-gardener from Boston—with due deference to your well-formed opinions, Mr. Dodge. I intend to mess around myself, and change my mind every other day about

36

all sorts of things. I want to work things out, not on paper in cold black and white; but in terms of growing things—wild things out of the woods. You understand, I'm sure."

The dawning light in his eyes told her that he did.

"But I've had no experience," he hesitated. "Besides, I've considerable farm-work of my own to do. I've been hoeing potatoes all day. Tomorrow I shall have to go into the cornfield, or lose my crop. Time, tide and weeds wait for no man."

"I supposed you were a hunter," she said. "I thought—"

He laughed unpleasantly.

"Oh, I see," he interrupted rudely: "you supposed, in other words, that I was an idle chap, addicted to wandering about the woods, a gun on my shoulder, a cur—quite as much of a ne'er-do-well as myself—at my heels. Of course Deacon Whittle and Mrs. Solomon Black have told you all about it. And since you've set about reforming Brookville, you thought you'd begin with me. Well, I'm obliged to you; but—"

The girl arose trembling to her feet.

"You are not kind!" she cried. "You are not kind!"

They stood for an instant, gazing into each other's eyes during one of those flashes of time which sometimes count for years.

"Forgive me," he muttered huskily. "I'm a brute at best; but I had no business to speak to you as I did."

"But why did you say—what made you ever think I'd set about reforming—that is what you said— *reforming*—Brookville? I never thought of such a thing! How could I?"

He hung his head, abashed by the lightning in her mild eyes.

She clasped her small, fair hands and bent toward him.

"And you said you wanted to be—friends. I hoped—"

"I do," he said gruffly. "I've told you I'm ashamed of myself."

She drew back, sighing deeply.

"I don't want you to feel—ashamed," she said, in a sweet, tired voice. "But I wish—"

"Tell me!" he urged, when she did not finish her sentence.

"Do you think everybody is going to misunderstand me, as you have?" she asked, somewhat piteously. "Is it so strange and unheard of a thing for a woman to want a home and—and friends? Isn't it allowable for a person who has money to want to pay fair wages? Why should I scrimp and haggle and screw, when I want most of all to be generous?"

"Because," he told her seriously, "scrimping, haggling and screwing have been the fashion for so long, the other thing rouses mean suspicions by its very novelty. It's too good to be true; that's all."

"You mean people will suspect—they'll think there's something—"

She stood before him, her hands fallen at her sides, her eyes downcast.

"I confess I couldn't believe that there wasn't an ulterior motive," he said honestly. "That's where I was less noble than you."

She flashed a sudden strange look at him.

"There is," she breathed. "I'm going to be honest—with you. I have—an ulterior motive."

"Will you tell me what it is?"

Her lips formed the single word of denial.

He gazed at her in silence for a moment.

"I'm going to accept the post you just offered me, Miss Orr; at any salary you think I'm worth," he said gravely.

"Thank you," she murmured.

Steps and the sound of voices floated across the picket fence. The gate rasped on its rusted hinges; then slammed shut.

"If I was you, Mr. Elliot," came the penetrating accents of Mrs. Solomon Black's voice, "I should hire a reg'lar reviv'list along in th' fall, after preservin' an' house-cleanin' time. We need an outpourin' of grace, right here in Brookville; and we can't get it no other way."

And the minister's cultured voice in reply:

"I shall give your suggestion the most careful consideration, Mrs. Black, between now and the autumn season."

"Great Scott!" exclaimed Jim Dodge; "this is no place for me! Good night, Miss Orr!"

She laid her hand in his.

"You can trust me," he said briefly, and became on the instant a flitting shadow among the lilac bushes, lightly vaulting over the fence and mingling with the darker shadows beyond.

Chapter IX

"Now, Henry," said Mrs. Daggett, as she smilingly set a plate of perfectly browned pancakes before her husband, which he proceeded to deluge with butter and maple syrup, "are you sure that's *so*, about the furniture? 'Cause if it is, we've got two or three o' them things right in this house: that chair you're settin' in, for one, an' upstairs there's that ol' fashioned brown bureau, where I keep the sheets 'n' pillow slips. You don't s'pose she'd want that, do you?"

Mrs. Daggett sank down in a chair opposite her husband, her large pink and white face damp with moisture. Above her forehead a mist of airy curls fluttered in the warm breeze from the open window.

"My, ain't it hot!" she sighed. "I got all het up a-bakin' them cakes. Shall I fry you another griddleful, papa?"

"They cer'nly do taste kind o' moreish, Abby," conceded Mr. Daggett thickly. "You do beat the Dutch, Abby, when it comes t' pancakes. Mebbe I could manage a few more of 'em."

Mrs. Daggett beamed sincerest satisfaction.

"Oh, I don't know," she deprecated happily. "Ann Whittle says I don't mix batter the way she does. But if *you* like 'em, Henry—"

"Couldn't be beat, Abby," affirmed Mr. Daggett sturdily, as he reached for his third cup of coffee.

The cook stove was only a few steps away, so the sizzle of the batter as it expanded into generous disks on the smoking griddle did not interrupt the conversation. Mrs. Daggett, in her blue and white striped gingham, a pancake turner in one plump hand, smiled through the odorous blue haze like a tutelary goddess. Mr. Daggett, in his shirt-sleeves, his scant locks brushed carefully over his bald spot, gazed at her with placid satisfaction. He was thoroughly accustomed to having Abby wait upon his appetite.

"I got to get down to the store kind of early this morning, Abby," he observed, frowning slightly at his empty plate.

"I'll have 'em for you in two shakes of a lamb's tail, papa," soothed Mrs. Daggett, to whom the above remark had come to signify not merely a statement of fact, but a gentle reprimand. "I know you like 'em good and hot; and cold buckwheat cakes certainly is about th' meanest vict'als.... There!"

And she transferred a neat pile of the delicate, crisp rounds from the griddle to her husband's plate with a skill born of long practice.

"About that furnitur'," remarked Mr. Daggett, gazing thoughtfully at the golden stream of sweetness, stolen from leaf and branch of the big sugar maples behind the house to supply the pewter syrup-jug he suspended above his cakes, "I guess it's a fact she wants it, all right."

"I should think she'd rather have new furniture; Henry, they do say the house is going to be handsome. But you say she wants the old stuff? Ain't that queer, for anybody with means."

"Well, that Orr girl beats me," Mr. Daggett acknowledged handsomely. "She seems kind of soft an' easy, when you talk to her; but she's got ideas of her own; an' you can't no more talk 'em out of her—"

"Why should you try to talk 'em out of her, papa?" inquired Mrs. Daggett mildly. "Mebbe her ideas is all right; and anyhow, s'long as she's paying out good money—"

"Oh, she'll pay! she'll pay!" said Mr. Daggett, with a large gesture. "Ain't no doubt about her paying for what she wants."

He shoved his plate aside, and tipped back in his chair with a heavy yawn.

"She's asked me to see about the wall paper, Abby," he continued, bringing down his chair with a resounding thump of its sturdy legs. "And she's got the most outlandish notions about it; asked me could I match up what was on the walls."

"Match it up? Why, ain't th' paper all moldered away, Henry, with the damp an' all?"

"'Course it is, Abby; but she says she wants to restore the house—fix it up just as 'twas. She says that's th' correct thing to do. 'Why, shucks!' I sez, 'the wall papers they're gettin' out now is a lot handsomer than them old style papers. You don't want no old stuff like that,' I sez. But, I swan! you can't tell that girl nothing, for all she seems so mild and meachin'. I was wonderin' if you couldn't shove some sense into her, Abby. Now, I'd like th' job of furnishin' up that house with new stuff. 'I don't carry a very big stock of furniture,' I sez to her; but—"

38

"Why, Hen-ery Daggett!" reproved his wife, "an' you a reg'lar professing member of the church! You ain't never carried no stock of furniture in the store, and you know it."

"That ain't no sign I ain't never goin' to, Abby," retorted Mr. Daggett with spirit. "We been stuck right down in the mud here in Brookville since that dratted bank failed. Nobody's moved, except to the graveyard. And here comes along a young woman with money ... I'd like mighty well to know just how much she's got an' where it come from. I asked the Judge, and he says, blamed if he knows.... But this 'ere young female spells op-per-tunity, Abby. We got to take advantage of the situation, Abby, same as you do in blackberrying season: pick 'em when they're ripe; if you don't, the birds and the bugs'll get 'em."

"It don't sound right to me, papa," murmured his wife, her kind face full of soft distress: "Taking advantage of a poor young thing, like her, an' all in mourning, too, fer a near friend. She told Lois so ... Dear, dear!"

Mr. Daggett had filled his morning pipe and was puffing energetically in his efforts to make it draw.

"I didn't *say* take advantage of *her*," he objected. "That's somethin' I never done yet in my business, Abby. Th' Lord knows I don't sand my sugar nor water my vinegar, the way some storekeepers do. I'm all for 'live an' let live.' What I says was—... Now, you pay attention to me, Abby, and quit sniffling. You're a good woman; but you're about as soft as that there butter! ..."

The article in question had melted to a yellow pool under the heat. Mrs. Daggett gazed at it with wide blue eyes, like those of a child.

"Why, Henry," she protested, "I never heerd you talk so before."

"And likely you won't again. Now you listen, Abby; all I want, is to do what honest business I can with this young woman. She's bound to spend her money, and she's kind of took to me; comes into th' store after her mail, and hangs around and buys the greatest lot o' stuff— 'Land!' I says to her: 'a body'd think you was getting ready to get married.'"

"Well, now I shouldn't wonder—" began Mrs. Daggett eagerly.

"Don't you get excited, Abby. She says she ain't; real pointed, too. But about this wall paper; I don't know as I can match up them stripes and figures. I wisht you'd go an' see her, Abby. She'll tell you all about it. An' her scheme about collecting all the old Bolton furniture is perfectly ridiculous. 'Twouldn't be worth shucks after kickin' 'round folk's houses here in Brookville for the last fifteen years or so."

"But you can't never find her at home, Henry," said Mrs. Daggett. "I been to see her lots of times; but Mis' Solomon Black says she don't stay in the house hardly long enough to eat her victuals."

"Why don't you take the buggy, Abby, and drive out to the old place?" suggested Mr. Daggett. "Likely you'll find her there. She appears to take an interest in every nail that's drove. I can spare the horse this afternoon just as well as not."

"'Twould be pleasant," purred Mrs. Daggett. "But, I suppose, by rights, I ought to take Lois along."

"Nope," disagreed her husband, shaking his head. "Don't you take Lois; she wouldn't talk confiding to Lois, the way she would to you. You've got a way with you, Abby. I'll bet you could coax a bird off a bush as easy as pie, if you was a mind to."

Mrs. Daggett's big body shook with soft laughter. She beamed rosily on her husband.

"How you do go on, Henry!" she protested. "But I ain't going to coax Lydia Orr off no bush she's set her heart on. She's got the sweetest face, papa; an' I know, without anybody telling me, whatever she does or wants to do is *all* right."

Mr. Daggett had by now invested his portly person in a clean linen coat, bearing on its front the shining mark of Mrs. Daggett's careful iron.

"Same here, Abby," he said kindly: "whatever you do, Abby, suits *me* all right."

The worthy couple parted for the morning: Mr. Daggett for the scene of his activities in the post office and store; Mrs. Daggett to set her house to rights and prepare for the noon meal, when her Henry liked to "eat hearty of good, nourishing victuals," after his light repast of the morning.

"Guess I'll wear my striped muslin," said Mrs. Daggett to herself happily. "Ain't it lucky it's all clean an' fresh? 'Twill be so cool to wear out buggy-ridin'."

Mrs. Daggett was always finding occasion for thus reminding herself of her astonishing good fortune. She had formed the habit of talking aloud to herself as she worked about the house and garden.

"'Tain't near as lonesome, when you can hear the sound of a voice—if it is only your own," she apologized, when rebuked for the practice by her friend Mrs. Maria Dodge. "Mebbe it does sound kind of crazy— You say lunatics does it constant—but, I don't know, Maria, I've a kind of a notion there's them that hears, even if you can't see 'em. And mebbe they answer, too—in your thought-ear."

"You want to be careful, Abby," warned Mrs. Dodge, shaking her head. "It makes the chills go up and down my back to hear you talk like that; and they don't allow no such doctrines in the church."

"The Apostle Paul allowed 'em," Mrs. Daggett pointed out, "so did the Psalmist. You read your Bible, Maria, with that in mind, and you'll see."

In the spacious, sunlighted chamber of her soul, devoted to the memory of her two daughters who had died in early childhood, Mrs. Daggett sometimes permitted herself to picture Nellie and Minnie, grown to angelic girlhood, and keeping her company about her lonely household tasks in the intervals not necessarily devoted to harp playing in the Celestial City. She laughed softly to herself as she filled two pies with sliced sour apples and dusted them plentifully with spice and sugar.

"I'd admire to see papa argufying with that sweet girl," she observed to the surrounding silence. "Papa certainly is set on having his own way. Guess bin' alone here with me so constant, he's got kind of willful. But it don't bother me any; ain't that lucky?"

She hurried her completed pies into the oven with a swiftness of movement she had never lost, her sweet, thin soprano soaring high in the words of a winding old hymn tune:

Lord, how we grovel here below,
Fond of these trifling toys;
Our souls can neither rise nor go
To taste supernal joys! ...

It was nearly two o'clock before the big brown horse, indignant at the unwonted invasion of his afternoon leisure, stepped slowly out from the Daggett barn. On the seat of the old-fashioned vehicle, to which he had been attached by Mrs. Daggett's skillful hands, that lady herself sat placidly erect, arrayed in her blue and white striped muslin. Mrs. Daggett conscientiously wore stripes at all seasons of the year: she had read somewhere that stripes impart to the most rotund of figures an appearance of slimness totally at variance with the facts. As for blue and white, her favorite combination of stripes, any fabric in those colors looked cool and clean; and there was a vague strain of poetry in Mrs. Daggett's nature which made her lift her eyes to a blue sky filled with floating white clouds with a sense of rapturous satisfaction wholly unrelated to the state of the weather.

"G'long, Dolly!" she bade the reluctant animal, with a gentle slap of leathern reins over a rotund back. "Git-ap!"

"Dolly," who might have been called Cæsar, both by reason of his sex and a stubbornly dominant nature, now fortunately subdued by years of chastening experience, strode slowly forward, his eyes rolling, his large hoofs stirring up heavy clouds of dust. There were sweet-smelling meadows stacked with newly-cured hay on either side of the road, and tufts of red clover blossoms exhaling delicious odors of honey almost under his saturnine nose; but he trotted ponderously on, sullenly aware of the gentle hand on the reins and the mild, persistent voice which bade him "Git-ap, Dolly!"

Miss Lois Daggett, carrying a black silk bag, which contained a prospectus of the invaluable work which she was striving to introduce to an unappreciative public, halted the vehicle before it had reached the outskirts of the village.

"Where you going, Abby?" she demanded, in the privileged tone of authority a wife should expect from her husband's female relatives.

"Just out in the country a piece, Lois," replied Mrs. Daggett evasively.

"Well, I guess I'll git in and ride a ways with you," said Lois Daggett. "Cramp your wheel, Abby," she added sharply. "I don't want to git my skirt all dust."

Miss Daggett was wearing a black alpaca skirt and a white shirtwaist, profusely ornamented with what is known as coronation braid. Her hair, very tightly frizzed, projected from beneath the brim of her straw hat on both sides.

"I'm going out to see if I can catch that Orr girl this afternoon," she explained, as she took a seat beside her sister-in-law. "She ought to want a copy of Famous People—in the best binding, too. I ain't sold a leather-bound yit, not even in Grenoble. They come in red with gold lettering. You'd ought to have one, Abby, now that Henry's gitting more business by the minute. I should think you might afford one, if you ain't too stingy."

"Mebbe we could, Lois," said Mrs. Daggett amiably. "I've always thought I'd like to know more about famous people: what they eat for breakfast, and how they do their back hair and—"

"Don't be silly, Abby," Miss Daggett bade her sharply. "There ain't any such nonsense in Famous People! *I* wouldn't be canvassing for it, if there was." And she shifted her pointed nose to one side with a slight, genteel sniff.

"Git-ap, Dolly!" murmured Mrs. Daggett, gently slapping the reins.

Dolly responded by a single swift gesture of his tail which firmly lashed the hated reminder of bondage to his hind quarters. Then wickedly pretending that he was not aware of what had happened he strolled to the side of the road nearest the hay field.

"Now, if he ain't gone and got his tail over the lines!" cried Mrs. Daggett indignantly. "He's got more resistin' strength in that tail of his'n—wonder if I can—"

She leaned over the dashboard and grasped the offending member with both hands.

"You hang onto the lines, Lois, and give 'em a good jerk the minute I loosen up his tail."

The subsequent failure of this attempt deflected the malicious Dolly still further from the path of duty. A wheel cramped and lifted perilously.

Miss Daggett squealed shrilly:

"He'll tip the buggy over—he'll tip the buggy over! For pity's sake, Abby!"

Mrs. Daggett stepped briskly out of the vehicle and seized the bridle.

"Ain't you ashamed?" she demanded sternly. "You loosen up that there tail o' yourn this minute!"

"I got 'em!" announced Miss Daggett, triumphantly. "He loosened right up."

She handed the recovered reins to her sister-in-law, and the two ladies resumed their journey and their conversation.

"I never was so scared in all my life," stated Lois Daggett, straightening her hat which had assumed a rakish angle over one ear. "I should think you'd be afraid to drive such a horse, Abby. What in creation would have happened to you if I hadn't been in the buggy?"

"As like as not he wouldn't have took a notion with his tail, Lois, if I'd been driving him alone," hazarded Mrs. Daggett mildly. "Dolly's an awful knowing horse.... Git-ap, Dolly!"

"Do you mean to tell me, Abby Daggett, that there horse of Henry's has took a spite against *me?*" demanded the spinster.... "Mebbe he's a mind-reader," she added darkly.

"You know I didn't mean nothin' like that, Lois," her sister-in-law assured her pacifically. "What I meant to say was: I got so interested in what you were saying, Lois, that I handled the reins careless, and he took advantage.... Git-ap, Dolly! Don't you see, Lois, even a horse knows the difference when two ladies is talking."

"You'd ought to learn to say exactly what you mean, Abby," commented Miss Daggett.

She glanced suspiciously at the fresh striped muslin, which was further enhanced by a wide crocheted collar and a light blue satin bow.

"Where'd you say you were goin' this afternoon, Abby?"

"I said out in the country a piece, Lois; it's such a nice afternoon."

"Well, *I* should think Henry'd be needing the horse for his business. I know *I'd* never think of asking him for it—and me a blood relation, too, trying to earn my bread and butter tramping around the country with Famous People."

Mrs. Daggett, thus convicted of heartless selfishness, sighed vaguely. Henry's sister always made her feel vastly uncomfortable, even sinful.

"You know, Lois, we'd be real glad to have you come and live with us constant," she said heroically.... "Git-ap, Dolly!"

Miss Daggett compressed her thin lips.

"No; I'm too independent for that, Abby, an' you know it. If poor Henry was to be left a widower, I might consider living in his house and doing for him; but you know, Abby, there's very few houses big enough for two women.... And that r'minds me; did you know Miss Orr has got a hired girl?"

"Has she?" inquired Mrs. Daggett, welcoming the change of subject with cordial interest. "A hired girl! ...Git-ap, Dolly!"

"Yes," confirmed Miss Daggett. "Lute Parsons was telling me she came in on th' noon train yesterday. She brought a trunk with her, and her check was from Boston."

"Well, I want to know!" murmured Mrs. Daggett. "Boston's where *she* came from, ain't it? It'll be real pleasant for her to have somebody from Boston right in the house.... G'long, Dolly!"

"I don't know why you should be so sure of that, Abby," sniffed Miss Daggett. "I should think a person from right here in Brookville would be more company. How can a hired girl from Boston view the passin' and tell her who's goin' by? I think it's a ridiculous idea, myself."

"I shouldn't wonder if it's somebody she knows," surmised Mrs. Daggett. "'Twould be real pleasant for her to have a hired girl that's mebbe worked for her folks."

41

"I intend to ask her, if she comes to the door," stated Lois Daggett. "You can drop me right at the gate; and if you ain't going too far with your buggy-riding, Abby, you might stop and take me up a spell later. It's pretty warm to walk far today."

"Well, I was thinkin' mebbe I'd stop in there, too, Lois," said Mrs. Daggett apologetically. "I ain't been to see Miss Orr for quite a spell, and—"

The spinster turned and fixed a scornfully, intelligent gaze upon the mild, rosy countenance of her sister-in-law.

"Oh, *I see!*" she sniffed. "That was where you was pointing for, all the while! And you didn't let on to me, oh, no!"

"Now, Lois, don't you get excited," exhorted Mrs. Daggett. "It was just about the wall papers. Henry, he says to me this mornin'—... Git-ap, Dolly!"

"*'Henry says—Henry says'!* Yes; I guess so! What do you know about wall papers, Abby? ...Well, all I got to say is: I don't want nobody looking on an' interfering when I'm trying to sell 'Lives of Famous People.' Folks, es a rule, ain't so interested in anything they got to pay out money fer, an' I want a clear field."

"I won't say a word till you're all through talkin', Lois," promised Mrs. Daggett meekly. "Mebbe she'd kind of hate to say 'no' before me. She's took a real liking to Henry.... Git-ap, Dolly.... And anyway, she's awful generous. I could say, kind of careless; 'If I was you, I'd take a leather-bound.' Couldn't I, Lois?"

"Well, you can come in, Abby, if you're so terrible anxious," relented Miss Daggett. "You might tell her, you and Henry was going to take a leather-bound; that might have some effect. I remember once I sold three Famous People in a row in one street. There couldn't one o' them women endure to think of her next door neighbor having something she didn't have."

"That's so, Lois," beamed Mrs. Daggett. "The most of folks is about like that. Why, I rec'lect once, Henry brought me up a red-handled broom from th' store. My! it wa'n't no time b'fore he was cleaned right out of red-handled brooms. Nobody wanted 'em natural color, striped, or blue. Henry, he says to me, 'What did you do to advertise them red-handled brooms, Abby?' 'Why, papa,' says I, 'I swept off my stoop and the front walk a couple of times, that's all.' 'Well,' he says, 'broom-handles is as catching as measles, if you only get 'em th' right color!' ... Git-ap, Dolly!"

"Well, did you *ever!*" breathed Miss Daggett excitedly, leaning out of the buggy to gaze upon the scene of activity displayed on the further side of the freshly-pruned hedge which divided Miss Lydia Orr's property from the road: "Painters and carpenters and masons, all going at once! And ain't that Jim Dodge out there in the side yard talking to her? 'Tis, as sure as I'm alive! I wonder what *he's* doing? Go right in, Abby!"

"I kind of hate to drive Dolly in on that fresh gravel," hesitated Mrs. Daggett. "He's so heavy on his feet he'll muss it all up. Mebbe I'd better hitch out in front."

"She sees us, Abby; go on in!" commanded Miss Daggett masterfully. "I guess when it comes to that, her gravel ain't any better than other folks' gravel."

Thus urged, Mrs. Daggett guided the sulky brown horse between the big stone gateposts and brought him to a standstill under the somewhat pretentious *porte-cochère* of the Bolton house.

Lydia Orr was beside the vehicle in a moment, her face bright with welcoming smiles.

"Dear Mrs. Daggett," she said, "I'm so glad you've come. I've been wanting to see you all day. I'm sure you can tell me—"

"You've met my husband's sister, Miss Lois Daggett, haven't you, Miss Orr? She's the lady that made that beautiful drawn-in mat you bought at the fair."

Miss Orr shook hands cordially with the author of the drawn-in mat.

"Come right in," she said. "You'll want to see what we're doing inside, though nothing is finished yet."

She led the way to a small room off the library, its long French windows opening on a balcony.

"This room used to be a kind of a den, they tell me; so I've made it into one, the first thing, you see."

There was a rug on the floor, a chair or two and a high mahogany desk which gave the place a semblance of comfort amid the general confusion. Miss Lois Daggett gazed about with argus-eyed curiosity.

"I don't know as I was ever in this room, when Andrew Bolton lived here," she observed, "but it looks real homelike now."

"Poor man! I often think of him," said kindly Mrs. Daggett. "'Twould be turrible to be shut away from the sunshine f'r even one year; but poor Andrew Bolton's been closed up in State's prison fer—l' me see, it mus' be goin' on—"

"It's fifteen years, come fall, since he got his sentence," stated the spinster. "His time must be 'most up."

42

Lydia Orr had seated herself in an old-fashioned chair, its tall carved back turned to the open windows.

"Did you—lose much in the bank failure, Miss Daggett?" she inquired, after a slight pause, during which the promoter of Famous People was loosening the strings of her black silk bag.

"About two hundred dollars I'd saved up," replied Miss Daggett. "By now it would be a lot more—with the interest."

"Yes, of course," assented their hostess; "one should always think of interest in connection with savings."

She appeared to be gazing rather attentively at the leather-bound prospectus Miss Daggett had withdrawn from her bag.

"That looks like something interesting, Miss Daggett," she volunteered.

"This volume I'm holdin' in my hand," began that lady, professionally, "is one of the most remarkable works ever issued by the press of any country. It is the life history of one thousand men and women of world-wide fame and reputation, in letters, art, science *an'* public life. No library nor parlor table is complete without this authoritative work of general information *an'* reference. It is a com-plete library in itself, and—"

"What is the price of the work, Miss Daggett?" inquired Lydia Orr.

"Just hold on a minute; I'm coming to that," said Miss Daggett firmly. "As I was telling you, this work is a complete library in itself. A careful perusal of the specimen pages will convince the most skeptical. Turning to page four hundred and fifty-six, we read:—"

" Just hold on a minute; I'm coming to that," said Miss Daggett firmly

"I'm sure I should like to buy the book, Miss Daggett."

"You ain't th' only one," said the agent. "Any person of even the most ordinary intelligence ought to own this work. Turning to page four hundred and fifty-six, we read: 'Snipeley, Samuel Bangs: lawyer ligislator *an'* author; born eighteen hundred fifty-nine, in the town of—'"

At this moment the door was pushed noiselessly open, and a tall, spare woman of middle age stood upon the threshold bearing a tray in her hands. On the tray were set forth silver tea things, flanked by thin bread and butter and a generous pile of sponge cake.

"You must be tired and thirsty after your drive," said Lydia Orr hospitably. "You may set the tray here, Martha."

The maid complied.

"Of course I must have that book, Miss Daggett," their hostess went on. "You didn't mention the title, nor the price. Won't you have a cup of tea, Mrs. Daggett?"

"That cup of tea looks real nice; but I'm afraid you've gone to a lot of trouble and put yourself out," protested Mrs. Daggett, who had not ventured to open her lips until then. What wonderful long words Lois had used; and how convincing had been her manner. Mrs. Daggett had resolved that "Lives of Famous People," in its best red leather binding, should adorn her own parlor table in the near future, if she could persuade Henry to consent.

"I think that book Lois is canvassing for is just lovely," she added artfully, as she helped herself to cake. "I'm awful anxious to own one; just think, I'd never even heard of Snipeley Samuel Bangs—"

Lois Daggett crowed with laughter.

"Fer pity sake, Abby! don't you know no better than that? It's Samuel Bangs Snipeley; he was County Judge, the author of 'Platform Pearls,' and was returned to legislature four times by his constituents, besides being—"

"Could you spare me five copies of the book, Miss Daggett?" inquired Lydia, handing her the sponge cake.

"Five copies!"

Miss Daggett swiftly controlled her agitation.

"I haven't told you the price, yet. You'd want one of them leather-bound, wouldn't you? They come high, but they wear real well, and I will say there's nothing handsomer for a parlor table."

"I want them all leather-bound," said Lydia, smiling. "I want one for myself, one for a library and the other three—"

"There's nothing neater for a Christmas or birthday present!" shrilled Lois Daggett joyously. "And so informing."

She swallowed her tea in short, swift gulps; her faded eyes shone. Inwardly she was striving to compute the agent's profit on five leather-bound copies of Famous People. She almost said aloud "I can have a new dress!"

"We've been thinking," Lydia Orr said composedly, "that it might be pleasant to open a library and reading room in the village. What do you think of the idea, Miss Daggett? You seem interested in books, and I thought possibly you might like to take charge of the work."

"Who, me?— Take charge of a library?"

Lois Daggett's eyes became on the instant watchful and suspicious. Lydia Orr had encountered that look before, on the faces of men and even of boys. Everybody was afraid of being cheated, she thought. Was this just in Brookville, and because of the misdeeds of one man, so long ago?

"Of course we shall have to talk it over some other day, when we have more time," she said gently.

"Wouldn't that be nice!" said Mrs. Daggett. "I was in a library once, over to Grenoble. Even school children were coming in constant to get books. But I never thought we could have one in Brookville. Where could we have it, my dear?"

"Yes; that's the trouble," chimed in Lois. "There isn't any place fit for anything like that in our town."

Lydia glanced appealingly from one to the other of the two faces. One might have thought her irresolute—or even afraid of their verdict.

"I had thought," she said slowly, "of buying the old Bolton bank building. It has not been used for anything, Judge Fulsom says, since—"

"No; it ain't," acquiesced Mrs. Daggett soberly, "not since—"

She fell silent, thinking of the dreadful winter after the bank failure, when scarlet fever raged among the impoverished homes.

"There's been some talk, off and on, of opening a store there," chimed in Lois Daggett, setting down her cup with a clash; "but I guess nobody'd patronize it. Folks don't forget so easy."

"But it's a good substantial building," Lydia went on, her eyes resting on Mrs. Daggett's broad, rosy face, which still wore that unwonted look of pain and sadness. "It seems a pity not to change the—the associations. The library and reading room could be on the first floor; and on the second, perhaps, a town hall, where—"

"For the land sake!" ejaculated Lois Daggett; "you cer'nly have got an imagination, Miss Orr. I haven't heard that town hall idea spoken of since Andrew Bolton's time. He was always talking about town improvements; wanted a town hall and courses of lectures, and a fountain playing in a park and a fire-engine, and the land knows what. He was a great hand to talk, Andrew Bolton was. And you see how he turned out!"

"And mebbe he'd have done all those nice things for Brookville, Lois, if his speculations had turned out different," said Mrs. Daggett, charitably. "I always thought Andrew Bolton *meant* all right. Of course he had to invest our savings; banks always do, Henry says."

"I don't know anything about *investing*, and don't want to, either—not the kind he did, anyhow," retorted Lois Daggett.

She arose as she spoke, brushing the crumbs of sponge cake from her skirt.

"I got to get that order right in," she said: "five copies—or was it six, you said?"

"I think I could use six," murmured Lydia.

"And all leather-bound! Well, now, I know you won't ever be sorry. It's one of those works any intelligent person would be proud to own."

"I'm sure it is," said the girl gently.

She turned to Mrs. Daggett.

"Can't you stay awhile longer? I—I should like—"

"Oh, I guess Abby'd better come right along with me," put in Lois briskly ... "and that reminds me, do you want to pay something down on that order? As a general thing, where I take a big order—"

"Of course—I'd forgotten; I always prefer to pay in advance."

The girl opened the tall desk and producing a roll of bills told off the price of her order into Miss Daggett's hand.

"I should think you'd be almost afraid to keep so much ready money by you, with all those men workin' outside," she commented.

"They're all Brookville men," said Lydia. "I have to have money to pay them with. Besides, I have Martha."

"You mean your hired girl, I suppose," inferred Miss Daggett, rubbing her nose thoughtfully.

"She isn't exactly—a servant," hesitated Lydia. "We give the men their noon meal," she added. "Martha helps me with that."

"You give them their dinner! Well, I never! Did you hear that, Abby? She gives them their dinner. Didn't you know men-folks generally bring their noonings in a pail? Land! I don't know how you get hearty victuals enough for all those men. Where do they eat?"

"In the new barn," said Lydia, smiling. "We have a cook stove out there."

"Ain't that just lovely!" beamed Mrs. Daggett, squeezing the girl's slim hand in both her own. "Most folks wouldn't go to the trouble of doing anything so nice. No wonder they're hustling."

"Mebbe they won't hustle so fast toward the end of the job," said Lois Daggett. "You'll find men-folks are always ready to take advantage of any kind of foolishness. Come, Abby; we must be going. You'll get those books in about two weeks, Miss Orr. A big order takes more time, I always tell people."

"Thank you, Miss Daggett. But wouldn't you—if you are in a hurry, you know; Mr. Dodge is going to the village in the automobile; we're expecting some supplies for the house. He'll be glad to take you."

"Who, Jim Dodge? You don't mean to tell me Jim Dodge can drive an auto! I never stepped foot inside of one of those contraptions. But I don't know but I might's well die for a sheep as a lamb."

Lois Daggett followed the girl from the room in a flutter of joyous excitement.

"You can come home when you get ready, Abby," she said over her shoulder. "But you want to be careful driving that horse of yours; he might cut up something scandalous if he was to meet an auto."

Chapter X

Mrs. Daggett was sitting by the window gazing dreamily out, when Lydia returned after witnessing the triumphant departure of the promoter of Famous People.

"It kind of brings it all back to me," said Mrs. Daggett, furtively wiping her eyes. "It's going t' look pretty near's it used to. Only I remember Mis' Bolton used to have a flower garden all along that stone wall over there; she was awful fond of flowers. I remember I gave her some roots of pinies and iris out of our yard, and she gave me a new kind of lilac bush—pink, it is, and sweet! My! you can smell it a mile off when it's in blow."

"Then you knew—the Bolton family?"

The girl's blue eyes widened wistfully as she asked the question.

"Yes, indeed, my dear. And I want to tell you—just betwixt ourselves—that Andrew Bolton was a real nice man; and don't you let folks set you t' thinking he wa'n't. Now that you're going to live right here in this house, my dear, seems to me it would be a lot pleasanter to know that those who were here before you were just good, kind folks that had made a mistake. I was saying to Henry this morning: 'I'm going to tell her some of the nice things folks has seemed to forget about the Boltons. It won't do any harm,' I said. 'And it'll be cheerfuller for her.' Now this room we're sitting in—I remember lots of pleasant things about this room. 'Twas here—right at that desk—he gave us a check to fix up the church. He was always doing things like that. But folks don't seem to remember."

"Thank you so much, dear Mrs. Daggett, for telling me," murmured Lydia. "Indeed it will be—cheerfuller for me to know that Andrew Bolton wasn't always—a thief. I've sometimes imagined him walking about these rooms.... One can't help it, you know, in an old house like this."

Mrs. Daggett nodded eagerly. Here was one to whom she might impart some of the secret thoughts and imaginings which even Maria Dodge would have called "outlandish":

"I know," she said. "Sometimes I've wondered if—if mebbe folks don't leave something or other after them— something you can't see nor touch; but you can sense it, just as plain, in your mind. But land! I don't know as I'd ought to mention it; of course you know I don't mean ghosts and like that."

"You mean their—their thoughts, perhaps," hesitated Lydia. "I can't put it into words; but I know what you mean."

Mrs. Daggett patted the girl's hand kindly.

"I've come to talk to you about the wall papers, dearie; Henry thought mebbe you'd like to see me, seeing I don't forget so easy's some. This room was done in a real pretty striped paper in two shades of buff. There's a little of it left behind that door. Mrs. Bolton was a great hand to want things cheerful. She said it looked kind of sunshiny, even on a dark day. Poor dear, it fell harder on her than on anybody else when the crash came. She died the same week they took him to prison; and fer one, I was glad of it."

Mrs. Daggett wiped her kind eyes.

"Mebbe you'll think it's a terrible thing for me to say," she added hastily. "But she was such a delicate, soft-hearted sort of a woman: I couldn't help feelin' th' Lord spared her a deal of bitter sorrow by taking her away. My! It does bring it all back to me so—the house and the yard, and all. We'd all got used to seeing it a ruin; and now— Whatever put it in your head, dearie, to want things put back just as they were? Papa was telling me this morning you was all for restoring the place. He thinks 'twould be more stylish and up-to-date if you was to put new-style paper on the walls, and let him furnish it up for you with nice golden oak. Henry's got real good taste. You'd ought to see our sideboard he gave me Chris'mas, with a mirror and all."

Having thus discharged her wifely duty, as it appeared to her, Mrs. Daggett promptly turned her back upon it.

"But you don't want any golden oak sideboards and like that in this house. Henry was telling me all about it, and how you were set on getting back the old Bolton furniture."

"Do you think I could?" asked the girl eagerly. "It was all sold about here, wasn't it? And don't you think if I was willing to pay a great deal for it people would—"

"'Course they would!" cried Mrs. Daggett, with cheerful assurance. "They'd be tickled half to death to get money for it. But, you see, dearie, it's a long time ago, and some folks have moved away, and there's been two or three fires, and I suppose some are not as careful as others; still—"

The smile faded on the girl's lips.

"But I can get some of it back; don't you think I can? I—I've quite set my heart on—restoring the house. I want it just as it used to be. The old furniture would suit the house so much better; don't you think it would?"

Mrs. Daggett clapped her plump hands excitedly.

"I've just thought of a way!" she exclaimed. "And I'll bet it'll work, too. You know Henry he keeps th' post office; an' 'most everybody for miles around comes after their mail to th' store. I'll tell him to put up a sign, right where everybody will see; something like this: 'Miss Lydia Orr wants to buy the old furniture of the Bolton house.' And you might mention casual you'd pay good prices for it. 'Twas real good, solid furniture, I remember.... Come to think of it, Mrs. Bolton collected quite a lot of it right 'round here. She was a city girl when she married Andrew Bolton, an' she took a great interest in queer old things. She bought a big tall clock out of somebody's attic, and four-posted beds, the kind folks used to sleep in, an' outlandish old cracked china plates with scenes on 'em. I recollect I gave her a blue and white teapot, with an eagle on the side that belonged to my grandmother. She thought it was perfectly elegant, and kept it full of rose-leaves and spice on the parlor mantelpiece. Land! I hadn't thought of that teapot for years and years. I don't know whatever became of it."

The sound of planes and hammers filled the silence that followed. Lydia was standing by the tall carved chair, her eyes downcast.

"I'm glad you thought of—that notice," she said at last. "If Mr. Daggett will see to it for me—I'll stop at the office tomorrow. And now, if you have time, I'd so like you to go over the house with me. You can tell me about the wall papers and—"

Mrs. Daggett arose with cheerful alacrity.

"I'd like nothing better," she declared. "I ain't been in the house for so long. Last time was the day of the auction; 'twas after they took the little girl away, I remember.... Oh, didn't nobody tell you? There was one child—a real, nice little girl. I forget her name; Mrs. Bolton used to call her Baby and Darling and like that. She was an awful pretty little girl, about as old as my Nellie. I've often wondered what became of her. Some of her relatives took her away, after her mother was buried. Poor little thing—her ma dead an' her pa shut up in prison—... Oh! yes; this was the parlor.... My! to think how the years have gone by, and me as slim as a match then. Now that's what I call a handsome mantel; and ain't the marble kept real pretty? There was all-colored rugs and a waxed floor in here, and a real old-fashioned sofa in that corner and a mahogany table with carved legs over here, and long lace curtains at the windows. I see they've fixed the ceilings as good as new and scraped all the old paper off the walls. There used to be some sort of patterned paper in here. I can't seem to think what color it was."

"I found quite a fresh piece behind the door," said Lydia. "See; I've put all the good pieces from the different rooms together, and marked them. I was wondering if Mr. Daggett could go to Boston for me? I'm sure he could match the papers there. You could go, too, if you cared to."

"To Boston!" exclaimed Mrs. Daggett; "me and Henry? Why, Miss Orr, what an idea! But Henry couldn't no more leave the post office—he ain't never left it a day since he was appointed postmaster. My, no! 'twouldn't do for Henry to take a trip clear to Boston. And me—I'm so busy I'd be like a fly trying t' get off sticky paper.... I do hate to see 'em struggle, myself."

She followed the girl up the broad stair, once more safe and firm, talking steadily all the way.

There were four large chambers, their windows framing lovely vistas of stream and wood and meadow, with the distant blue of the far horizon melting into the summer sky. Mrs. Daggett stopped in the middle of the wide hall and looked about her wonderingly.

"Why, yes," she said slowly. "You certainly did show good sense in buying this old house. They don't build them this way now-a-days. That's what I said to Mrs. Deacon Whittle— You know some folks thought you were kind of foolish not to buy Mrs. Solomon Black's house down in the village. But if you're going to live here all alone, dearie, ain't it going to be kind of lonesome—all these big rooms for a little body like you?"

"Tell me about it, please," begged Lydia. "I—I've been wondering which room was his."

"You mean Andrew Bolton's, I s'pose," said Mrs. Daggett reluctantly. "But I hope you won't worry any over what folks tells you about the day he was taken away. My! seems as if 'twas yesterday."

She moved softly into one of the spacious, sunny rooms and stood looking about her, as if her eyes beheld once more the tragedy long since folded into the past.

"I ain't going to tell you anything sad," she said under her breath. "It's best forgot. This was their room; ain't it nice an' cheerful? I like a southwest room myself. And 'tain't a bit warm here, what with the breeze sweeping in at the four big windows and smelling sweet of clover an' locust blooms. And ain't it lucky them trees didn't get blown over last winter?"

She turned abruptly toward the girl.

"Was you thinking of sleeping in this room, dearie? It used to have blue and white paper on it, and white paint as fresh as milk. It'd be nice and pleasant for a young lady, I should think."

Lydia shook her head.

"Not," she said slowly, "if it was *his* room. I think I'd rather—which was the little girl's room? You said there was a child?"

"Now, I'm real sorry you feel that way," sympathized Mrs. Daggett, "but I don't know as I blame you, the way folks talk. You'd think they'd have forgot all about it by now, wouldn't you? But land! it does seem as if bad thoughts and mean thoughts, and like that, was possessed to fasten right on to folks; and you can't seem to shake 'em off, no more than them spiteful little stick-tights that get all over your clo'es.... This room right next belonged to their baby. Let me see; she must have been about three and a half or four years old when they took her away. See, there's a door in between, so Mrs. Bolton could get to her quick in the night. I used to be that

47

way, too, with my children.... You know we lost our two little girls that same winter, three and five, they were. But I know I wanted 'em right where I could hear 'em if they asked for a drink of water, or like that, in the night. Folks has a great notion now-a-days of putting their babies off by themselves and letting them cry it out, as they say. But I couldn't ever do that; and Mrs. Andrew Bolton she wa'n't that kind of a parent, either— I don't know as they ought to be called *mothers*. No, she was more like me—liked to tuck the blankets around her baby in the middle of th' night an' pat her down all warm and nice. I've often wondered what became of that poor little orphan child. We never heard. Like enough she died. I shouldn't wonder."

And Mrs. Daggett wiped the ready tears from her eyes.

"But I guess you'll think I'm a real old Aunty Doleful, going on this way," she made haste to add.

"There's plenty of folks in Brookville as 'll tell you how stuck-up an' stylish Mrs. Andrew Bolton was, always dressed in silk of an afternoon and driving out with a two-horse team, an' keeping two hired girls constant, besides a man to work in her flower garden and another for the barn. But of course she supposed they were really rich and could afford it. *He* never let on to *her*, after things begun to go to pieces; and folks blamed her for it, afterwards. Her heart was weak, and he knew it, all along. And then I suppose he thought mebbe things would take a turn.... Yes; the paper in this room was white with little wreaths of pink roses tied up with blue ribbons all over it. 'Twas furnished up real pretty with white furniture, and there was ruffled muslin curtains with dots on 'em at the windows and over the bed; Mrs. Andrew Bolton certainly did fix things up pretty, and to think you're going to have it just the same way. Well, I will say you couldn't do any better.... But, land! if there isn't the sun going down behind the hill, and me way out here, with Henry's supper to get, and Dolly champing his bit impatient. There's one lucky thing, though; he'll travel good, going towards home; he won't stop to get his tail over the lines, neither."

An hour later, when the long summer twilight was deepening into gloom, Jim Dodge crossed the empty library and paused at the open door of the room beyond. The somber light from the two tall windows fell upon the figure of the girl. She was sitting before Andrew Bolton's desk, her head upon her folded arms. Something in the spiritless droop of her shoulders and the soft dishevelment of her fair hair suggested weariness—sleep, perhaps. But as the young man hesitated on the threshold the sound of a muffled sob escaped the quiet figure. He turned noiselessly and went away, sorry and ashamed, because unwittingly he had stumbled upon the clew he had long been seeking.

Chapter XI

"Beside this stone wall I want flowers," Lydia was saying to her landscape-gardener, as she persisted in calling Jim Dodge. "Hollyhocks and foxgloves and pinies—I shall never say peony in Brookville—and pansies, sweet williams, lads' love, iris and sweetbrier. Mrs. Daggett has promised to give me some roots."

He avoided her eyes as she faced him in the bright glow of the morning sunlight.

"Very well, Miss Orr," he said, with cold respect. "You want a border here about four feet wide, filled with old-fashioned perennials."

He had been diligent in his study of the books she had supplied him with.

"A herbaceous border of that sort in front of the stone wall will give quite the latest effect in country-house decoration," he went on professionally. "Ramblers of various colors might be planted at the back, and there should be a mixture of bulbs among the taller plants to give color in early spring."

She listened doubtfully.

"I don't know about the ramblers," she said. "Were there ramblers—twenty years ago? I want it as nearly as possible just as it was. Mrs. Daggett told me yesterday about the flower-border here. You—of course you don't remember the place at all; do you?"

He reddened slightly under her intent gaze.

"Oh, I remember something about it," he told her; "the garden was a long time going down. There were flowers here a few years back; but the grass and weeds got the better of them."

"And do you—remember the Boltons?" she persisted. "I was so interested in what Mrs. Daggett told me about the family yesterday. It seems strange to think no one has lived here since. And now that I—it is to be my home, I can't help thinking about them."

"You should have built a new house," said Jim Dodge. "A new house would have been better and cheaper, in the end."

He thrust his spade deep, a sign that he considered the conversation at an end.

"Tell one of the other men to dig this," she objected. "I want to make a list of the plants we need and get the order out."

"I can do that tonight, Miss Orr," he returned, going on with his digging. "The men are busy in the orchards this morning."

"You want me to go away," she inferred swiftly.

He flung down his spade.

"It is certainly up to me to obey orders," he said. "Pardon me, if I seem to have forgotten the fact. Shall we make the list now?"

Inwardly he was cursing himself for his stupidity. Perhaps he had been mistaken the night before. His fancy had taken a swift leap in the dark and landed—where? There was a sort of scornful honesty in Jim Dodge's nature which despised all manner of shams and petty deceits. His code also included a strict minding of his own business. He told himself rather sharply that he was a fool for suspecting that Lydia Orr was other than she had represented herself to be. She had been crying the night before. What of that? Other girls cried over night and smiled the next morning—his sister Fanny, for example. It was an inexplicable habit of women. His mother had once told him, rather vaguely, that it did her good to have a regular crying-spell. It relieved her nerves, she said, and sort of braced her up....

"Of course I didn't mean that," Lydia was at some pains to explain, as the two walked toward the veranda where there were chairs and a table.

She was looking fair and dainty in a gown of some thin white stuff, through which her neck and arms showed slenderly.

"It's too warm to dig in the ground this morning," she decided. "And anyway, planning the work is far more important."

"Than doing it?" he asked quizzically. "If we'd done nothing but plan all this; why you see—"

He made a large gesture which included the carpenters at work on the roof, painters perilously poised on tall ladders and a half dozen men busy spraying the renovated orchards.

"I see," she returned with a smile, "—now that you've so kindly pointed it out to me."

He leveled a keen glance at her. It was impossible not to see her this morning in the light of what he thought he had discovered the night before.

"I've done nothing but make plans all my life," she went on gravely. "Ever since I can remember I've been thinking—thinking and planning what I should do when I grew up. It seemed such a long, long time—being just a little girl, I mean, and not able to do what I wished. But I kept on thinking and planning, and all the while I *was* growing up; and then at last—it all happened as I wished."

She appeared to wait for his question. But he remained silent, staring at the blue rim of distant hills.

"You don't ask me—you don't seem to care what I was planning," she said, her voice timid and uncertain.

He glanced quickly at her. Something in her look stirred him curiously. It did not occur to him that her appeal and his instant response to it were as old as the race.

"I wish you would tell me," he urged. "Tell me everything!"

She drew a deep breath, her eyes misty with dreams.

"For a long time I taught school," she went on, "but I couldn't save enough that way. I never could have saved enough, even if I had lived on bread and water. I wanted—I needed a great deal of money, and I wasn't clever nor particularly well educated. Sometimes I thought if I could only marry a millionaire—"

He stared at her incredulously.

"You don't mean that," he said with some impatience.

She sighed.

"I'm telling you just what happened," she reminded him. "It seemed the only way to get what I wanted. I thought I shouldn't mind that, or—anything, if I could only have as much money as I needed."

A sense of sudden violent anger flared up within him. Did the girl realize what she was saying?

She glanced up at him.

"I never meant to tell any one about that part of it," she said hurriedly. "And—it wasn't necessary, after all; I got the money another way."

He bit off the point of a pencil he had been sharpening with laborious care.

"I should probably never have had a chance to marry a millionaire," she concluded reminiscently. "I'm not beautiful enough."

With what abominable clearness she understood the game: the marriage-market; the buyer and the price.

"I—didn't suppose you were like that," he muttered, after what seemed a long silence.

She seemed faintly surprised.

"Of course you don't know me," she said quickly. "Does any man know any woman, I wonder?"

"They think they do," he stated doggedly; "and that amounts to the same thing."

His thoughts reverted for an uncomfortable instant to Wesley Elliot and Fanny. It was only too easy to see through Fanny.

"Most of them are simple souls, and thank heaven for it!"

His tone was fervently censorious.

She smiled understandingly.

"Perhaps I ought to tell you further that a rich man—not a millionaire; but rich enough—actually did ask me to marry him, and I refused."

"H'mph!"

"But," she added calmly, "I think I should have married him, if I had not had money left me first—before he asked me, I mean. I knew all along that what I had determined to do, I could do best alone."

He stared at her from under gathered brows. He still felt that curious mixture of shame and anger burning hotly within.

"Just why are you telling me all this?" he demanded roughly.

She returned his look quietly.

"Because," she said, "you have been trying to guess my secret for a long time and you have succeeded; haven't you?"

He was speechless.

"You have been wondering about me, all along. I could see that, of course. I suppose everybody in Brookville has been wondering and—and talking. I meant to be frank and open about it—to tell right out who I was and what I came to do. But—somehow—I couldn't.... It didn't seem possible, when everybody—you see I thought it all happened so long ago people would have forgotten. I supposed they would be just glad to get their money back. I meant to give it to them—all, every dollar of it. I didn't care if it took all I had.... And then—I heard you last night when you crossed the library. I hoped—you would ask me why—but you didn't. I thought, first, of telling Mrs. Daggett; she is a kind soul. I had to tell someone, because he is coming home soon, and I may need—help."

Her eyes were solemn, beseeching, compelling.

His anger died suddenly, leaving only a sort of indignant pity for her unfriended youth.

"You are—" he began, then stopped short. A painter was swiftly descending his ladder, whistling as he came.

"My name," she said, without appearing to notice, "is Lydia Orr Bolton. No one seems to remember—perhaps they didn't know my mother's name was Orr. My uncle took me away from here. I was only a baby. It seemed best to—"

"Where are they now?" he asked guardedly.

The painter had disappeared behind the house. But he could hear heavy steps on the roof over their heads.

"Both are dead," she replied briefly. "No one knew my uncle had much money; we lived quite simply and unpretentiously in South Boston. They never told me about the money; and all those years I was praying for it! Well, it came to me—in time."

His eyes asked a pitying question.

"Oh, yes," she sighed. "I knew about father. They used to take me to visit him in the prison. Of course I didn't understand, at first. But gradually, as I grew older, I began to realize what had happened—to him and to me. It was then I began to make plans. He would be free, sometime; he would need a home. Once he tried to escape, with some other men. A guard shot my father; he was in the prison-hospital a long time. They let me see him then without bars between, because they were sure he would die."

"For God's sake," he interrupted hoarsely. "Was there no one—?"

She shook her head.

"That was after my aunt died: I went alone. They watched me closely at first; but afterward they were kinder. He used to talk about home—always about home. He meant this house, I found. It was then I made up my mind to do anything to get the money.... You see I knew he could never be happy here unless the old wrongs were

50

righted first. I saw I must do all that; and when, after my uncle's death, I found that I was rich—really rich, I came here as soon as I could. There wasn't any time to lose."

She fell silent, her eyes shining luminously under half closed lids. She seemed unconscious of his gaze riveted upon her face. It was as if a curtain had been drawn aside by her painful effort. He was seeing her clearly now and without cloud of passion—in all her innocence, her sadness, set sacredly apart from other women by the long devotion of her thwarted youth. An immense compassion took possession of him. He could have fallen at her feet praying her forgiveness for his mean suspicions, his harsh judgment.

The sound of hammers on the veranda roof above their heads appeared to rouse her.

"Don't you think I ought to tell—everybody?" she asked hurriedly.

He considered her question in silence for a moment. The bitterness against Andrew Bolton had grown and strengthened with the years into something rigid, inexorable. Since early boyhood he had grown accustomed to the harsh, unrelenting criticisms, the brutal epithets applied to this man who had been trusted with money and had defaulted. Even children, born long after the failure, reviled the name of the man who had made their hard lot harder. It had been the juvenile custom to throw stones at the house he had lived in. He remembered with fresh shame the impish glee with which, in company with other boys of his own age, he had trampled the few surviving flowers and broken down the shrubs in the garden. The hatred of Bolton, like some malignant growth, had waxed monstrous from what it preyed upon, ruining and distorting the simple kindly life of the village. She was waiting for his answer.

"It would seem so much more honest," she said in a tired voice. "Now they can only think me eccentric, foolishly extravagant, lavishly generous—when I am trying— I didn't dare to ask Deacon Whittle or Judge Fulsom for a list of the creditors, so I paid a large sum—far more than they would have asked—for the house. And since then I have bought the old bank building. I should like to make a library there."

"Yes, I know," he said huskily.

"Then the furniture—I shall pay a great deal for that. I want the house to look just as it used to, when father comes home. You see he had an additional sentence for trying to escape and for conspiracy; and since then his mind—he doesn't seem to remember everything. Sometimes he calls me Margaret. He thinks I am—mother."

Her voice faltered a little.

"You mustn't tell them," he said vehemently. "You mustn't!"

He saw with terrible clearness what it would be like: the home-coming of the half-imbecile criminal, and the staring eyes, the pointing fingers of all Brookville leveled at him. She would be overborne by the shame of it all—trampled like a flower in the mire.

She seemed faintly disappointed.

"But I would far rather tell," she persisted. "I have had so much to conceal—all my life!"

She flung out her hands in a gesture of utter weariness.

"I was never allowed to mention father to anyone," she went on. "My aunt was always pointing out what a terrible thing it would be for any one to find out—who I was. She didn't want me to know; but uncle insisted. I think he was sorry for—father.... Oh, you don't know what it is like to be in prison for years—to have all the manhood squeezed out of one, drop by drop! I think if it hadn't been for me he would have died long ago. I used to pretend I was very gay and happy when I went to see him. He wanted me to be like that. It pleased him to think my life had not been clouded by what he called his *mistake*.... He didn't intend to wreck the bank, Mr. Dodge. He thought he was going to make the village rich and prosperous."

She leaned forward. "I have learned to smile during all these years. But now, I want to tell everybody—I long to be free from pretending! Can't you see?"

Something big and round in his throat hurt him so that he could not answer at once. He clenched his hands, enraged by the futility of his pity for her.

"Mrs. Daggett seems a kind soul," she murmured. "She would be my friend. I am sure of it. But—the others—"

She sighed.

"I used to fancy how they would all come to the station to meet him—after I had paid everybody, I mean—how they would crowd about him and take his hand and tell him they were glad it was all over; then I would bring him home, and he would never even guess it had stood desolate during all these years. He has forgotten so much already; but he remembers home—oh, quite perfectly. I went to see him last week, and he spoke of the gardens and orchards. That is how I knew how to have things planted: he told me."

He got hastily to his feet: her look, her voice—the useless smart of it all was swiftly growing unbearable.

"You must wait—I must think!" he said unsteadily. "You ought not to have told me."

51

"Do you think I should have told the minister, instead?" she asked rather piteously. "He has been very kind; but somehow—"

"What! Wesley Elliot?"

His face darkened.

"Thank heaven you did not tell him! I am at least no—"

He checked himself with an effort.

"See here," he said: "You—you mustn't speak to any one of what you have told me—not for the present, anyway. I want you to promise me."

Her slight figure sagged wearily against the back of her chair. She was looking up at him like a child spent with an unavailing passion of grief.

"I have promised that so many times," she murmured: "I have concealed everything so long—it will be easier for me."

"It will be easier for you," he agreed quickly; "and—perhaps better, on the whole."

"But they will not know they are being paid—they won't understand—"

"That makes no difference," he decided. "It would make them, perhaps, less contented to know where the money was coming from. Tell me, does your servant—this woman you brought from Boston; does she know?"

"You mean Martha? I—I'm not sure. She was a servant in my uncle's home for years. She wanted to live with me, so I sent for her. I never spoke to her about—father. She seems devoted to me. I have thought it would be necessary to tell her—before— He is coming in September. Everything will be finished by then."

His eyes were fixed blankly on the hedge; something—a horse's ears, perhaps—was bobbing slowly up and down; a faint rattle of wheels came to their ears.

"Don't tell anyone, yet," he urged, and stepped down from the veranda, his unseeing gaze still fixed upon the slow advance of those bobbing ears.

"Someone is coming," she said.

He glanced at her, marveling at the swift transition in her face. A moment before she had been listless, sad, disheartened by his apparent disapproval of her plans. Now all at once the cloud had vanished; she was once more cheerful, calm, even smiling.

She too had been looking and had at once recognized the four persons seated in the shabby old carryall which at that moment turned in at the gate.

"I am to have visitors," she said tranquilly.

His eyes reluctantly followed hers. There were four women in the approaching vehicle.

As on another occasion, the young man beat a swift retreat.

Chapter XII

"I am sure I don't know what you'll think of us gadding about in the morning so," began Mrs. Dix, as she caught sight of Lydia.

Mrs. Dix was sitting in the back seat of the carryall with Mrs. Dodge. The two girls were in front. Lydia noticed mechanically that both were freshly gowned in white and that Fanny, who was driving, eyed her with haughty reserve from under the brim of her flower-laden hat. Ellen Dix had turned her head to gaze after Jim Dodge's retreating figure; her eyes returned to Lydia with an expression of sulky reluctance.

"I'm so glad to see you," said Lydia. "Won't you come in?"

"I should like to," said Mrs. Dodge. "Jim has been telling us about the improvements, all along."

"It certainly does look nice," chimed in Mrs. Dix. "I wouldn't have believed it possible, in such a little time, too. Just cramp that wheel a little more, Fanny."

The two older women descended from the carryall and began looking eagerly around.

"Just see how nice the grass looks," said Mrs. Dodge. "And the flowers! My! I didn't suppose Jim was that smart at fixing things up.... Aren't you going to get out, girls?"

The two girls still sat on the high front seat of the carryall; both were gazing at Lydia in her simple morning frock. There were no flowers on Lydia's Panama hat; nothing but a plain black band; but it had an air of style and elegance. Fanny was wishing she had bought a plain hat without roses. Ellen tossed her dark head:

"I don't know," she said. "You aren't going to stay long; are you, mother?"

"For pity sake, Ellen!" expostulated Mrs. Dodge briskly. "Of course you'll get out, and you, too, Fanny. The horse'll stand."

"Please do!" entreated Lydia.

Thus urged, the girls reluctantly descended. Neither was in the habit of concealing her feelings under the convenient cloak of society observance, and both were jealously suspicious of Lydia Orr. Fanny had met her only the week before, walking with Wesley Elliot along the village street. And Mrs. Solomon Black had told Mrs. Fulsom, and Mrs. Fulsom had told Mrs. Deacon Whittle, and Mrs. Whittle had told another woman, who had felt it to be her Christian duty (however unpleasant) to inform Fanny that the minister was "payin' attention to Miss Orr."

"Of course," the woman had pointed out, "it wasn't to be wondered at, special, seeing the Orr girl had every chance in the world to catch him—living right in the same house with him." Then she had further stated her opinions of men in general for Fanny's benefit. All persons of the male sex, according to this woman, were easily put upon, deceived and otherwise led astray by artful young women from the city, who were represented as perpetually on the lookout for easy marks, like Wesley Elliot.

"He ain't any different from other men, if he *is* a minister," said she with a comprehensive sniff. "They're all alike, as far as I can find out: anybody that's a mind to soft-soap them and flatter them into thinkin' they're something great can lead them right around by the nose. And besides, *she's* got *money!*"

Fanny had affected a haughty indifference to the doings of Wesley Elliot, which did not for a moment deceive her keen-eyed informer.

"Of course, anybody with eyes in their heads can see what's taken place," compassionated she, impaling the unfortunate Fanny on the prongs of her sympathy. "My! I was telling George only yesterday, I thought it was a *perfect shame!* and somebody ought to speak out real plain to the minister."

Whereat Fanny had been goaded into wishing the woman would mind her own business! She did wish everybody would leave her and her affairs alone! People had no right to talk! As for speaking to the minister; let any one dare—!

As for Ellen Dix, she had never quite forgiven Lydia for innocently acquiring the fox skin and she had by now almost persuaded herself that she was passionately in love with Jim Dodge. She had always liked him—at least, she had not actively disliked him, as some of the other girls professed to do. She had found his satirical tongue, his keen eyes and his real or affected indifference to feminine wiles pleasantly stimulating. There was some fun in talking to Jim Dodge. But of late she had not been afforded the opportunity. Fanny had explained to Ellen that Jim was working terribly hard, often rising at three and four in the morning to work on his own farm, and putting in long days at the Bolton place.

"She seems to have most of the men in Brookville doing for her," Ellen had remarked coldly.

Then the girls had exchanged cautious glances.

"There's something awfully funny about her coming here, anyway," said Ellen. "Everybody thinks it's queer."

"I expect she had a reason," said Fanny, avoiding Ellen's eyes.

After which brief interchange of opinion they had twined their arms about each other's waists and squeezed wordless understanding and sympathy. Henceforth, it was tacitly understood between the two girls that singly and collectively they did not "like" Lydia Orr.

Lydia understood without further explanation that she was not to look to her nearest neighbors for either friendship or the affection she so deeply craved. Both Ellen and Fanny had passed the place every day since its restoration began; but not once had either betrayed the slightest interest or curiosity in what was going on beyond the barrier of the hedge. To be sure, Fanny had once stopped to speak to her brother; but when Lydia had hurried hopefully out to greet her it was only to catch a glimpse of the girl's back as she walked quickly away.

Jim Dodge had explained, with some awkwardness, that Fanny was in a hurry....

"Well, now, I'll tell you, Miss Orr," Mrs. Dix was saying, as all five women walked slowly toward the house. "I was talking with Abby Daggett, and she was telling me about your wanting to get back the old furniture that used to be in the house. It seems Henry Daggett has put up a notice in the post office; but so far, he says, not very many pieces have been heard from. You know the men-folks generally go after the mail, and men are slow; there's no denying that. As like as not they haven't even mentioned seeing the notice to the folks at home."

"That's so," confirmed Mrs. Dodge, nodding her head. "I don't know as Jim would ever tell us anything that happened from morning till night. We just have to pump things out of him; don't we, Fanny? He'd never tell without we did. His father was just the same."

Fanny looked annoyed, and Ellen squeezed her arm with an amused giggle.

"I didn't know, mother, there was anything we wanted to know, particularly," she said coldly.

"Well, you know both of us have been real interested in the work here," protested Mrs. Dodge, wonderingly. "I remember you was asking Jim only last night if Miss Orr was really going to—"

"I hope you'll like to see the house," said Lydia, as if she had not heard; "of course, being here every day I don't notice the changes as you might."

"You aren't living here yet, are you?" asked Mrs. Dix. "I understood Mrs. Solomon Black to say you weren't going to leave her for awhile yet."

"No; I shall be there nights and Sundays till everything is finished here," said Lydia. "Mrs. Black makes me very comfortable."

"Well, I think most of us ladies had ought to give you a vote of thanks on account of feeding the men-folks, noons," put in Mrs. Dodge. "It saves a lot of time not to have to look after a dinner-pail."

"Mother," interrupted Fanny in a thin, sharp voice, quite unlike her own, "you know Jim always comes home to his dinner."

"Well, what if he does; I was speaking for the rest of th' women," said Mrs. Dodge. "I'm sure it's very kind of Miss Orr to think of such a thing as cooking a hot dinner for all those hungry men."

Mrs. Dodge had received a second check from the assignees that very morning from the sale of the old bank building, and she was proportionately cheerful and content.

"Well; if this isn't handsome!" cried Mrs. Dix, pausing in the hall to look about her. "I declare I'd forgotten how it used to look. This is certainly better than having an old ruin standing here. But, of course it brings back old days."

She sighed, her dark, comely face clouding with sorrow.

"You know," she went on, turning confidentially to Lydia, "that dreadful bank failure was the real cause of my poor husband's death. He never held up his head after that. They suspected at first he was implicated in the steal. But Mr. Dix wasn't anything like Andrew Bolton. No; indeed! He wouldn't have taken a cent that belonged to anybody else—not if he was to die for it!"

"That's so," confirmed Mrs. Dodge. "What Andrew Bolton got was altogether too good for him. Come right down to it, he wasn't no better than a murderer!"

And she nodded her head emphatically.

Fanny and Ellen, who stood looking on, reddened impatiently at this:

"I'm sick and tired of hearing about Andrew Bolton," complained Ellen. "I've heard nothing else since I can remember. It's a pity you bought this house, Miss Orr: I heard Mr. Elliot say it was like stirring up a horrid, muddy pool. Not very complimentary to Brookville; but then—"

"Don't you think people will—forget after a while?" asked Lydia, her blue eyes fixed appealingly on the two young faces. "I don't see why everybody should—"

"Well, if you'd fixed the house entirely different," said Mrs. Dix. "But having it put back, just as it was, and wanting the old furniture and all—whatever put that into your head, my dear?"

"I heard it was handsome and old—I like old things. And, of course, it was—more in keeping to restore the house as it was, than to—"

"Well, I s'pose that's so," conceded Mrs. Dodge, her quick dark eyes busy with the renovated interior. "I'd sort of forgot how it did look when the Boltons was livin' here. But speaking of furniture; I see Mrs. Judge Fulsom let you have the old sofa. I remember she got it at the auction; she's kept it in her parlor ever since."

"Yes," said Lydia. "I was only too happy to give a hundred dollars for the sofa. It has been excellently preserved."

"A hundred dollars!" echoed Mrs. Dix. "Well!"

Mrs. Dodge giggled excitedly, like a young girl.

"A hundred dollars!" she repeated. "Well, I want to know!"

The two women exchanged swift glances.

"You wouldn't want to buy any pieces that had been broke, I s'pose," suggested Mrs. Dodge.

"If they can be repaired, I certainly do," replied Lydia.

"Mother!" expostulated Fanny, in a low but urgent tone. "Ellen and I—we really ought to be going."

The girl's face glowed with shamed crimson. She felt haughty and humiliated and angry all at once. It was not to be borne.

Mrs. Dix was not listening to Fanny Dodge.

"I bid in the big, four-post mahogany bed at the auction," she said, "and the bureau to match; an' I believe there are two or three chairs about the house."

"We've got a table," chimed in Mrs. Dodge; "but one leg give away, an' I had it put up in the attic years ago. And Fanny's got a bed and bureau in her room that was painted white, with little pink flowers tied up with blue ribbons. Of course the paint is pretty well rubbed off; but—"

"Oh, might I have that set?" cried Lydia, turning to Fanny. "Perhaps you've grown fond of it and won't want to give it up. But I—I'd pay almost anything for it. And of course I shall want the mahogany, too."

"Well, we didn't know," explained Mrs. Dix, with dignity. "We got those pieces instead of the money we'd ought to have had from the estate. There was a big crowd at the auction, I remember; but nobody really wanted to pay anything for the old furniture. A good deal of it had come out of folks' attics in the first place."

"I shall be glad to pay three hundred dollars for the mahogany bed and bureau," said Lydia. "And for the little white set—"

"I don't care to part with my furniture," said Fanny Dodge, her pretty round chin uplifted.

She was taller than Lydia, and appeared to be looking over her head with an intent stare at the freshly papered wall beyond.

"For pity sake!" exclaimed her mother sharply. "Why, Fanny, you could buy a brand new set, an' goodness knows what-all with the money. What's the matter with you?"

"I know just how Fanny feels about having her room changed," put in Ellen Dix, with a spirited glance at the common enemy. "There are things that money can't buy, but some people don't seem to think so."

Lydia's blue eyes had clouded swiftly.

"If you'll come into the library," she said, "we'll have some lemonade. It's so very warm I'm sure we are all thirsty."

She did not speak of the furniture again, and after a little the visitors rose to go. Mrs. Dodge lingered behind the others to whisper:

"I'm sure I don't know what got into my Fanny. Only the other day she was wishing she might have her room done over, with new furniture and all. I'll try and coax her."

But Lydia shook her head.

"Please don't," she said. "I want that furniture very much; but—I know there are things money can't buy."

"Mebbe you wouldn't want it, if you was t' see it," was Mrs. Dodge's honest opinion. "It's all turned yellow, an' the pink flowers are mostly rubbed off. I remember it was real pretty when we first got it. It used to belong to Mrs. Bolton's little girl. I don't know as anybody's told you, but they had a little girl. My! what an awful thing for a child to grow up to! I've often thought of it. But mebbe she didn't live to grow up. None of us ever heard."

"Mother!" called Fanny, from the front seat of the carryall. "We're waiting for you."

"In a minute, Fanny," said Mrs. Dodge.... "Of course you can have that table I spoke of, Miss Orr, and anything else I can find in the attic, or around. An' I was thinking if you was to come down to the Ladies' Aid on Friday afternoon—it meets at Mrs. Mixter's this week, at two o'clock; you know where Mrs. Mixter lives, don't you? Well; anyway, Mrs. Solomon Black does, an' she generally comes. But I know lots of the ladies has pieces of that furniture; and most of them would be mighty glad to get rid of it. But they are like my Fanny— kind of contrary, and backward about selling things. I'll talk to Fanny when we get home. Why, she don't any more want that old painted set—"

"Mother!" Fanny's sweet angry voice halted the rapid progress of her mother's speech for an instant.

"I shouldn't wonder if the flies was bothering th' horse," surmised Mrs. Dodge; "he does fidget an' stamp somethin' terrible when the flies gets after him; his tail ain't so long as some.... Well, I'll let you know; and if you could drop around and see the table and all— Yes, some day this week. Of course I'll have to buy new furniture to put in their places; so will Mrs. Dix. But I will say that mahogany bed is handsome; they've got it in their spare room, and there ain't a scratch on it. I can guarantee that.... Yes; I guess the flies are bad today; looks like rain. Good-by!"

Lydia stood watching the carryall, as it moved away from under the milk-white pillars of the restored portico. Why did Fanny Dodge and Ellen Dix dislike her, she wondered, and what could she do to win their friendship? Her troubled thoughts were interrupted by Martha, the taciturn maid.

"I found this picture on the floor, Miss Lydia," said Martha; "did you drop it?"

Lydia glanced at the small, unmounted photograph. It was a faded snapshot of a picnic party under a big tree. Her eyes became at once riveted upon the central figures of the little group; the pretty girl in the middle was Fanny Dodge; and behind her—yes, surely, that was the young clergyman, Wesley Elliot. Something in the attitude of the man and the coquettish upward tilt of the girl's face brought back to her mind a forgotten remark of Mrs. Solomon Black's. Lydia had failed to properly understand it, at the time. Mrs. Solomon Black was given to cryptic remarks, and Lydia's mind had been preoccupied by the increasing difficulties which threatened the accomplishment of her purpose:

"A person, coming into a town like Brookville to live, by rights had ought to have eyes in the backs of their heads," Mrs. Black had observed.

It was at breakfast time, Lydia now remembered, and the minister was late, as frequently happened.

"I thought like's not nobody would mention it to you," Mrs. Black had further elucidated. "Of course *he* wouldn't say anything, men-folks are kind of sly and secret in their doings—even the best of 'em; and you'll find it's so, as you travel along life's path-way."

Mrs. Black had once written a piece of poetry and it had actually been printed in the Grenoble *News*; since then she frequently made use of figures of speech.

"A married woman and a widow can speak from experience," she went on. "So I thought I'd just tell you: he's as good as engaged, already."

"Do you mean Mr. Elliot?" asked Lydia incuriously.

Mrs. Black nodded.

"I thought you ought to know," she said.

Mr. Elliot had entered the room upon the heels of this warning, and Lydia had promptly forgotten it. Now she paused for a swift review of the weeks which had already passed since her arrival. Mr. Elliot had been unobtrusively kind and helpful from the first, she remembered. Later, he had been indefatigable in the matter of securing workmen for the restoration of the old house, when she made it clear to him that she did not want an architect and preferred to hire Brookville men exclusively. As seemed entirely natural, the minister had called frequently to inspect the progress of the work. Twice in their rounds together they had come upon Jim Dodge; and although the clergyman was affable in his recognition and greeting, Lydia had been unpleasantly surprised by the savage look on her landscape-gardener's face as he returned the polite salutation.

"Don't you like Mr. Elliot?" she had ventured to inquire, after the second disagreeable incident of the sort.

Jim Dodge had treated her to one of his dark-browed, incisive glances before replying.

"I'm afraid I can't answer that question satisfactorily, Miss Orr," was what he said.

And Lydia, wondering, desisted from further question.

"That middle one looks some like one of the young ladies that was here this morning," observed Martha, with the privileged familiarity of an old servant.

"She must have dropped it," said Lydia, slowly.

"The young ladies here in the country has very bad manners," commented Martha, puckering her lips primly. "I wouldn't put myself out for them, if I was you, mem."

Lydia turned the picture over and gazed abstractedly at the three words written there: "Lest we forget!" Beneath this pertinent quotation appeared the initials "W. E."

"If it was for *me* to say," went on Martha, in an injured tone, "I'd not be for feedin' up every man, woman and child that shows their face inside the grounds. Why, they don't appreciate it no more than—"

The woman's eloquent gesture appeared to include the blue-bottle fly buzzing noisily on the window-pane:

"Goodness gracious! if these flies ain't enough to drive a body crazy—what with the new paint and all...."

Chapter XIII

Lydia laid the picture carefully away in a pigeonhole of her desk. She was still thinking soberly of the subtle web of prejudices, feelings and conditions into which she had obtruded her one fixed purpose in life. But if Mr. Elliot had been as good as engaged to Fanny Dodge, as Mrs. Solomon Black had been at some pains to imply, in what way had she (Lydia) interfered with the dénouement?

She shook her head at last over the intricacies of the imperfectly stated problem. The idea of coquetting with a man had never entered Lydia's fancy. Long since, in the chill spring of her girlhood, she had understood her position in life as compared with that of other girls. She must never marry. She must never fall in love, even. The inflexible Puritan code of her uncle's wife had found ready acceptance in Lydia's nature. If not an active participant in her father's crime, she still felt herself in a measure responsible for it. He had determined to grow rich and powerful for her sake. More than once, in the empty rambling talk which he poured forth in a turgid stream during their infrequent meetings, he had told her so, with extravagant phrase and gesture. And so, at last, she had come to share his punishment in a hundred secret, unconfessed ways. She ate scant food, slept on the hardest of beds, labored unceasingly, with the great, impossible purpose of some day making things right: of restoring the money they—she no longer said *he*—had stolen; of building again the waste places desolated by the fire of his ambition for her. There had followed that other purpose, growing ever stronger with the years, and deepening with the deepening stream of her womanhood: her love, her vast, unavailing pity for the broken and aging man, who would some day be free. She came at length to the time when she saw clearly that he would never leave the prison alive, unless in some way she could contrive to keep open the clogging springs of hope and desire. She began deliberately and with purpose to call back memories of the past: the house in which he had lived, the gardens and orchards in which he once had taken pride, his ambitious projects for village improvement.

"You shall have it all back, father!" she promised him, with passionate resolve. "And it will only be a little while to wait, now."

Thus encouraged, the prisoner's horizon widened, day by day. He appeared, indeed, to almost forget the prison, so busy was he in recalling trivial details and unimportant memories of events long since past. He babbled incessantly of his old neighbors, calling them by name, and chuckling feebly as he told her of their foibles and peculiarities.

"But we must give them every cent of the money, father," she insisted; "we must make everything right."

"Oh, yes! Oh, yes, we'll fix it up somehow with the creditors," he would say.

Then he would scowl and rub his shorn head with his tremulous old hands.

"What did they do with the house, Margaret?" he asked, over and over, a furtive gleam of anxiety in his eyes. "They didn't tear it down; did they?"

He waxed increasingly anxious on this point as the years of his imprisonment dwindled at last to months. And then her dream had unexpectedly come true. She had money—plenty of it—and nothing stood in the way. She could never forget the day she told him about the house. Always she had tried to quiet him with vague promises and imagined descriptions of a place she had completely forgotten.

"The house is ours, father," she assured him, jubilantly. "And I am having it painted on the outside."

"You are having it painted on the outside, Margaret? Was that necessary, already?"

"Yes, father.... But I am Lydia. Don't you remember? I am your little girl, grown up."

"Yes, yes, of course. You are like your mother— And you are having the house painted? Who's doing the job?"

She told him the man's name and he laughed rather immoderately.

"He'll do you on the white lead, if you don't watch him," he said. "I know Asa Todd. Talk about frauds— You must be sure he puts honest linseed oil in the paint. He won't, unless you watch him."

"I'll see to it, father."

"But whatever you do, don't let 'em into my room," he went on, after a frowning pause.

"You mean your library, father? I'm having the ceiling whitened. It—it needed it."

"I mean my bedroom, child. I won't have workmen pottering about in there."

"But you won't mind if they paint the woodwork, father? It—has grown quite yellow in places."

"Nonsense, my dear! Why, I had all the paint upstairs gone over—let me see—"

And he fell into one of his heavy moods of introspection which seemed, indeed, not far removed from torpor.

When she had at last roused him with an animated description of the vegetable garden, he appeared to have forgotten his objections to having workmen enter his chamber. And Lydia was careful not to recall it to his mind.

She was still sitting before his desk, ostensibly absorbed in the rows of incomprehensible figures Deacon Whittle, as general contractor, had urged upon her attention, when Martha again parted the heavy cloud of her thoughts.

"The minister, come to see you again," she announced, with a slight but mordant emphasis on the ultimate word.

"Yes," said Lydia, rousing herself, with an effort. "Mr. Elliot, you said?"

"I s'pose that's his name," conceded Martha ungraciously. "I set him in the dining room. It's about the only place with two chairs in it; an' I shan't have no time to make more lemonade, in case you wanted it, m'm."

Chapter XIV

The Reverend Wesley Elliot, looking young, eager and pleasingly worldly in a blue serge suit of unclerical cut, rose to greet her as she entered.

"I haven't been here in two or three days," he began, as he took the hand she offered, "and I'm really astonished at the progress you've been making."

He still retained her hand, as he smiled down into her grave, preoccupied face.

"What's the trouble with our little lady of Bolton House?" he inquired. "Any of the workmen on strike, or—"

She withdrew her hand with a faint smile.

"Everything is going very well, I think," she told him.

He was still scrutinizing her with that air of intimate concern, which inspired most of the women of his flock to unburden themselves of their manifold anxieties at his slightest word of encouragement.

"It's a pretty heavy burden for you," he said gravely. "You need some one to help you. I wonder if I couldn't shoulder a few of the grosser details?"

"You've already been most kind," Lydia said evasively. "But now— Oh, I think everything has been thought of. You know Mr. Whittle is looking after the work."

He smiled, a glimmer of humorous understanding in his fine dark eyes. "Yes, I know," he said.

A silence fell between them. Lydia was one of those rare women who do not object to silence. It seemed to her that she had always lived alone with her ambitions, which could not be shared, and her bitter knowledge, which was never to be spoken of. But now she stirred uneasily in her chair, aware of the intent expression in his eyes. Her troubled thoughts reverted to the little picture which had fluttered to the floor from somebody's keeping only an hour before.

"I've had visitors this morning," she told him, with purpose.

"Ah! people are sure to be curious and interested," he commented.

"They were Mrs. Dodge and her daughter and Mrs. Dix and Ellen," she explained.

"That must have been pleasant," he murmured perfunctorily. "Are you—do you find yourself becoming at all interested in the people about here? Of course it is easy to see you come to us from quite another world."

She shook her head.

"Oh, no," she said quickly. "—If you mean that I am superior in any way to the people of Brookville; I'm not, at all. I am really a very ordinary sort of a person. I've not been to college and—I've always worked, harder than most, so that I've had little opportunity for—culture."

His smile broadened into a laugh of genuine amusement.

"My dear Miss Orr," he protested, "I had no idea of intimating—"

Her look of passionate sincerity halted his words of apology.

"I am very much interested in the people here," she declared. "I want—oh, so much—to be friends with them! I want it more than anything else in the world! If they would only like me. But—they don't."

"How can they help it?" he exclaimed. "Like you? They ought to worship you! They shall!"

She shook her head sadly.

"No one can compel love," she said.

"Sometimes the love of one can atone for the indifference—even the hostility of the many," he ventured.

But she had not stooped to the particular, he perceived. Her thoughts were ranging wide over an unknown country whither, for the moment, he could not follow. He studied her abstracted face with its strangely aloof expression, like that of a saint or a fanatic, with a faint renewal of previous misgivings.

"I am very much interested in Fanny Dodge," she said abruptly.

"In—Fanny Dodge?" he repeated.

He became instantly angry with himself for the dismayed astonishment he had permitted to escape him, and increasingly so because of the uncontrollable tide of crimson which invaded his face.

She was looking at him, with the calm, direct gaze which had more than once puzzled him.

"You know her very well, don't you?"

"Why, of course, Miss Dodge is—she is—er—one of our leading young people, and naturally— She plays our little organ in church and Sunday School. Of course you've noticed. She is most useful and—er—helpful."

Lydia appeared to be considering his words with undue gravity.

"But I didn't come here this morning to talk to you about another woman," he said, with undeniable hardihood. "I want to talk to you—*to you*—and what I have to say—"

58

Lydia got up from her chair rather suddenly.

"Please excuse me a moment," she said, quite as if he had not spoken.

He heard her cross the hall swiftly. In a moment she had returned.

"I found this picture on the floor—after they had gone," she said, and handed him the photograph.

He stared at it with unfeigned astonishment.

"Oh, yes," he murmured. "Well—?"

"Turn it over," she urged, somewhat breathlessly.

He obeyed, and bit his lip angrily.

"What of it?" he demanded. "A quotation from Kipling's Recessional—a mere commonplace.... Yes; I wrote it."

Then his anger suddenly left him. His mind had leaped to the solution of the matter, and the solution appeared to Wesley Elliot as eminently satisfying; it was even amusing. What a transparent, womanly little creature she was, to be sure! He had not been altogether certain of himself as he walked out to the old Bolton place that morning. But oddly enough, this girlish jealousy of hers, this pretty spite—he found it piquantly charming.

"I wrote it," he repeated, his indulgent understanding of her mood lurking in smiling lips and eyes, "on the occasion of a particularly grubby Sunday School picnic: I assure you I shall not soon forget the spiders which came to an untimely end in my lemonade, nor the inquisitive ants which explored my sandwiches."

She surveyed him unsmilingly.

"But you did not mean that," she said. "You were thinking of something—quite different."

He frowned thoughtfully. Decidedly, this matter should be settled between them at once and for ever. A clergyman, he reflected, must always be on friendly—even confidential terms with a wide variety of women. His brief experience had already taught him this much. And a jealous or unduly suspicious wife might prove a serious handicap to future success.

"Won't you sit down," he urged. "I—You must allow me to explain. We—er—must talk this over."

She obeyed him mechanically. All at once she was excessively frightened at what she had attempted. She knew nothing of the ways of men; but she felt suddenly sure that he would resent her interference as an unwarrantable impertinence.

"I thought—if you were going there today—you might take it—to her," she hesitated. "Or, I could send it. It is a small matter, of course."

"I think," he said gravely, "that it is a very serious matter."

She interpreted uncertainly the intent gaze of his beautiful, somber eyes.

"I came here," she faltered, "to—to find a home. I had no wish—"

"I understand," he said, his voice deep and sympathetic; "people have been talking to you—about me. Am I right?"

She was silent, a pink flush slowly staining her cheeks.

"You have not yet learned upon what slight premises country women, of the type we find in Brookville, arrive at the most unwarrantable conclusions," he went on carefully. "I did not myself sufficiently realize this, at first. I may have been unwise."

"No, you were not!" she contradicted him unexpectedly.

His lifted eyebrows expressed surprise.

"I wish you would explain to me—" he began.

Then stopped short. How indeed could she explain, when as yet he had not made clear to her his own purpose, which had grown steadily with the passing weeks?

"You will let me speak, first," he concluded inadequately.

He hastily reviewed the various phrases which arose to his lips and rejected them one by one. There was some peculiar quality of coldness, of reserve—he could not altogether make it clear to himself: it might well be the knowledge of her power, her wealth, which lent that almost austere expression to her face. It was evident that her wonted composure had been seriously disturbed by the unlucky circumstance of the photograph. He had permitted the time and occasion which had prompted him to write those three fatefully familiar words on the back of the picture altogether to escape him. If he chose to forget, why should Fanny Dodge, or any one else, persist in remembering?

And above all, why should the girl have chosen to drop this absurd memento of the most harmless of flirtations at the feet of Lydia? There could be but one reasonable explanation.... Confound women, anyway!

"I had not meant to speak, yet," he went on, out of the clamoring multitude of his thoughts. "I felt that we ought—"

He became suddenly aware of Lydia's eyes. There was no soft answering fire, no maidenly uncertainty of hope and fear in those clear depths.

"It is very difficult for me to talk of this to you," she said slowly. "You will think me over-bold—unmannerly, perhaps. But I can't help that. I should never have thought of your caring for me—you will at least do me the justice to believe that."

"Lydia!" he interrupted, poignantly distressed by her evident timidity—her exquisite hesitation, "let me speak! I understand—I know—"

She forbade him with a gesture, at once pleading and peremptory.

"No," she said. "No! I began this, I must go on to the end. What you ought to understand is this: I am not like other women. I want only friendship from every one. I shall never ask more. I can never accept more—from any one. I want you to know this—now."

"But I—do you realize—"

"I want your friendship," she went on, facing him with a sort of desperate courage; "but more than any kindness you can offer me, Mr. Elliot, I want the friendship of Fanny Dodge, of Ellen Dix—of all good women. I need it! Now you know why I showed you the picture. If you will not give it to her, I shall. I want her—I want every one—to understand that I shall never come between her and the slightest hope she may have cherished before my coming to Brookville. All I ask is—leave to live here quietly—and be friendly, as opportunity offers."

Her words, her tone were not to be mistaken. But even the sanest and wisest of men has never thus easily surrendered the jealously guarded stronghold of sex. Wesley Elliot's youthful ideas of women were totally at variance with the disconcerting conviction which strove to invade his mind. He had experienced not the slightest difficulty, up to the present moment, in classifying them, neatly and logically; but there was no space in his mental files for a woman such as Lydia Orr was representing herself to be. It was inconceivable, on the face of it! All women demanded admiration, courtship, love. They always had; they always would. The literature of the ages attested it. He had been too precipitate—too hasty. He must give her time to recover from the shock she must have experienced from hearing the spiteful gossip about himself and Fanny Dodge. On the whole, he admired her courage. What she had said could not be attributed to the mere promptings of vulgar sex-jealousy. Very likely Fanny had been disagreeable and haughty in her manner. He believed her capable of it. He sympathized with Fanny; with the curious mental aptitude of a sensitive nature, he still loved Fanny. It had cost him real effort to close the doors of his heart against her.

"I admire you more than I can express for what you have had the courage to tell me," he assured her. "And you will let me see that I understand—more than you think."

"It is impossible that you should understand," she said tranquilly. "But you will, at least, remember what I have said?"

"I will," he promised easily. "I shall never forget it!"

A slight humorous smile curved the corners of his handsome mouth.

"Now this—er—what shall we call it?—'bone of contention' savors too strongly of wrath and discomfiture; so we'll say, simply and specifically, this photograph—which chances to have a harmless quotation inscribed upon its reverse: Suppose I drop it in the waste-basket? I can conceive that it possesses no particular significance or value for any one. I assure you most earnestly that it does not—for me."

He made as though he would have carelessly torn the picture across, preparatory to making good his proposal.

She stopped him with a swift gesture.

"Give it to me," she said. "It is lost property, and I am responsible for its safe-keeping."

She perceived that she had completely failed in her intention.

"What are you going to do with it?" he inquired, with an easy assumption of friendliness calculated to put her more completely at her ease with him.

"I don't know. For the present, I shall put it back in my desk."

"Better take my advice and destroy it," he persisted. "It—er—is not valuable evidence. Or—I believe on second thought I shall accept your suggestion and return it myself to its probable owner."

He was actually laughing, his eyes brimming with boyish mischief.

"I think it belongs to Miss Dix," he told her audaciously.

"To Miss Dix?" she echoed.

60

"Yes; why not? Don't you see the fair Ellen among the group?"

Her eyes blazed suddenly upon him; her lips trembled.

"Forgive me!" he cried, aghast at his own folly.

She retreated before his outstretched hands.

"I didn't mean to—to make light of what appears so serious a matter to you," he went on impetuously. "It is only that it is *not* serious; don't you see? It is such a foolish little mistake. It must not come between us, Lydia!"

"Please go away, at once," she interrupted him breathlessly, "and—and *think* of what I have said to you. Perhaps you didn't believe it; but you *must* believe it!"

Then, because he did not stir, but instead stood gazing at her, his puzzled eyes full of questions, entreaties, denials, she quietly closed a door between them. A moment later he heard her hurrying feet upon the stair.

Chapter XV

August was a month of drought and intense heat that year; by the first week in September the stream had dwindled to the merest silver thread, its wasted waters floating upward in clouds of impalpable mist at dawn and evening to be lost forever in the empty vault of heaven. Behind the closed shutters of the village houses, women fanned themselves in the intervals of labor over superheated cookstoves. Men consulted their thermometers with incredulous eyes. Springs reputed to be unfailing gradually ceased their cool trickle. Wells and cisterns yielded little save the hollow sound of the questing bucket. There was serious talk of a water famine in Brookville. At the old Bolton house, however, there was still water in abundance. In jubilant defiance of blazing heavens and parching earth the Red-Fox Spring—tapped years before by Andrew Bolton and piped a mile or more down the mountain side, that his household, garden and stock might never lack of pure cold water—gushed in undiminished volume, filling and overflowing the new cement reservoir, which had been one of Lydia Orr's cautious innovations in the old order of things.

The repairs on the house were by now finished, and the new-old mansion, shining white amid the chastened luxuriance of ancient trees, once more showed glimpses of snowy curtains behind polished windowpanes. Flowers, in a lavish prodigality of bloom the Bolton house of the past had never known, flanked the old stone walls, bordered the drives, climbed high on trellises and arbors, and blazed in serried ranks beyond the broad sweep of velvet turf, which repaid in emerald freshness its daily share of the friendly water.

Mrs. Abby Daggett gazed at the scene in rapt admiration through the clouds of dust which uprose from under Dolly's scuffling feet.

"Ain't that place han'some, now she's fixed it up?" she demanded of Mrs. Deacon Whittle, who sat bolt upright at her side, her best summer hat, sparsely decorated with purple flowers, protected from the suffocating clouds of dust by a voluminous brown veil. "I declare I'd like to stop in and see the house, now it's all furnished up—if only for a minute."

"We ain't got time, Abby," Mrs. Whittle pointed out. "There's work to cut out after we get to Mis' Dix's, and it was kind of late when we started."

Mrs. Daggett relinquished her random desire with her accustomed amiability. Life consisted mainly in giving up things, she had found; but being cheerful, withal, served to cast a mellow glow over the severest denials; in fact, it often turned them into something unexpectedly rare and beautiful.

"I guess that's so, Ann," she agreed. "Dolly got kind of fractious over his headstall when I was harnessin'. He don't seem to like his sun hat, and I dunno's I blame him. I guess if our ears stuck up through the top of our bunnits like his we wouldn't like it neither."

Mrs. Whittle surveyed the animal's grotesquely bonneted head with cold disfavor.

"What simple ideas you do get into your mind, Abby," said she, with the air of one conscious of superior intellect. "A horse ain't human, Abby. He ain't no idea he's wearing a hat.... The Deacon says their heads get hotter with them rediculous bunnits on. He favors a green branch."

"Well," said Mrs. Daggett, foiling a suspicious movement of Dolly's switching tail, "mebbe that's so; I feel some cooler without a hat. But 'tain't safe to let the sun beat right down, the way it does, without something between. Then, you see, Henry's got a lot o' these horse hats in the store to sell. So of course Dolly, he has to wear one."

Mrs. Whittle cautiously wiped the dust from her hard red cheeks.

"My! if it ain't hot," she observed. "You're so fleshy, Abby, I should think you'd feel it something terrible."

"Oh, I don't know," said Mrs. Daggett placidly. "Of course I'm fleshy, Ann; I ain't denying that; but so be you. You don't want to think about the heat so constant, Ann. Our thermometer fell down and got broke day before yesterday, and Henry says 'I'll bring you up another from the store this noon.' But he forgot all about it. I didn't say a word, and that afternoon I set out on the porch under the vines and felt real cool—not knowing it was so hot—when along comes Mrs. Fulsom, a-pantin' and fannin' herself. 'Good land, Abby!' says she; 'by the looks, a body'd think you didn't know the thermometer had risen to ninety-two since eleven o'clock this morning.' 'I didn't,' I says placid; 'our thermometer's broke.' 'Well, you'd better get another right off,' says she, wiping her face and groaning. 'It's an awful thing, weather like this, not to have a thermometer right where you can see it.' Henry brought a real nice one home from the store that very night; and I hung it out of sight behind the sitting room door; I told Henry I thought 'twould be safer there."

"That sounds exactly like you, Abby," commented Mrs. Whittle censoriously. "I should think Henry Daggett would be onto you, by now."

"Well, he ain't," said Mrs. Daggett, with mild triumph. "He thinks I'm real cute, an' like that. It does beat all, don't it? how simple menfolks are. I like 'em all the better for it, myself. If Henry'd been as smart an' penetrating as some folks, I don't know as we'd have made out so well together. Ain't it lucky for me he ain't?"

Ann Whittle sniffed suspiciously. She never felt quite sure of Abby Daggett: there was a lurking sparkle in her demure blue eyes and a suspicious dimple near the corner of her mouth which ruffled Mrs. Whittle's temper, already strained to the breaking point by the heat and dust of their midday journey.

"Well, I never should have thought of such a thing, as going to Ladies' Aid in all this heat, if you hadn't come after me, Abby," she said crossly. "I guess flannel petticoats for the heathen could have waited a spell."

"Mebbe they could, Ann," Mrs. Daggett said soothingly. "It's kind of hard to imagine a heathen wanting any sort of a petticoat this weather, and I guess they don't wear 'em before they're converted; but of course the missionaries try to teach 'em better. They go forth, so to say, with the Bible in one hand and a petticoat in the other."

"I should hope so!" said Mrs. Whittle, with vague fervor.

The sight of a toiling wagon supporting a huge barrel caused her to change the subject rather abruptly.

"That's Jacob Merrill's team," she said, craning her neck. "What on earth has he got in that hogs-head?"

"He's headed for Lydia Orr's spring, I shouldn't wonder," surmised Mrs. Daggett. "She told Henry to put up a notice in the post office that folks could get all the water they wanted from her spring. It's running, same as usual; but, most everybody else's has dried up."

"I think the minister ought to pray for rain regular from the pulpit on Sunday," Mrs. Whittle advanced. "I'm going to tell him so."

"She's going to do a lot better than that," said Mrs. Daggett.... "For the land sake, Dolly! I ain't urged you beyond your strength, and you know it; but if you don't g'long—"

A vigorous slap of the reins conveyed Mrs. Daggett's unuttered threat to the reluctant animal, with the result that both ladies were suddenly jerked backward by an unlooked for burst of speed.

"I think that horse is dangerous, Abby," remonstrated Mrs. Whittle, indignantly, as she settled her veil. "You ought to be more careful how you speak up to him."

"I'll risk him!" said Mrs. Daggett with spirit. "It don't help him none to stop walking altogether and stand stock still in the middle of the road, like he was a graven image. I'll take the whip to him, if he don't look out!"

Mrs. Whittle gathered her skirts about her, with an apprehensive glance at the dusty road.

"If you das' to touch that whip, Abby Daggett," said she, "I'll git right out o' this buggy and walk, so there!"

Mrs. Daggett's broad bosom shook with merriment.

"Fer pity sake, Ann, don't be scared," she exhorted her friend. "I ain't never touched Dolly with the whip; but he knows I mean what I say when I speak to him like that! ...I started in to tell you about the Red-Fox Spring, didn't I?"

Mrs. Whittle coughed dryly.

"I wish I had a drink of it right now," she said. "The idea of that Orr girl watering her flowers and grass, when everybody else in town is pretty near burnt up. Why, we ain't had water enough in our cistern to do the regular wash fer two weeks. I said to Joe and the Deacon today: 'You can wear them shirts another day, for I don't know where on earth you'll get clean ones.'"

"There ain't nothing selfish about Lydia Orr," proclaimed Mrs. Daggett joyfully. "What *do* you think she's going to do now?"

"How should I know?"

Mrs. Whittle's tone implied a jaded indifference to the doings of any one outside of her own immediate family circle.

"She's going to have the Red-Fox piped down to the village," said Mrs. Daggett. "She's had a man from Boston to look at it; and he says there's water enough up there in the mountains to supply two or three towns the size of Brookville. She's going to have a reservoir: and anybody that's a mind to can pipe it right into their kitchens."

Mrs. Whittle turned her veiled head to stare incredulously at her companion.

"Well, I declare!" she said; "that girl certainly does like to make a show of her money; don't she? If 'tain't one thing it's another. How did a girl like her come by all that money, I'd like to know?"

"I don't see as that's any of our particular affairs," objected Mrs. Daggett warmly. "Think of havin' nice cool spring water, just by turning a faucet. We're going to have it in our house. And Henry says mebbe he'll put in a tap and a drain-pipe upstairs. It'd save a lot o' steps."

"Huh! like enough you'll be talkin' about a regular nickel-plated bathroom like hers, next," suspicioned Mrs. Whittle. "The Deacon says he did his best to talk her out of it; but she stuck right to it. And one wa'n't enough, at that. She's got three of 'em in that house. That's worse'n Andrew Bolton."

"Do you mean *worse*, Ann Whittle, or do you mean *better*? A nice white bathtub is a means o' grace, I think!"

"I mean what I said, Abby; and you hadn't ought to talk like that. It's downright sinful. *Means o' grace! a bathtub!* Well, I never!"

The ladies of the Aid Society were already convened in Mrs. Dix's front parlor, a large square room, filled with the cool green light from a yard full of trees, whose deep-thrust roots defied the drought. Ellen Dix had just brought in a glass pitcher, its frosted sides proclaiming its cool contents, when the late comers arrived.

"Yes," Mrs. Dix was saying, "Miss Orr sent over a big piece of ice this morning and she squeezed out juice of I don't know how many lemons. Jim Dodge brought 'em here in the auto; and she told him to go around and gather up all the ladies that didn't have conveyances of their own."

"And that's how I came to be here," said Mrs. Mixter. "Our horse has gone lame."

"Well now, wa'n't that lovely?" crowed Mrs. Daggett, cooling her flushed face with slow sweeps of the big turkey-feather fan Mrs. Dix handed her. "Ain't she just the sweetest girl—always thinking of other folks! I never see anything like her."

A subtle expression of reserve crept over the faces of the attentive women. Mrs. Mixter tasted the contents of her glass critically.

"I don't know," she said dryly, as if the lemonade had failed to cool her parched throat, "that depends on how you look at it."

Mrs. Whittle gave vent to a cackle of rather discordant laughter.

"That's just what I was telling Abby on the way over," she said. "Once in a while you do run across a person that's bound to make a show of their money."

Mrs. Solomon Black, in a green and white sprigged muslin dress, her water-waves unusually crisp and conspicuous, bit off a length of thread with a meditative air.

"Well," said she, "that girl lived in my house, off an' on, for more than two months. I can't say as I think she's the kind that wants to show off."

Fifteen needles paused in their busy activities, and twice as many eyes were focused upon Mrs. Solomon Black. That lady sustained the combined attack with studied calm. She even smiled, as she jerked her thread smartly through a breadth of red flannel.

"I s'pose you knew a lot more about her in the beginning than we did," said Mrs. Dodge, in a slightly offended tone.

"You must have known something about her, Phoebe," put in Mrs. Fulsom. "I don't care what anybody says to the contrary, there's something queer in a young girl, like her, coming to a strange place, like Brookville, and doing all the things she's done. It ain't natural: and that's what I told the Judge when he was considering the new waterworks. There's a great deal of money to be made on waterworks, the Judge says."

The eyes were now focused upon Mrs. Fulsom.

"Well, I can tell you, she ain't looking to make money out of Brookville," said Abby Daggett, laying down her fan and taking an unfinished red flannel petticoat from the basket on the table. "Henry knows all about her plans, and he says it's the grandest idea! The water's going to be piped down from the mountain right to our doors—an' it'll be just as free as the Water of Life to anybody that'll take it."

"Yes; but who's going to pay for digging up the streets and putting 'em back?" piped up an anxious voice from a corner.

"We'd ought to, if she does the rest," said Mrs. Daggett; "but Henry says—"

"You can be mighty sure there's a come-back in it somewhere," was Mrs. Whittle's opinion. "The Deacon says he don't know whether to vote for it or not. We'll have rain before long; and these droughts don't come every summer."

Ellen Dix and Fanny Dodge were sitting outside on the porch. Both girls were sewing heart-shaped pieces of white cloth upon squares of turkey-red calico.

"Isn't it funny nobody seems to like her?" murmured Ellen, tossing her head. "I shouldn't be surprised if they wouldn't let her bring the water in, for all she says she'll pay for everything except putting it in the houses."

Fanny gazed at the white heart in the middle of the red square.

"It's awfully hard to sew these hearts on without puckering," she said.

"Fan," said Ellen cautiously, "does the minister go there much now?"

Fanny compressed her lips.

"I'm sure I don't know," she replied, her eyes and fingers busy with an unruly heart, which declined to adjust itself to requirements. "What are they going to do with this silly patchwork, anyway?"

"Make an autograph quilt for the minister's birthday; didn't you know?"

Fanny dropped her unfinished work.

"I never heard of anything so silly!" she said sharply.

"Everybody is to write their names in pencil on these hearts," pursued Ellen mischievously; "then they're to be done in tracing stitch in red cotton. In the middle of the quilt is to be a big white square, with a large red heart in it; that's supposed to be Wesley Elliot's. It's to have his monogram in stuffed letters, in the middle of it. Lois Daggett's doing that now. I think it's a lovely idea—so romantic, you know."

Fanny did not appear to be listening; her pretty white forehead wore a frowning look.

"Ellen," she said abruptly, "do you ever see anything of Jim nowadays?"

"Oh! so you thought you'd pay me back, did you?" cried Ellen angrily. "I never said I cared a rap for Jim Dodge; but you told me a whole lot about Wesley Elliot: don't you remember that night we walked home from the fair, and you—"

Fanny suddenly put her hand over her friend's.

"Please don't talk so loud, Ellen; somebody will be sure to hear. I'd forgotten what you said—truly, I had. But Jim—"

"Well?" interrogated Ellen impatiently, arching her slender black brows.

"Let's walk down in the orchard," proposed Fanny. "Somebody else can work on these silly old hearts, if they want to. My needle sticks so I can't sew, anyway."

"I've got to help mother cut the cake, in a minute," objected Ellen.

But she stepped down on the parched grass and the two friends were soon strolling among the fallen fruit of a big sweet apple tree behind the house, their arms twined about each other's waists, their pretty heads bent close together.

Chapter XVI

"The reason I spoke to you about Jim just now," said Fanny, "was because he's been acting awfully queer lately. I thought perhaps you knew—I know he likes you better than any of the other girls. He says you have some sense, and the others haven't."

"I guess that must have been before Lydia Orr came to Brookville," said Ellen, in a hard, sweet voice.

"Yes; it was," admitted Fanny reluctantly. "Everything seems to be different since then."

"What has Jim been doing that's any queerer than usual?" inquired Ellen, with some asperity.

Fanny hesitated.

"You won't tell?"

"Of course not, if it's a secret."

"Cross your heart an' hope t' die?" quoted Fanny from their childhood days.

Ellen giggled.

64

"Cross m' heart an' hope t' die," she repeated.

"Well, Jim's been off on some sort of a trip," said Fanny.

"I don't see anything so very queer about that."

"Wait till I tell you— You must be sure and not breathe a word, even to your mother; you won't, will you?"

"Fan, you make me mad! Didn't I just say I wouldn't?"

"Well, then; he went with *her* in the auto; they started about five o'clock in the morning, and Jim didn't get home till after twelve that night."

Ellen laughed, with studied indifference.

"Pity they couldn't have asked us to go along," she said. "I'm sure the car's plenty big enough."

"I don't think it was just for fun," said Fanny.

"You don't? What for, then?"

"I asked Jim, and he wouldn't tell me."

"When did you ask him?"

"The morning they went. I came down about half past four: mother doesn't get up as early as that, we haven't much milk to look after now; but I wake up awfully early sometimes, and I'd rather be doing something than lying there wide awake."

Ellen squeezed Fanny's arm sympathetically. She herself had lost no moments of healthy sleep over Jim Dodge's fancied defection; but she enjoyed imagining herself to be involved in a passionate romance.

"Isn't it *awful* to lie awake and think—*and think*, and not be able to do a single thing!" she said, with a tragic gesture.

Fanny bent down to look into Ellen's pretty face.

"Why, Ellen," she said, "is it as bad as that? I didn't suppose you really cared."

She clasped Ellen's slender waist closer and kissed her fervently.

Ellen coaxed two shining tears into sparkling prominence on her long lashes.

"Oh, don't mind me, Fan," she murmured; "but I *can* sympathize with you, dear. I know *exactly* how you feel—and to think it's the same girl!"

Ellen giggled light-heartedly:

"Anyway, she can't marry both of them," she finished.

Fanny was looking away through the boles of the gnarled old trees, her face grave and preoccupied.

"Perhaps I oughtn't to have told you," she said.

"Why, you haven't told me anything, yet," protested Ellen. "You're the funniest girl, Fan! I don't believe you know how to—really confide in anybody. If you'd tell me more how you feel about *him*, you wouldn't care half so much."

Fanny winced perceptibly. She could not bear to speak of the secret—which indeed appeared to be no secret—she strove daily to bury under a mountain of hard work, but which seemed possessed of mysterious powers of resurrection in the dark hours between sunset and sunrise.

"But there's nothing to—to talk about, Ellen," she said; and in spite of herself her voice sounded cold, almost menacing.

"Oh, very well, if you feel that way," retorted Ellen. "But I can tell you one thing—or, I *might* tell you something; but I guess I won't."

"Please, Ellen,—if it's about—"

"Well, it is."

Fanny's eyes pleaded hungrily with the naughty Ellen.

"You haven't finished your account of that interesting pleasure excursion of Jim's and Miss Orr's," said Ellen. "Isn't it lovely Jim can drive her car? Is he going to be her regular chauffeur? And do you get an occasional joy-ride?"

"Of course not," Fanny said indignantly. "Oh, Ellen, how can you go on like that! I'm sure you don't care a bit about Jim or me, either."

"I do!" declared Ellen. "I love you with all my heart, Fan; but I don't know about Jim. I—I might have—you know; but if he's crazy over that Orr girl, what's the use? There are other men, just as good-looking as Jim Dodge and not half so sarcastic and disagreeable."

"Jim can be disagreeable, if he wants to," conceded Jim's sister. "When I asked him where he was going with the car so early in the morning—you know he's been bringing the car home nights so as to clean it and fix the engine, till she can get somebody—I was surprised to find him putting in oil and tightening up screws and things, when it was scarcely daylight; and I said so. He wouldn't tell me a thing. 'You just 'tend to your own knitting, Fan,' was all he said; 'perhaps you'll know some day; and then again, perhaps you won't.'"

"And didn't you find out?" cried Ellen, her dark eyes alight with curiosity. "If that doesn't sound exactly like Jim Dodge! But you said you heard him when he came in that night; didn't he tell you anything then?—You don't think they ran off to get married? Oh, Fan!"

"Of course not, you goose! Do you suppose he'd have come back home alone, if it had been anything like that?"

Ellen heaved a sigh of exaggerated relief.

"'Be still, my heart'!" she murmured.

"No; they went to get somebody from somewhere," pursued Fanny.

"To get somebody from somewhere," repeated Ellen impatiently. "How thrilling! Who do you suppose it was?"

Fanny shook her head:

"I haven't the slightest idea."

"How perfectly funny! ...Is the somebody there, now?"

"I don't know. Jim won't tell me a thing that goes on there. He says if there's anything on top of the earth he absolutely despises it's a gossiping man. He says a gossiping woman is a creation of God—must be, there's so many of 'em; but a gossiping man—he can't find any word in the dictionary mean enough for that sort of a low-down skunk."

Ellen burst into hysterical laughter.

"What an idea!" she gasped. "Oh, but he's almost too sweet to live, Fan. Somebody ought to take him down a peg or two. Fan, if he proposes to that girl, I hope she won't have him. 'Twould serve him right!"

"Perhaps she won't marry anybody around here," mused Fanny. "Did you ever notice she wears a thin gold chain around her neck, Ellen?"

Ellen nodded.

"Perhaps there's a picture of somebody on it."

"I shouldn't wonder."

Ellen impatiently kicked a big apple out of her way, to the manifest discomfiture of two or three drunken wasps who were battening on the sweet juices.

"I've got to go back to the house," she said. "Mother'll be looking for me."

"But, Ellen—"

"Well?"

"You said you knew something—"

Ellen yawned.

"Did I?"

"You know you did, Ellen! Please—"

"'Twasn't much."

"What was it?"

"Oh, nothing, only I met the minister coming out of Lydia Orr's house one day awhile ago, and he was walking along as if he'd been sent for— Never even saw me. I had a good mind to speak to him, anyway; but before I could think of anything cute to say he'd gone by—two-forty on a plank road!"

Fanny was silent. She was wishing she had not asked Ellen to tell. Then instantly her mind began to examine this new aspect of her problem.

"He didn't look so awfully pleased and happy," Ellen went on, "his head was down—so, and he was just scorching up the road. Perhaps they'd been having a scrap."

"Oh, no!" burst from Fanny's lips. "It wasn't that."

"Why, what do you know about Wesley Elliot and Lydia Orr?" inquired Ellen vindictively. "You're a whole lot like Jim—as close-mouthed as a molasses jug, when you don't happen to feel like talking.... It isn't fair," she went on crossly. "I tell you everything—every single thing; and you just take it all in without winking an eyelash. It isn't fair!"

66

"Oh, Ellen, please don't—I can't bear it from you!"

Fanny's proud head drooped to her friend's shoulder, a stifled sob escaped her.

"There now, Fan; I didn't mean a word of it! I'm sorry I told you about him—only I thought he looked so kind of cut up over something that maybe— Honest, Fan, I don't believe he likes her."

"You don't know," murmured Fanny, wiping her wet eyes. "I didn't tell you she came to see me."

"She did!"

"Yes; it was after we had all been there, and mother was going on so about the furniture. It all seemed so mean and sordid to me, as if we were trying to—well, you know."

Ellen nodded:

"Of course I do. That's why you wouldn't let her have your furniture. I gloried in your spunk, Fan."

"But I did let her have it, Ellen."

"You did? Well!"

"I'll tell you how it happened. Mother'd gone down to the village, and Jim was off somewhere—he's never in the house day-times any more; I'd been working on the new curtains all day, and I was just putting them up in the parlor, when she came.... Ellen, sometimes I think perhaps we don't understand that girl. She was just as sweet— If it wasn't for— If I hadn't hardened my heart against her almost the first thing, you know, I don't believe I could help loving her."

"Fanny!" cried Ellen protestingly. "She certainly is a soft-soap artist. My mother says she is so refined; and Mrs. Daggett is always chanting her praises."

"Think of all she's done for the village," urged Fanny. "I want to be just, even if—"

"Well, I don't!" cried Ellen. "I just enjoy being real spiteful sometimes—especially when another girl gobbles all the men in sight; and I know I'm prettier than she is. It's just because she's new and—and stylish and rich. What made you give in about your furniture, Fan?"

"Because I—"

Fanny stopped short, puckering her forehead.

"I don't know whether I can explain it, Ellen; but I notice it every time I am with her. There's something—"

"Good gracious, Fan! She must have hypnotized you."

"Be quiet, Ellen, I'm trying to think just how it happened. She didn't say so very much—just sat down and watched me, while I sewed rings on the curtains. But the first thing I knew, I piped up and said: 'Do you really want that old furniture of mine so much?' And she said— Well, no matter what she said; it was more the way she looked. I guess I'd have given her the eyes out of my head, or any old thing."

"That's just what I told you," interrupted Ellen. "There are people like that. Don't you remember that horrid old what's-his-name in 'Trilby'?"

"Don't be silly, Ellen," said Fanny rebukingly. "Well, I took her up to my room and showed her my bed and bureau and washstand. There were some chairs, too; mother got them all for my room at that old auction we've heard so much about; I was just a baby then. I told her about it. She sat down in my rocking-chair by the window and just looked at the things, without saying a word, at first. After a while, she said: 'Your mother used to come in and tuck the blankets around you nice and warm in the night; didn't she?'"

"'Why, I suppose she did,' I told her. 'Mother's room is right next to mine.' ... Ellen, there was a look in her eyes—I can't tell you about it—you wouldn't understand. And, anyway, I didn't care a bit about the furniture. 'You can have it,' I said. 'I don't want it, and I don't see why you do; it isn't pretty any more.' I thought she was going to cry, for a minute. Then such a soft gladness came over her face. She came up to me and took both my hands in hers; but all she said was 'Thank you.'"

"And did she pay you a whole lot for it?" inquired Ellen sordidly.

"I didn't think anything about that part of it," said Fanny. "Jim carried it all over the next day, with a lot of old stuff mother had. Jim says she's had a man from Grenoble working in the barn for weeks and weeks, putting everything in order. My old set was painted over, with all the little garlands and blue ribbons, like new."

"But how much—" persisted Ellen. "She must have paid you a lot for it."

"I didn't ask mother," said Fanny. "I didn't want to know. I've got a new set; it's real pretty. You must come over and see my room, now it's all finished."

What Fanny did not tell Ellen was that after Lydia's departure she had unexpectedly come upon the photograph of the picnic group under a book on her table. The faded picture with its penciled words had meant much to Fanny. She had not forgotten, she told herself, she could never forget, that day in June, before the unlooked-for arrival of the strange girl, whose coming had changed everything. Once more she lived over in imagination that perfect day, with its white clouds floating high in the blue, and the breath of clover on the wind. She and Wesley Elliot had gone quietly away into the woods after the boisterous merriment of the picnic luncheon.

"It's safe enough, as long as we follow the stream," Fanny had assured him, piloting the way over fallen logs and through dense thickets of pine and laurel, further and further away from the sounds of shrill laughter and the smoky smell of the camp fire, where the girls were still busy toasting marshmallows on long sticks for the youths who hovered in the rear.

The minister had expressed a keen desire to hear the rare notes of the hermit thrush; and this romantic quest led them deep into the forest. The girl paused at last on the brink of a pool, where they could see the shadowy forms of brook trout gliding through the clear, cold water.

"If we are quiet and listen," she told him, "I think we shall hear the hermit."

On a carpet of moss, thicker and softer than a deep-piled rug, they sat down. Not a sound broke the stillness but the gurgle of water and the soft soughing of the wind through great tree tops. The minister bared his head, as if aware of the holy spirit of solitude in the place. Neither spoke nor stirred; but the girl's heart beat loud—so loud she feared he might hear, and drew her little cape closer above her breast. Then all at once, ringing down the somber aisles of the forest came the song of the solitary bird, exquisite, lonely, filled with an indescribable, yearning sweetness. The man's eloquent eyes met her own in a long look.

"Wonderful!" he murmured.

His hand sought and closed upon hers for an instant. Then without further speech they returned to the picnickers. Someone—she thought it was Joyce Fulsom—snapped the joyous group at the moment of the departure. It had been a week later, that he had written the words "Lest we forget"—with a look and smile which set the girl's pulses fluttering. But that was in June. Now it was September. Fanny, crouched by the window where Lydia Orr had been that afternoon, stared coldly at the picture. It was downright silly to have carried it about with her. She had lost it somewhere—pulling out her handkerchief, perhaps. Had Lydia Orr found and brought it back? She ardently wished she knew; but in the meanwhile—

She tore the picture deliberately across, thereby accomplishing unhindered what Wesley Elliot had attempted several days before; then she burned the fragments in the quick spurt of a lighted match.... Lest we forget, indeed!

Chapter XVII

The day after the sewing society Ellen Dix went up to her room, after hurriedly washing the dinner dishes. It was still hot, but a vague haze had crept across the brazen sky since morning. Ellen's room looked out into cool green depths of trees, so that on a cloudy day it was almost too dark to examine the contents of the closet opposite its two east windows.

It was a pretty room, freshly papered and painted, as were many rooms in Brookville since the sale of the old Bolton properties. Nearly every one had scrimped and saved and gone without so long that the sudden influx of money into empty pockets had acted like wine in a hungry stomach. Henry Daggett had thrice replenished his stock of wall papers; window shades and curtaining by the yard had been in constant demand for weeks; bright colored chintzes and gay flowered cretonnes were apparently a prime necessity in many households. As for paper hangers and painters, few awaited their unhurried movements. It was easy for anybody with energy and common sense to wield a paintbrush; and old paper could be scraped off and fresh strips applied by a simple application of flour paste and the fundamental laws of physics. One improvement clamors loudly for another, and money was still coming in from the most unexpected sources, so new furniture was bought to take the place of unprized chairs and tables long ago salvaged from the Bolton wreck. And since Mrs. Deacon Whittle's dream parlor, with its marble-tops and plush-upholstered furniture, had become a solid reality, other parlors burgeoned forth in multi-colored magnificence. Scraggy old shrubs were trimmed; grass was cut in unkempt dooryards; flowers were planted—and all because of the lavish display of such improvements at Bolton House, as "that queer Orr girl" persisted in calling it; thereby flying in the face of public opinion and local prejudice in a way which soured the milk of human kindness before the cream of gratitude could rise.

Everybody agreed that there was something mysterious, if not entirely unnatural in the conduct of the young woman. Nobody likes unsolved riddles for long. The moment or century of suspense may prove interesting—even exciting; but human intelligence resents the Sphynx.

Ellen Dix was intensely human. She was, moreover, jealous—or supposed she was, which often amounts to the same thing. And because of this she was looking over the dresses, hanging on pegs along her closet wall, with a demurely puckered brow. The pink muslin was becoming, but old-fashioned; the pale yellow trimmed with black velvet might get soiled with the dust, and she wasn't sure it would wash. She finally selected a white dress of a new and becoming style, attired in which she presently stood before her mirror adjusting a plain Panama hat, trimmed simply with a black ribbon. Not for nothing had Ellen used her handsome dark eyes. She set the hat over her black hair at exactly the right angle, skewering it securely in place with two silver pins, also severely simple in their style and quite unlike the glittering rhinestone variety offered for sale in Henry Daggett's general store.

"I'm going out for a while, mother," she said, as she passed the room where Mrs. Dix was placidly sewing carpet rags out of materials prodigiously increased of late, since both women had been able to afford several new dresses.

"Going to Fanny's?" inquired Mrs. Dix.... "Seems to me you're starting out pretty early, dear, in all this heat. If you'll wait till sundown, I'll go with you. I haven't seen their parlor since they got the new curtains up."

"I'm not going to Fanny's, right off," said Ellen evasively. "Maybe I'll stop on the way back, though. 'Tisn't very hot; it's clouded up some."

"Better taken an umbrella," her mother sent after her. "We might get a thunder storm along towards four o'clock. My shoulder's been paining me all the morning."

But Ellen had already passed out of hearing, her fresh skirts held well away from the dusty wayside weeds.

She was going, with intentions undefined, to see Lydia Orr. Perhaps (she was thinking) she might see Jim Dodge. Anyway, she wanted to go to Bolton House. She would find out for herself wherein lay the curious fascination of which Fanny had spoken. She was surprised at Fanny for so easily giving in about the furniture. Secretly, she considered herself to be possibly a bit shrewder than Fanny. In reality she was not as easily influenced, and slower at forming conclusions. She possessed a mind of more scope.

Ellen walked along, setting her pointed feet down very carefully so as not to raise the dust and soil her nice skirts. She was a dainty creature. When she reached the hedge which marked the beginning of the Bolton estate, she started, not violently, that was not her way, but anybody is more startled at the sudden glimpse of a figure at complete rest, almost rigidity, than of a figure in motion. Had the old man whom Ellen saw been walking along toward her, she would not have started at all. She might have glanced at him with passing curiosity, since he was a stranger in Brookville, then that would have been the end of it. But this old man, standing as firmly fixed as a statue against the hedge, startled the girl. He was rather a handsome old man, but there was something peculiar about him. For one thing he was better dressed than old men in Brookville generally were. He wore a light Palm Beach cloth suit, possibly too young for him, also a Panama hat. He did not look altogether tidy. He did not wear his up-to-date clothes very well. He had a rumpled appearance. He was very pale almost with the paleness of wax. He did not stand strongly, but rested his weight first on one foot, then on the other. Ellen recovered her composure, but as she was passing, he spoke suddenly. His tone was eager and pitiful. "Why Ann Eliza Dix," he said. "How do you do? You are not going to pass without speaking to me?"

"My name is Dix, but not Ann Eliza," said Ellen politely; "my name is Ellen."

"You are Cephas Dix's sister, Ann Eliza," insisted the old man. His eyes looked suddenly tearful. "I know I am right," he said. "You are Ann Eliza Dix."

The girl felt a sudden pity. Her Aunt Ann Eliza Dix had been lying in her grave for ten years, but she could not contradict the poor man. "Of course," she said. "How do you do?"

The old man's face lit up. "I knew I was right," he said. "I forget, you see, sometimes, but this time I was sure. How are you, Ann Eliza?"

"Very well, thank you."

"How is Cephas?"

"He is well, too."

"And your father?"

Ellen shivered a little. It was rather bewildering. This strange old man must mean her grandfather, who had died before her Aunt Ann Eliza. She replied faintly that he was well, and hoped, with a qualm of ghastly mirth, that she was speaking the truth. Ellen's grandfather had not been exactly a godly man, and the family seldom mentioned him.

"He means well, Ann Eliza, if sometimes you don't exactly like the way he does," said the living old man, excusing the dead one for the faults of his life.

"I know he does," said Ellen. The desire to laugh grew upon her.

She was relieved when the stranger changed the subject. She felt that she would become hysterical if this forcible resurrection of her dead relatives continued.

"Do you like an automobile?" asked the old man.

"I don't know, I never had one."

The stranger looked at her confidingly. "My daughter has one," he said, "and I know she bought it for me, and she has me taken out in it, but I am afraid. It goes too fast. I can't get over being afraid. But you won't tell her, will you, Ann Eliza?"

"Of course I won't."

Ellen continued to gaze at him, but she did not speak.

"Let me see, what is your name, my dear?" the man went on. He was leaning on his stick, and Ellen noticed that he trembled slightly, as though with weakness. He breathed hard. The veinous hands folded on top of the stick were almost as white as his ears.

"My name is Ellen Dix," she said.

"Dix—Dix?" repeated the man. "Why, I know that name, certainly, of course! You must be the daughter of Cephas Dix. Odd name, Cephas, eh?"

Ellen nodded, her eyes still busy with the details of the stranger's appearance. She was sure she had never seen him before, yet he knew her father's name.

"My father has been dead a long time," she said; "ever since I was a little girl."

The man appeared singularly disquieted by this intelligence. "I hadn't heard that," he said. "Dead—a long time? Well!"

He scowled, flourishing his stick as if to pass on; then settled to his former posture, his pale hands folded on its handsome gold top.

"Cephas Dix wasn't an old man," he muttered, as if talking to himself. "Not old. He should be hale and hearty, living in this good country air. Wonderful air this, my dear."

And he drew a deep breath, his wandering gaze returning swiftly to the girl's face.

"I was just walking out," he said, nodding briskly. "Great treat to be able to walk out. I shall walk out whenever I like. Don't care for automobiles—get you over the road too fast. No, no; I won't go out in the automobile, unless I feel like it! No, I won't; and there's an end of it!"

He brought his stick down heavily in the dust, as if emphasizing this statement.

"Guess your father left you pretty well off, eh, my dear?" he went on presently. "Glad to see you looking so fresh and neat. Always like to see a pretty girl well dressed."

The man's eyes, extraordinarily bright and keen, roved nimbly over her face and figure.

"No, he did not," replied Ellen. "My father used to be rich," she went on. "I've heard mother tell about it hundreds of times. We had horses and a carriage and plenty of money; but when the bank went to pieces my father lost everything. Then he died."

The man was peering at her from under his shaggy gray brows.

"But not because the bank failed? Surely not because he lost his money? That sort of thing doesn't kill a man, my dear. No, no!"

"It did," declared Ellen firmly.

The man at once seemed to grow smaller; to huddle together in his clothes. He muttered something unintelligible, then turned squarely about, so that Ellen could see only his hunched back and the glistening white hair cut close behind his waxen ears.

The girl walked thoughtfully on, but when she paused to look back she saw that he had resumed his slow walk in the opposite direction, his stick describing odd flourishes in the air, as before.

When she reached Bolton House she was ushered into a beautiful parlor by a prim maid in a frilled cap and apron. The maid presented to her attention a small silver tray, and Ellen, blushing uncomfortably because she had no card, asked for Miss Orr.

Soon the frilled maid reappeared. "I'm sorry, Miss," she said, "I thought Miss Lydia was at home, but I can't find her anywheres about."

She eyed Ellen's trim figure doubtfully. "If there was any message—"

"No," said Ellen. "I only came to call."

"I'm real sorry, Miss," repeated the maid. "Miss Lydia'll be sorry, too. Who shall I say, please?"

"Miss Dix," replied Ellen. She walked past the maid, who held the door wide for her exit. Then she paused. A surprising sight met her eyes. Lydia Orr, hatless, flushed as if by rapid flight, was just reaching the steps, convoying the strange old man Ellen had met on the road a short time before.

The maid at her back gave a little cry. Ellen stood staring. So this was the person Jim Dodge had gone to fetch from somewhere!

"But it isn't too warm for me to be walking out to take the air," she heard, in the heavy mumble of the man's voice. "I don't like being watched, Lydia; and I won't stand it, either. I might as well be—"

Lydia interrupted him with a sharp exclamation. She had caught sight of Ellen Dix standing under the deep portico, the scared face of the maid looking over her shoulder.

Ellen's face crimsoned slowly. All at once she felt unaccountably sorry and ashamed. She wished she had not come. She felt that she wanted nothing so much as to hurry swiftly away.

But Lydia Orr, still holding the strange old man by the arm, was already coming up the steps.

"I'll not go in the automobile, child," he repeated, with an obstinate flourish of his stick. "I don't like to ride so fast. I want to see things. I want—"

He stopped short, his mouth gaping, his eyes staring at Ellen.

"That girl!" he almost shouted. "She told me—I don't want her here.... Go away, girl, you make my head hurt!"

Lydia flashed a beseeching look at Ellen, as she led the old man past.

"Please come in," she said; "I shall be at liberty in just a moment.... Come, father!"

Ellen hesitated.

"Perhaps I'd better not, today," she murmured, and slowly descended the steps.

The discreet maid closed the door behind her.

Chapter XVIII

Ellen did not at once return home. She walked on reflecting. So the old man was Lydia Orr's father! And she was the first to know it!

The girl had never spoken of her father, Ellen was sure. Had she done so, Mrs. Solomon Black would certainly have told Mrs. Whittle, and Mrs. Whittle would have informed Mrs. Daggett, and thence, by way of Mrs. Dodge and Fanny, the news would long ago have reached Ellen and her mother.

Before she had covered a quarter of a mile of the dusty road, Ellen heard the muffled roar of an over-taking motor car. She glanced up, startled and half choked with the enveloping cloud of dust. Jim Dodge was driving the car. He slowed down and stopped.

"Hello, Ellen. Going down to the village? Get in and I'll take you along," he called out.

"All right," said Ellen, jumping in.

"I haven't seen you for an age, Jim," said Ellen after awhile.

The young man laughed. "Does it seem that long to you, Ellen?"

"No, why should it?" she returned.

"I say, Ellen," said Jim, "I saw you when you came out of Bolton House just now."

"Did you?"

"Yes." He looked sharply at Ellen, who smiled evasively.

"I was going to call," she said with an innocent air, "but Miss Orr had—a visitor."

"Look here, Ellen; don't let's beat about the bush. Nobody knows he's there, yet, except myself and—you. You met him on the road; didn't you?"

"Yes," said Ellen, "I met him on the road."

"Did he talk to you?"

"He asked me what my name was. He's crazy, isn't he, Jim?"

The young man frowned thoughtfully at his steering wheel.

"Not exactly," he said, after a pause. "He's been sick a long time and his mind is—well, I think it has been somewhat affected. Did he— He didn't talk to you about himself, did he?"

"What do you want to know for?"

"Oh, he appeared rather excited, and—"

"Yes; I noticed that." She laughed mischievously.

Jim frowned. "Come, Ellen, quit this nonsense! What did he say to you?"

"If you mean Mr. Orr—"

He turned his eyes from the road to stare at her for an instant.

"Did he tell you his name was Orr?" he asked sharply.

It was Ellen's turn to stare.

"Why, if he is Miss Orr's father—" she began.

"Oh, of course," said Jim hurriedly. "I was just wondering if he had introduced himself."

Ellen was silent. She was convinced that there was some mystery about the pale old man.

"He said a lot of awfully queer things to me," she admitted, after a pause during which Jim turned the car into a side road.... "I thought you were going to the village."

"This will take us to the village—give you a longer ride, Ellen. I'll take you home afterwards."

"After what?"

"Why, after we've got the mail—or whatever you want."

"Don't you think Miss Orr and that queer old Mr. —— If his name isn't Orr, Jim, what is it?" She shot a quick glance at him.

"Good Lord!" muttered Jim profanely.

He drew the car up at the side of the road and stopped it.

"What are you going to do?" inquired Ellen, in some alarm. "Won't it go?"

"When I get ready," said Jim.

He turned and faced her squarely:

"We'll have this out, before we go a foot further! I won't have the whole town talking," he said savagely.

Ellen said nothing. She was rather angry.

"The devil!" cried Jim Dodge. "What's the matter with you, Ellen?"

"With me?" she repeated.

"Yes. Why can't you talk?"

She shrugged her shoulders. "I want to go home," she said.

He seized her roughly by the wrist. "Ellen," he said, "I believe you know more than you are willing to tell." He stared down into her eyes. "What did he say to you, anyway?"

"Who?"

"You know well enough. The old man. Lord, what a mess!"

"Please let me go, Jim," said Ellen. "Now look here, I know absolutely nothing except what I have told you, and I want to go home."

"Ellen!"

"Well?"

"Can you keep a secret?"

"Of course I can, Jim!" She met his dark gaze squarely.

"Well, rather than have you spreading a piece of damnable gossip over the village— Of course you would have told everybody."

"You mean about meeting the old man? But won't everybody know? If he goes out and talks to people as he did to me?"

"You haven't told me what he said."

Ellen raised her brows with a mischievous air.

"I didn't care to spread any—what sort of gossip did you say, Jim?"

"Confound it! I didn't mean that."

"Of course I could see he was some one who used to live here," she went on. "He knew father."

Jim had thrust his hands deep into his trousers' pockets. He uttered an impatient ejaculation.

"And he said he should go out whenever he felt like it. He doesn't like the automobile."

"Oh, it's an impossible proposition. I see that plainly enough!" Jim said, as if to himself. "But it seems a pity—"

He appeared to plunge into profound meditation.

"I say, Ellen, you like her; don't you? ...Don't see how you can help it. She's a wonder!"

"Who? Miss Orr?"

"Of course! Say, Ellen, if you knew what that girl has gone through, without a murmur; and now I'm afraid— By George! we ought to spare her."

"We?"

"Yes; you and I. You can do a lot to help, Ellen, if you will. That old man you saw is sick, hardly sane. And no wonder."

He stopped short and stared fixedly at his companion.

"Did you guess who he was?" he asked abruptly.

Ellen reflected. "I can guess—if you'll give me time."

Jim made an impatient gesture. "That's just what I thought," he growled. "There'll be the devil to pay generally."

"Jim," said Ellen earnestly, "if we are to help her, you must tell me all about that old man."

"*She* wanted to tell everybody," he recollected gloomily. "And why not you? Imagine an innocent child set apart from the world by another's crime, Ellen. See, if you can, that child growing up, with but one thought, one ideal—the welfare of that other person. Picture to yourself what it would be like to live solely to make a great wrong right, and to save the wrongdoer. Literally, Ellen, she has borne that man's grief and carried his sorrow, as truly as any vaunted Saviour of the world. Can you see it?"

"Do you mean—? Is *that* why she calls it *Bolton* House? Of course! And that dreadful old man is— But, Jim, everybody will find it out."

"You're right," he acknowledged. "But they mustn't find it out just yet. We must put it off till the man can shake that hang-dog air of his. Why, he can't even walk decently. Prison is written all over him. Thank God, she doesn't seem to see it!"

"I'm so glad you told me, Jim," said Ellen gently.

"You won't say a word about this, will you, Ellen?" he asked anxiously. "I can depend on you?"

"Give me a little credit for decency and common sense," replied Ellen.

Jim bent over the wheel and kissed her.

Chapter XIX

Rain was falling in torrents, slanting past the windows of the old parsonage in long gray lines, gurgling up between loosened panes, and drip-dropping resoundingly in the rusty pan the minister had set under a broken spot in the ceiling. Upstairs a loosened shutter banged intermittently under the impact of the wind, which howled past, to lose itself with great commotion in the tops of the tall evergreens in the churchyard. It was the sort of day when untoward events, near and far, stand out with unpleasant prominence against the background of one's everyday life. A day in which a man is led, whether he will or not, to take stock of himself and to balance with some care the credit and debit sides of his ledger.

Wesley Elliot had been working diligently on his sermon since nine o'clock that morning, at which hour he had deserted Mrs. Solomon Black's comfortable tight roof, to walk under the inadequate shelter of a leaking umbrella to the parsonage.

Three closely written pages in the minister's neat firm handwriting attested his uninterrupted diligence. At the top of the fourth page he set a careful numeral, under it wrote "Thirdly," then paused, laid down his pen, yawned wearily and gazed out at the dripping shrubbery. The rain had come too late to help the farmers, he was thinking. It was always that way: too much sunshine and dry weather; then too much rain—floods of it, deluges of it.

He got up from his chair, stretched his cramped limbs and began marching up and down the floor. He had fully intended to get away from Brookville before another winter set in. But there were reasons why he felt in no hurry to leave the place. He compelled himself to consider them.

Was he in love with Lydia Orr? Honestly, he didn't know. He had half thought he was, for a whole month, during which Lydia had faced him across Mrs. Solomon Black's table three times a day.

As he walked up and down, he viewed the situation. Lydia had declared, not once but often, that she wanted friends. Women always talked that way, and meant otherwise. But did she? The minister shook his head dubiously. He thought of Lydia Orr, of her beauty, of her elusive sweetness. He was ashamed to think of her money, but he owned to himself that he did.

Then he left his study and rambled about the chill rooms of the lower floor. From the windows of the parlor, where he paused to stare out, he could look for some distance up the street. He noticed dully the double row of maples from which yellowed leaves were already beginning to fall and the ugly fronts of houses, behind their shabby picket fences. A wagon was creaking slowly through a shallow sea of mud which had been dust the day before: beyond the hunched figure of the teamster not a human being was in sight. Somewhere, a dog barked fitfully and was answered by other dogs far away; and always the shutter banged at uncertain intervals upstairs. This nuisance, at least, could be abated. He presently located the shutter and closed it; then, because its fastening had rusted quite away, sought for a bit of twine in his pocket and was about to tie it fast when the wind wrenched it again from his hold. As he thrust a black-coated arm from the window to secure the unruly disturber of the peace he saw a man fumbling with the fastening of the parsonage gate. Before he could reach the foot of the stairs the long unused doorbell jangled noisily.

He did not recognize the figure which confronted him on the stoop, when at last he succeeded in undoing the door. The man wore a raincoat turned up about his chin and the soft brim of a felt hat dripped water upon its close-buttoned front.

"Good-morning, good-morning, sir!" said the stranger, as if his words had awaited the opening of the door with scant patience. "You are the—er—local clergyman, I suppose?"

At uncertain periods Wesley Elliot had been visited by a migratory *colporteur*, and less frequently by impecunious persons representing themselves to be fellow warriors on the walls of Zion, temporarily out of ammunition. In the brief interval during which he convoyed the stranger from the chilly obscurity of the hall to the dubious comfort of his study, he endeavored to place his visitor in one of these two classes, but without success.

"Didn't stop for an umbrella," explained the man, rubbing his hands before the stove, in which the minister was striving to kindle a livelier blaze.

Divested of his dripping coat and hat he appeared somewhat stooped and feeble; he coughed slightly, as he gazed about the room.

"What's the matter here?" he inquired abruptly; "don't they pay you your salary?"

The minister explained in brief his slight occupancy of the parsonage; whereat the stranger shook his head:

"That's wrong—all wrong," he pronounced: "A parson should be married and have children—plenty of them. Last time I was here, couldn't hear myself speak there was such a racket of children in the hall. Mother sick upstairs, and the kids sliding down the banisters like mad. I left the parson a check; poor devil!"

He appeared to fall into a fit of musing, his eyes on the floor.

"I see you're wondering who I am, young man," he said presently. "Well, we're coming to that, presently. I want some advice; so I shall merely put the case baldly.... I wanted advice, before; but the parson of that day couldn't give me the right sort. Good Lord! I can see him yet: short man, rather stout and baldish. Meant well, but his religion wasn't worth a bean to me that day.... Religion is all very well to talk about on a Sunday; broadcloth coat, white tie and that sort of thing; good for funerals, too, when a man's dead and can't answer back. Sometimes I've amused myself wondering what a dead man would say to a parson, if he could sit up in his coffin and talk five minutes of what's happened to him since they called him dead. Interesting to think of— eh? ...Had lots of time to think.... Thought of most everything that ever happened; and more that didn't."

"You are a stranger in Brookville, sir?" observed Wesley Elliot, politely.

He had already decided that the man was neither a *colporteur* nor a clerical mendicant; his clothes were too good, for one thing.

The man laughed, a short, unpleasant sound which ended in a fit of coughing.

"A stranger in Brookville?" he echoed. "Well; not precisely.... But never mind that, young man. Now, you're a clergyman, and on that account supposed to have more than ordinary good judgment: what would you advise a man to do, who had—er—been out of active life for a number of years. In a hospital, we'll say, incapacitated, very much so. When he comes out, he finds himself quite pleasantly situated, in a way; good home, and all that sort of thing; but not allowed to—to use his judgment in any way. Watched—yes, watched, by a person who ought to know better. It's intolerable—intolerable! Why, you'll not believe me when I tell you I'm obliged to sneak out of my own house on the sly—on the sly, you understand, for the purpose of taking needful exercise."

He stopped short and wiped his forehead with a handkerchief, the fineness of which the minister noted mechanically—with other details which had before escaped him; such as the extreme, yellowish pallor of the man's face and hands and the extraordinary swiftness and brightness of his eyes. He was conscious of growing uneasiness as he said:

"That sounds very unpleasant, sir; but as I am not in possession of the facts—"

"But I just told you," interrupted the stranger. "Didn't I say—"

"You didn't make clear to me what the motives of this person who tries to control your movements are. You didn't tell me—"

The man moved his hand before his face, like one trying to brush away imaginary flies.

"I suppose she has her motives," he said fretfully. "And very likely they're good. I'll not deny that. But I can't make her see that this constant espionage—this everlasting watchfulness is not to be borne. I want freedom, and by God I'll have it!"

He sprang from his chair and began pacing the room.

Wesley Elliot stared at his visitor without speaking. He perceived that the man dragged his feet, as if from excessive fatigue or weakness.

"I had no thought of such a thing," the stranger went on. "I'd planned, as a man will who looks forward to release from—from a hospital, how I'd go about and see my old neighbors. I wanted to have them in for dinners and luncheons—people I haven't seen for years. She knows them. She can't excuse herself on that ground. She knows you."

He stopped short and eyed the minister, a slow grin spreading over his face.

"The last time you were at my house I had a good mind to walk in and make your acquaintance, then and there. I heard you talking to her. You admire my daughter: that's easy to see; and she's not such a bad match, everything considered."

"Who are you?" demanded the young man sharply.

"I am a man who's been dead and buried these eighteen years," replied the other. "But I'm alive still—very much alive; and they'll find it out."

An ugly scowl distorted the man's pale face. For an instant he stared past Wesley Elliot, his eyes resting on an irregular splotch of damp on the wall. Then he shook himself.

"I'm alive," he repeated slowly. "And I'm free!"

"Who are you?" asked the minister for the second time.

For all his superior height and the sinewy strength of his young shoulders he began to be afraid of the man who had come to him out of the storm. There was something strangely disconcerting, even sinister, in the ceaseless movements of his pale hands and the sudden lightning dart of his eyes, as they shifted from the defaced wall to his own perturbed face.

By way of reply the man burst into a disagreeable cackle of laughter:

"Stopped in at the old bank building on my way," he said. "Got it all fixed up for a reading room and library. Quite a nice idea for the villagers. I'd planned something of the sort, myself. Approve of that sort of thing for a rural population. Who—was the benefactor in this case—eh? Take it for granted the villagers didn't do it for themselves. The women in charge there referred me to you for information.... Don't be in haste, young man. I'll answer your question in good time. Who gave the library, fixed up the building and all that? Must have cost something."

The minister sat down with an assumption of ease he did not feel, facing the stranger who had already possessed himself of the one comfortable chair in the room.

"The library," he said, "was given to the village by a Miss Orr, a young woman who has recently settled in Brookville. She has done a good deal for the place, in various ways."

"What ways?" asked the stranger, with an air of interest.

Wesley Elliot enumerated briefly the number of benefits: the purchase and rebuilding of the old Bolton house, the construction of the waterworks, at present under way, the library and reading room, with the town hall above. "There are," he stated, "other things which might be mentioned; such as the improvement of the village green, repairs on the church, the beginning of a fund for lighting the streets, as well as innumerable smaller benefactions, involving individuals in and around Brookville."

The man listened alertly. When the minister paused, he said:

"The young woman you speak of appears to have a deep pocket."

The minister did not deny this. And the man spoke again, after a period of frowning silence:

"What was her idea?— Orr, you said her name was?—in doing all this for Brookville? Rather remarkable— eh?"

His tone, like his words, was mild and commonplace; but his face wore an ugly sneering look, which enraged the minister.

"Miss Orr's motive for thus benefiting a wretched community, well-nigh ruined years ago by the villainy of one man, should be held sacred from criticism," he said, with heat.

"Well, let me tell you the girl had a motive—or thought she had," said the stranger unpleasantly. "But she had no right to spend her money that way. You spoke just now of the village as being ruined years ago by the villainy of one man. That's a lie! The village ruined the man.... Never looked at it that way; did you? Andrew Bolton had the interests of this place more deeply at heart than any other human being ever did. He was the one public-spirited man in the place.... Do you know who built your church, young man? I see you don't. Well, Andrew Bolton built it, with mighty little help from your whining, hypocritical church members. Every Tom, Dick and Harry, for miles about; every old maid with a book to sell; every cause—as they call the thousand and one pious schemes to line their own pockets—every damned one of 'em came to Andrew Bolton for money, and he gave it to them. He was no hoarding skinflint; not he. Better for him if he had been. When luck went against him, as it did at last, these precious villagers turned on him like a pack of wolves. They killed his wife; stripped his one child of everything—even to the bed she slept in; and the man himself they buried alive under a mountain of stone and iron, where he rotted for eighteen years!"

The stranger's eyes were glaring with maniacal fury; he shook a tremulous yellow finger in the other's face.

"Talk about ruin!" he shouted. "Talk about one man's villainy! This damnable village deserves to be razed off the face of the earth! ...But I meant to forgive them. I was willing to call the score even."

A nameless fear had gripped the younger man by the throat.

"Are you—?" he began; but could not speak the words.

"My name," said the stranger, with astonishing composure, in view of his late fury, "is Andrew Bolton; and the girl you have been praising and—courting—is my daughter. Now you see what a sentimental fool a woman can be. Well; I'll have it out with her. I'll live here in Brookville on equal terms with my neighbors. If there was ever a debt between us, it's been paid to the uttermost farthing. I've paid it in flesh and blood and manhood. Is there any money—any property you can name worth eighteen years of a man's life? And such years— God! such years!"

Wesley Elliot stared. At last he understood the girl, and as he thought of her shrinking aloofness standing guard over her eager longing for friends—for affection, something hot and wet blurred his eyes. He was scarcely conscious that the man, who had taken to himself the name with which he had become hatefully familiar during his years in Brookville, was still speaking, till a startling sentence or two aroused him.

"There's no reason under heaven why you should not marry her, if you like. Convict's daughter? Bah! I snap my fingers in their faces. My girl shall be happy yet. I swear it! But we'll stop all this sickly sentimentality about the money. We'll—"

The minister held up a warning hand.

An immense yearning pity for Lydia had taken possession of him; but for the man who had thus risen from a dishonorable grave to blight her girlhood he felt not a whit.

"You'd better keep quiet," he said sternly. "You'd far better go away and leave her to live her life alone."

"You'd like that; wouldn't you?" said Bolton dryly.

He leaned forward and stared the young man in the eyes.

"But she wouldn't have it that way. Do you know that girl of mine wouldn't hear of it. She expects to make it up to me.... Imagine making up eighteen years of hell with a few pet names, a soft bed and—"

"Stop!" cried Wesley Elliot, with a gesture of loathing. "I can't listen to you."

"But you'll marry her—eh?"

Bolton's voice again dropped into a whining monotone. He even smiled deprecatingly.

"You'll excuse my ranting a bit, sir. It's natural after what I've gone through. You've never been in a prison, maybe. And you don't know what it's like to shake the bars of a cell at midnight and howl out of sheer madness to be off and away—somewhere, anywhere!"

He leaned forward and touched the minister on the knee.

"And that brings me back to my idea in coming to see you. I'm a level-headed man, still—quite cool and collected, as you see—and I've been thinking the situation over."

He drew his brows together and stared hard at the minister.

"I've a proposition to make to you—as man to man. Can't talk reason to a woman; there's no reason in a woman's make-up—just sentiment and affection and imagination: an impossible combination, when there are hard realities to face.... I see you don't agree with me; but never mind that; just hear what I have to say."

But he appeared in no haste to go on, for all the eagerness of his eyes and those pallid, restless hands. The minister got quickly to his feet. The situation was momentarily becoming intolerable; he must have time to think it over, he told himself, and determine his own relations to this new and unwelcome parishioner.

"I'm very sorry, sir," he began; "but—"

"None of that," growled Bolton. "Sit down, young man, and listen to what I have to say to you. We may not have another chance like this."

His assumption of a common interest between them was most distasteful; but for all that the minister resumed his chair.

"Now, as I've told you, my daughter appears unwilling to allow me out of her sight. She tries to cover her watchfulness under a pretense of solicitude for my health. I'm not well, of course; was knocked down and beaten about the head by one of those devils in the prison— Can't call them men: no decent man would choose to earn his living that way. But cosseting and coddling in a warm house will never restore me. I want freedom— nothing less. I must be out and away when the mood seizes me night or day. Her affection stifles me at times.... You can't understand that, of course; you think I'm ungrateful, no doubt; and that I ought—"

"You appear to me, a monster of selfishness," Wesley Elliot broke in. "You ought to stop thinking of yourself and think of her."

Bolton's face drew itself into the mirthless wrinkles which passed for a smile.

"I'm coming to that," he said with some eagerness. "I do think of her; and that's why— Can't you see, man, that eighteen years of prison don't grow the domestic virtues? A monster of selfishness? You're dead right. I'm all of that; and I'm too old to change. I can't play the part of a doting father. I thought I could, before I got out; but I can't. Twice I've been tempted to knock her down, when she stood between me and the door.... Keep cool; I didn't do it! But I'm afraid of myself, I tell you. I've got to have my liberty. She can have hers.... Now here's my proposition: Lydia's got money. I don't know how much. My brother-in-law was a close man. Never even knew he was rich. But she's got it—all but what she's spent here trying to square accounts, as she thought. Do they thank her for it? Not much. I know them! But see here, you marry Lydia, whenever you like; then give me ten thousand dollars, and I'll clear out. I'm not a desirable father-in-law; I know that, as well as you do. But I'll guarantee to disappear, once my girl is settled. Is it a bargain?"

Elliot shook his head.

"Your daughter doesn't love me," he said.

Bolton flung up his hand in an impatient gesture of dissent.

"I stood in the way," he said. "She was thinking of me, don't you see? But if I get out— Oh, I promise you I'll make myself scarce, once this matter is settled."

"What you propose is impossible, on the face of it," the minister said slowly. "I am sorry—"

"Impossible! Why impossible?" shouted Bolton, in a sudden fury. "You've been courting my daughter—don't try to crawl out of it, now you know what I am. I'll not stand in the way, I tell you. Why, the devil—"

He stopped short, his restless eyes roving over the young man's face and figure:

"Oh, I see!" he sneered. "I begin to understand: 'the sanctity of the cloth'—'my sacred calling'— Yes, yes! And perhaps my price seems a bit high: ten thousand dollars—"

Elliot sprang from his chair and stood over the cringing figure of the ex-convict.

"I could strike you," he said in a smothered voice; "but you are an old man and—not responsible. You don't understand what you've said, perhaps; and I'll not try to make you see it as I do."

"I supposed you were fond of my girl," mumbled Bolton. "I heard you tell her—"

But the look in the younger man's eyes stopped him. His hand sought his heart in an uncertain gesture.

"Have you any brandy?" he asked feebly. "I—I'm not well.... No matter; I'll go over to the tavern. I'll have them take me home. Tired, after all this; don't feel like walking."

Chapter XX

The minister from the doorstep of the parsonage watched the stooped figure as it shambled down the street. The rain was still falling in torrents. The thought crossed his mind that the old man might not be able to compass the two miles or more of country road. Then he got into his raincoat and followed.

"My umbrella isn't of the best," he said, as he overtook the toiling figure; "but I should have offered it."

Andrew Bolton muttered something unintelligible, as he glanced up at the poor shelter the young man held over him. As he did not offer to avail himself of it the minister continued to walk at his side, accommodating his long free stride to the curious shuffling gait of the man who had spent eighteen years in prison. And so they passed the windowed fronts of the village houses, peering out from the dripping autumnal foliage like so many watchful eyes, till the hoarse signal of a motor car halted them, as they were about to cross the street in front of the Brookville House.

From the open door of the car Lydia Orr's pale face looked out.

"Oh, father," she said. "I've been looking for you everywhere!"

She did not appear to see the minister.

Bolton stepped into the car with a grunt.

"Glad to see the old black Maria, for once," he chuckled. "Don't you recognize the parson, my dear? Nice fellow—the parson; been having quite a visit with him at the manse. Old stamping-ground of mine, you know. Always friendly with the parson."

Wesley Elliot had swept the hat from his head. Lydia's eyes, blue and wide like those of a frightened child, met his with an anguished question.

He bowed gravely.

"I should have brought him home quite safe," he told her. "I intended ordering a carriage."

The girl's lips shaped formal words of gratitude. Then the obedient humming of the motor deepened to a roar and the car glided swiftly away.

On the opposite corner, her bunched skirts held high, stood Miss Lois Daggett.

"Please wait a minute, Mr. Elliot," she called. "I'll walk right along under your umbrella, if you don't mind."

Wesley Elliot bowed and crossed the street. "Certainly," he said.

"I don't know why I didn't bring my own umbrella this morning," said Miss Daggett with a keen glance at Elliot. "That old man stopped in the library awhile ago, and he rather frightened me. He looked very odd and talked so queer. Did he come to the parsonage?"

"Yes," said Wesley Elliot. "He came to the parsonage?"

"Did he tell you who he was?"

He had expected this question. But how should he answer it?

"He told me he had been ill for a long time," said the minister evasively.

"Ill!" repeated Miss Daggett shrilly. Then she said one word: "Insane."

"People who are insane are not likely to mention it," said Elliot.

"Then he is insane," said Miss Daggett with conviction.

Wesley looked at her meditatively. Would the truth, the whole truth, openly proclaimed, be advisable at this juncture, he wondered. Lydia could not hope to keep her secret long. And there was danger in her attempt. He shuddered as he remembered the man's terrible words, "Twice I have been tempted to knock her down when she stood between me and the door." Would it not be better to abandon this pretense sooner, rather than later? If the village knew the truth, would not the people show at least a semblance of kindness to the man who had expiated so bitterly the wrong he had done them?

"If the man is insane," Miss Daggett said, "it doesn't seem right to me to have him at large."

"I wish I knew what to do," said Elliot.

"I think you ought to tell what you know if the man is insane."

"Well, I will tell," said Elliot, almost fiercely. "That man is Andrew Bolton. He has come home after eighteen years of imprisonment, which have left him terribly weak in mind and body. Don't you think people will forgive him now?"

A swift vindictiveness flashed into the woman's face. "I don't know," said she.

"Why in the world don't you know, Miss Daggett?"

Then the true reason for the woman's rancor was disclosed. It was a reason as old as the human race, a suspicion as old as the human race, which she voiced. "I have said from the first," she declared, "that nobody would come here, as that girl did, and do so much unless she had a motive."

Elliot stared at her. "Then you hate that poor child for trying to make up for the wrong her father did; and that, and not his wrongdoing, influences you?"

Miss Daggett stared at him. Her face slowly reddened. "I wouldn't put it that way," she said.

"What way would you put it?" demanded Elliot mercilessly. He was so furious that he forgot to hold the umbrella over Miss Daggett, and the rain drove in her hard, unhappy face. She did not seem to notice. She had led a poisoned life, in a narrow rut of existence, and toxic emotions had become as her native atmosphere of mind. Now she seemed to be about to breathe in a better air of humanity, and she choked under it.

"If—" she stammered, "that was—her reason, but—I always felt—that nobody ever did such things without—as they used to say—an ax to grind."

"This seems to me a holy sort of ax," said Elliot grimly, "and one for which a Christian woman should certainly not fling stones."

They had reached the Daggett house. The woman stopped short. "You needn't think I'm going around talking, any more than you would," she said, and her voice snapped like a whip. She went up the steps, and Elliot went home, not knowing whether he had accomplished good or mischief.

Chapter XXI

Much to Mrs. Solomon Black's astonishment, Wesley Elliot ate no dinner that day. It was his habit to come in from a morning's work with a healthy young appetite keen-set for her beef and vegetables. He passed directly up to his room, although she called to him that dinner was ready. Finally she went upstairs and knocked smartly on his door.

"Dinner's ready, Mr. Elliot," she called out.

"I don't want any today, thank you, Mrs. Black," was his reply.

"You ain't sick?"

"Oh, no, only not hungry."

Mrs. Black was alarmed when, later in the afternoon, she heard the front door slam, and beheld from a front window Elliot striding down the street. The rain had ceased falling, and there were ragged holes in the low-hanging clouds which revealed glimpses of dazzling blue.

"I do hope he ain't coming down with a fever or something," Mrs. Black said aloud. Then she saw Mrs. Deacon Whittle, Lois Daggett, Mrs. Fulsom, and the wife of the postmaster approaching her house in the opposite direction. All appeared flushed and agitated, and Mrs. Black hastened to open her door, as she saw them hurrying up her wet gravel path.

"Is the minister home?" demanded Lois Daggett breathlessly. "I want he should come right down here and tell you what he told me this noon. Abby Daggett seems to think I made it up out of whole cloth. Don't deny it, Abby. You know very well you said.... I s'pose of course he's told you, Mrs. Black."

"Mr. Elliot has gone out," said Mrs. Black rather coldly.

"Where's he gone?" demanded Lois.

Mrs. Black was being devoured with curiosity; still she felt vaguely repelled.

"Ladies," she said, her air of reserve deepening. "I don't know what you are talking about, but Mr. Elliot didn't eat any dinner, and he is either sick or troubled in his mind."

"There! Now you c'n all see from that!" triumphed Lois Daggett.

Mrs. Deacon Whittle and Mrs. Judge Fulsom gazed incredulously at Mrs. Solomon Black, then at one another.

Abby Daggett, the soft round of her beautiful, kind face flushed and tremulous, murmured: "Poor man—poor man!"

Mrs. Solomon Black with a masterly gesture headed the women toward her parlor, where a fire was burning in a splendidly nickeled stove full five feet high.

"Now," said she; "we'll talk this over, whatever it is."

Chapter XXII

A mile from town, where the angry wind could be seen at work tearing the purple rainclouds into rags and tatters, through which the hidden sun shot long rays of pale splendor, Wesley Elliot was walking rapidly, his head bent, his eyes fixed and absent.

He had just emerged from one of those crucial experiences of life, which, more than the turning of the earth upon its axis, serve to age a human being. For perhaps the first time in the brief span of his remembrance, he had scrutinized himself in the pitiless light of an intelligence higher than his own everyday consciousness; and the sight of that meaner self, striving to run to cover, had not been pleasant. Just why his late interview with Andrew Bolton should have precipitated this event, he could not possibly have explained to any one—and least of all to himself. He had begun, logically enough, with an illuminating review of the motives which led him into the ministry; they were a sorry lot, on the whole; but his subsequent ambitions appeared even worse. For the first time, he perceived his own consummate selfishness set over against the shining renunciations of his mother. Then, step by step, he followed his career in Brookville: his smug satisfaction in his own good looks; his shallow pride and vanity over the vapid insincerities he had perpetrated Sunday after Sunday in the shabby pulpit of the Brookville church; his Pharisaical relations with his people; his utter misunderstanding of their needs. All this proved poignant enough to force the big drops to his forehead.... There were other aspects of himself at which he scarcely dared look in his utter abasement of spirit; those dark hieroglyphics of the beast-self which appear on the whitest soul. He had supposed himself pure and saintly because, forsooth, he had concealed the arena of these primal passions beneath the surface of this outward life, chaining them there like leashed tigers in the dark.... Two faces of women appeared to be looking on, while he strove to unravel the snarl of his self-knowledge. Lydia's unworldly face, wearing a faint nimbus of unimagined self-immolation, and Fanny's—full of love and solicitude, the face which he had almost determined to forget.

He was going to Lydia. Every newly awakened instinct of his manhood bade him go.

She came to him at once, and without pretense of concealment began to speak of her father. She trembled a little as she asked:

"He told you who he was?"

Without waiting for his answer she gravely corrected herself.

"I should have said, who *we* are."

She smiled a faint apology:

"I have always been called Lydia Orr; it was my mother's name. I was adopted into my uncle's family, after father—went to prison."

Her blue eyes met his pitying gaze without evasion.

"I am glad you know," she said. "I think I shall be glad—to have every one know. I meant to tell them all, at first. But when I found—"

"I know," he said in a low voice.

Then because as yet he had said nothing to comfort her, or himself; and because every word that came bubbling to the surface appeared banal and inadequate, he continued silent, gazing at her and marveling at her perfect serenity—her absolute poise.

"It will be a relief," she sighed, "When every one knows. He dislikes to be watched. I have been afraid—I could not bear to have him know how they hate him."

"Perhaps," he forced himself to say, "they will not hate him, when they know how you— Lydia, you are wonderful!"

She looked up startled and put out her hand as if to prevent him from speaking further.

But the words came in a torrent now:

"How you must despise me! I despise myself. I am not worthy, Lydia; but if you can care—"

"Stop!" she said softly, as if she would lay the compelling finger of silence upon his lips. "I told you I was not like other women. Can't you see—?"

"You must marry me," he urged, in a veritable passion of self-giving. "I want to help you! You will let me, Lydia?"

She shook her head.

"You could not help me; I am better alone."

She looked at him, the glimmer of a smile dawning in her eyes.

"You do not love me," she said; "nor I you. You are my friend. You will remain my friend, I hope?"

She arose and held out her hand. He took it without a word. And so they stood for a moment; each knowing without need of speech what the other was thinking; the man sorry and ashamed because he could not deny the truth of her words; and she compassionately willing to draw the veil of a soothing silence over his hurts.

"I ought to tell you—" he began.

But she shook her head:

"No need to tell me anything."

"You mean," he said bitterly, "that you saw through my shallow pretenses all the while. I know now how you must have despised me."

"Is it nothing that you have asked me—a convict's daughter—to be your wife?" she asked. "Do you think I don't know that some men would have thanked heaven for their escape and never spoken to me again? I can't tell you how it has helped to hearten me for what must come. I shall not soon forget that you offered me your self—your career; it would have cost you that. I want you to know how much I—appreciate what you have done, in offering me the shelter of an honest name."

He would have uttered some unavailing words of protest, but she checked him.

"We shall both be glad of this, some day," she predicted gravely.... "There is one thing you can do for me," she added: "Tell them. It will be best for both of us, now."

It was already done, he said, explaining his motives in short, disjointed sentences.

Then with a feeling of relief which he strove to put down, but which nevertheless persisted in making itself felt in a curious lightening of his spirits, he was again walking rapidly and without thought of his destination. Somber bars of crimson and purple crossed the west, and behind them, flaming up toward the zenith in a passionate splendor of light, streamed long, golden rays from out the heart of that glory upon which no human eye may look. The angry wind had fallen to quiet, and higher up, floating in a sea of purest violet, those despised and flouted rags of clouds were seen, magically changed to rose and silver.

Chapter XXIII

Fanny Dodge sat by the pleasant west window of the kitchen, engaged in reading those aimless shreds of local information which usually make up the outside pages of the weekly newspaper. She could not possibly feel the slightest interest in the fact that Mr. and Mrs. James M. Snider of West Schofield were entertaining a daughter, whose net weight was reported to be nine and three quarters pounds; or that Miss Elizabeth Wardwell of Eltingville had just issued beautifully engraved invitations to her wedding, which was to take place on the seventeenth day of October—yet she went on reading. Everybody read the paper. Sometimes they talked about what they read. Anyway, her work was over for the day—all except tea, which was negligible; so she went on, somewhat drearily suppressing a yawn, to a description of the new water-works, which were being speedily brought to completion in "our neighboring enterprising town of Brookville."

Fanny already knew all there was to tell concerning the concrete reservoir on the mountain, the big conduit leading to the village and the smaller pipes laid wherever there were householders desiring water. These were surprisingly few, considering the fact that there would be no annual charge for the water, beyond the insignificant sum required for its up-keep. People said their wells were good enough for them; and that spring water wasn't as good as cistern water, when it came to washing. Some were of the opinion that Lydia Orr was in a fool's hurry to get rid of her money; others that she couldn't stand it to be out of the limelight; and still other sagacious individuals felt confident there was something in it for "that girl." Fanny had heard these various views of Miss Orr's conduct. She was still striving with indifferent success to rise above her jealousy, and to this end she never failed to champion Lydia's cause against all comers. Curiously enough, this course had finally brought her tranquillity of a sort and an utter unprotesting acquiescence.

Mrs. Whittle had been overheard saying to Mrs. Fulsom that she guessed, after all, Fanny Dodge didn't care so much about the minister.

Fanny, deep once more in the absorbing consideration of the question which had once been too poignant to consider calmly, and the answer to which she was never to know, permitted the paper to slide off her knee to the floor: Why had Wesley Elliot so suddenly deserted her? Surely, he could not have fallen in love with another woman; she was sure he had been in love with her. However, to kiss and forget might be one of the inscrutable ways of men. She was really afraid it was. But Wesley Elliot had never kissed her; had never even held her hand for more than a minute at a time. But those minutes loomed large in retrospect.

The clock struck five and Fanny, roused from her reverie by the sudden sound, glanced out of the window. At the gate she saw Elliot. He stood there, gazing at the house as if uncertain whether to enter or not. Fanny put up a tremulous hand to her hair, which was pinned fast in its accustomed crisp coils; then she glanced down at her blue gown.... Yes; he was coming in! The bell hanging over the passage door jangled shrilly. Fanny stood stock-still in the middle of the floor, staring at it. There was no fire in the parlor. She would be forced to bring him out to the kitchen. She thought of the wide, luxuriously furnished rooms of Bolton house and unconsciously her face hardened. She might pretend she did not hear the bell. She might allow him to go away, thinking none of the family were at home. She pictured him, standing there on the doorstep facing the closed door; and a perverse spirit held her silent, while the clock ticked resoundingly. Then all at once with a smothered cry she hurried through the hall, letting the door fall to behind her with a loud slam.

He was waiting patiently on the doorstep, as she had pictured him; and before a single word had passed between them she knew that the stone had been rolled away. His eyes met hers, not indeed with the old look, but with another, incomprehensible, yet wonderfully soul-satisfying.

"I wanted to tell you about it, before it came to you from the outside," he said, when they had settled themselves in the warm, silent kitchen.

His words startled Fanny. Was he going to tell her of his approaching marriage to Lydia? Her color faded, and a look of almost piteous resignation drooped the corners of her mouth. She strove to collect her scattered wits, to frame words of congratulation with which to meet the dreaded avowal.

He appeared in no hurry to begin; but bent forward, his eyes upon her changing face.

"Perhaps you know, already," he reflected. "She may have told your brother."

"Are you speaking of Miss Orr?"

Her voice sounded strange in her own ears.

"Yes," he said slowly. "But I suppose one should give her her rightful name, from now on."

"I—I hadn't heard," said Fanny, feeling her hard-won courage slipping from her. "Jim didn't tell me. But of course I am not—surprised."

He evidently experienced something of the emotion she had just denied.

"No one seemed to have guessed it," he said. "But now everything is plain. Poor girl!"

He fell into a fit of musing, which he finally broke to say:

"I thought you would go to see her. She sorely needs friends."

"She has—you," said Fanny in a smothered voice.

For the life of her she could not withhold that one lightning flash out of her enveloping cloud.

He disclaimed her words with a swift gesture.

"I'm not worthy to claim her friendship, nor yours," he said humbly; "but I hope you—sometime you may be able to forgive me, Fanny."

"I don't think I understand what you have come to tell me," she said with difficulty.

"The village is ringing with the news. She wanted every one to know; her father has come home."

"Her father!"

"Ah, you didn't guess, after all. I think we were all blind. Andrew Bolton has come back to Brookville, a miserable, broken man."

"But you said—her father. Do you mean that Lydia Orr—"

"It wasn't a deliberate deception on her part," he interrupted quickly. "She has always been known as Lydia Orr. It was her mother's name."

Fanny despised herself for the unreasoning tumult of joy which surged up within her. He could not possibly marry Andrew Bolton's daughter!

He was watching her closely.

"I thought perhaps, if she consented, I would marry Lydia Orr," he forced himself to tell her. "I want you to know this from me, now. I decided that her money and her position would help me.... I admired her; I even thought at one time I—loved her. I tried to love her.... I am not quite so base as to marry without love.... But she knew. She tried to save me.... Then her father—that wretched, ruined man came to me. He told me everything.... Fanny, that girl is a saint!"

His eyes were inscrutable under their somber brows. The girl sitting stiffly erect, every particle of color drained from her young face, watched him with something like terror. Why was he telling her this?—Why? Why?

His next words answered her:

"I can conceive of no worse punishment than having you think ill of me." ... And after a pause: "I deserve everything you may be telling yourself."

But coherent thought had become impossible for Fanny.

"Why don't you marry her?" she asked clearly.

"Oh, I asked her. I knew I had been a cad to both of you. I asked her all right."

Fanny's fingers, locked rigidly in her lap, did not quiver. Her blue eyes were wide and strange, but she tried to smile.

His voice, harsh and hesitating, went on: "She refused me, of course. She had known all along what I was. She said she did not love me; that I did not love her—which was God's truth. I wanted to atone. You see that, don't you?"

He looked at Fanny and started.

"My God, Fanny!" he cried. "I have made you suffer too!"

"Never mind me."

"Fanny, can you love me and be my wife after all this?"

"I am a woman," said Fanny. Her eyes blazed angrily at him. Then she laughed and put up her mouth to be kissed.

"Men will make fools of women till the Day of Judgment," said she, and laughed again.

Chapter XXIV

When the afternoon mail came in that day, Mr. Henry Daggett retired behind his official barrier according to his wont, leaving the store in charge of Joe Whittle, the Deacon's son. It had been diligently pointed out to Joe by his thrifty parents that all rich men began life by sweeping out stores and other menial tasks, and for some time Joe had been working for Mr. Daggett with doubtful alacrity.

Joe liked the store. There was a large stock of candy, dried fruit, crackers and pickles; Joe was a hungry boy, and Mr. Daggett had told him he could eat what he wished. He was an easy-going man with no children of his own, and he took great delight in pampering the Deacon's son. "I told him he could eat candy and things, and he looked tickled to death," he told his wife.

"He'll get his stomach upset," objected Mrs. Daggett.

"He can't eat the whole stock," said Daggett, "and upsetting a boy's stomach is not much of an upset anyway. It don't take long to right it."

Once in a while Daggett would suggest to Joe that if he were in his place he wouldn't eat too much of that green candy. He supposed it was pure; he didn't mean to sell any but pure candy if he knew it, but it might be just as well for him to go slow. Generally he took a paternal delight in watching the growing boy eat his stock in trade.

That afternoon Joe was working on a species of hard sweet which distended his cheeks, and nearly deprived him temporarily of the power of speech, while the people seeking their mail came in. There was never much custom while mail-sorting was going on, and Joe sucked blissfully.

Then Jim Dodge entered and spoke to him. "Hullo, Joe," he said.

Joe nodded, speechless.

Jim seated himself on a stool, and lit his pipe.

Joe eyed him. Jim was a sort of hero to him on account of his hunting fame. As soon as he could control his tongue, he addressed him:

"Heard the news?" said he, trying to speak like a man.

"What news?"

"Old Andrew Bolton's got out of prison and come back. He's crazy, too."

"How did you get hold of such nonsense?"

"Heard the women talking."

Jim pondered a moment. Then he said "Damn," and Joe admired him as never before. When Jim had gone out, directly, Joe shook his fist at a sugar barrel, and said "Damn," in a whisper.

Jim in the meantime was hurrying along the road to the Bolton house. He made up his mind that he must see Lydia. He must know if she had authorized the revelation that had evidently been made, and if so, through whom. He suspected the minister, and was hot with jealousy. His own friendship with Lydia seemed to have suffered a blight after that one confidential talk of theirs, in which she had afforded him a glimpse of her sorrowful past. She had not alluded to the subject a second time; and, somehow, he had not been able to get behind the defenses of her smiling cheerfulness. Always she was with her father, it seemed; and the old man, garrulous enough when alone, was invariably silent and moody in his daughter's company. One might almost have said he hated her, from the sneering impatient looks he cast at her from time to time. As for Lydia, she was all love and brooding tenderness for the man who had suffered so long and terribly.

"He'll be better after a while," she constantly excused him. "He needs peace and quiet and home to restore him to himself."

"You want to look out for him," Jim had ventured to warn the girl, when the two were alone together for a moment.

"Do you mean father?" Lydia asked. "What else should I do? It is all I live for—just to look out for father."

Had she been a martyr bound to the stake, the faggots piled about her slim body, her face might have worn just that expression of high resignation and contempt for danger and suffering.

The young man walked slowly on. He wanted time to think. Besides—he glanced down with a quick frown of annoyance at his mud-splashed clothing—he certainly cut a queer figure for a call.

Some one was standing on the doorstep talking to Fanny, as he approached his own home. Another instant and he had recognized Wesley Elliot. He stopped behind a clump of low-growing trees, and watched. Fanny, framed in the dark doorway, glowed like a rose. Jim saw her bend forward, smiling; saw the minister take both her hands in his and kiss them; saw Fanny glance quickly up and down the empty road, as if apprehensive of a chance passerby. Then the minister, his handsome head bared to the cold wind, waved her farewell and started at a brisk pace down the road.

Jim waited till the door had closed lingeringly on the girl; then he stepped forth from his concealment and waited.

Abreast of him Elliot stopped; aware, it would seem, of the menace in the other man's eyes.

"You wished to speak with me?" he began.

"Speak with you—no! I want to kick you."

The minister eyed him indignantly. "What do you mean?"

"You sneaking hypocrite! do you think I don't know what has happened? You threw Fanny down, when Lydia Orr came to town; you thought my sister wasn't good enough—nor rich enough for a handsome, eloquent clergyman like you. But when you learned her father was a convict—"

"Stop!" cried Elliot. "You don't understand!"

"I don't? Well, I guess I come pretty near it. And not content with telling Lydia's pitiful secret to all the busybodies in town, you come to Fanny with your smug explanations. My God! I could kill you!"

The minister's face had hardened during this speech.

"See here," he said. "You are going too far."

"Do you deny that you've made love to both my sister and Miss Orr?" demanded Jim.

Physically the minister was no coward. He measured the slight, wiry figure of his wrathful opponent with a coolly appraising eye.

"My relations with Miss Orr are none of your business," he reminded Jim. "As for your sister—"

"Damn you!" cried Jim.

The minister shrugged his shoulders.

"If you'll listen to reason," he suggested pacifically.

"I saw you kiss my sister's hand! I tell you I'll not have you hanging around the place, after what's gone. You may as well understand it."

Wesley Elliot reflected briefly.

"There's one thing you ought to know," he said, controlling his desire to knock Fanny's brother into the bushes.

A scornful gesture bade him to proceed.

"Andrew Bolton came to see me in the parsonage this morning. He is a ruined man, in every sense of the word. He will never be otherwise."

Jim Dodge thrust both hands deep in his trousers' pockets, his eyes fixed and frowning.

"Well," he murmured; "what of that?"

"That being the case, all we can do is to make the best of things—for her.... She requested me to make the facts known in the village. They would have found out everything from the man himself. He is—perhaps you are aware that Bolton bitterly resents his daughter's interference. She would have been glad to spare him the pain of publicity."

The minister's tone was calm, even judicial; and Jim Dodge suddenly experienced a certain flat humiliation of spirit.

"I didn't know she asked you to tell," he muttered, kicking a pebble out of the way. "That puts a different face on it."

He eyed the minister steadily.

"I'll be hanged if I can make you out, Elliot," he said at last. "You can't blame me for thinking— Why did you come here this afternoon, anyway?"

A sudden belated glimmer of comprehension dawned upon the minister.

"Are you in love with Miss Orr?" he parried.

"None of your damned business!"

"I was hoping you were," the minister said quietly. "She needs a friend—one who will stand close, just now."

"Do you mean—?"

"I am going to marry Fanny."

"The devil you are!"

The minister smiled and held out his hand.

"We may as well be friends, Jim," he said coolly, "seeing we're to be brothers."

The young man turned on his heel.

"I'll have to think that proposition over," he growled. "It's a bit too sudden—for me."

Without another glance in the direction of the minister he marched toward the house. Fanny was laying the table, a radiant color in her face. A single glance told her brother that she was happy. He threw himself into a chair by the window.

"Where's mother?" he asked presently, pretending to ignore the excited flutter of the girl's hands as she set a plate of bread on the table.

"She hasn't come back from the village yet," warbled Fanny. She couldn't keep the joy in her soul from singing.

"Guess I'll eat my supper and get out. I don't want to hear a word of gossip."

Fanny glanced up, faltered, then ran around the table and threw her arms about Jim's neck.

"Oh, Jim!" she breathed, "you've seen him!"

"Worse luck!" grumbled Jim.

He held his sister off at arm's length and gazed at her fixedly.

"What you see in that chap," he murmured. "Well—"

"Oh, Jim, he's wonderful!" cried Fanny, half laughing, half crying, and altogether lovely.

"I suppose you think so. But after the way he's treated you— By George, Fan! I can't see—"

Fanny drew herself up proudly.

"Of course I haven't talked much about it, Jim," she said, with dignity; "but Wesley and I had a—a little misunderstanding. It's all explained away now."

And to this meager explanation she stubbornly adhered, through subsequent soul-searching conversations with her mother, and during the years of married life that followed. In time she came to believe it, herself; and the "little misunderstanding with Wesley" and its romantic dénouement became a well-remembered milestone, wreathed with sentiment.

But poised triumphant on this pinnacle of joy, she yet had time to think of another than herself.

"Jim," said she, a touch of matronly authority already apparent in her manner. "I've wanted for a long time to talk to you seriously about Ellen."

Jim stared.

"About Ellen?" he repeated.

"Jim, she's awfully fond of you. I think you've treated her cruelly."

"Look here, Fan," said Jim, "don't you worry yourself about Ellen Dix. She's not in love with me, and never was."

Having thus spoken, Jim would not say another word. He gulped down his supper and was off. He kissed Fanny when he went.

"Hope you'll be happy, and all that," he told her rather awkwardly. Fanny looked after him swinging down the road. "I guess it's all right between him and Ellen," she thought.

Chapter XXV

Jim had no definite plan as he tramped down the road in the falling darkness. He felt uncertain and miserable as he speculated with regard to Lydia. She could not guess at half the unkind things people must be saying; but she would ask for the bread of sympathy and they would give her a stone. He wished he might carry her away, shielding her and comforting her against the storm. He knew he would willingly give his life to make her happier. Of course she did not care for him. How could she? Who was he—Jim Dodge—to aspire to a girl like Lydia?

The wind had risen again and was driving dark masses of cloud across the sky; in the west a sullen red flared up from behind the hills, touching the lower edges of the vaporous mountains with purple. In a small, clear space above the red hung the silver sickle of the new moon, and near it shone a single star.... Lydia was like that star, he told himself—as wonderful, as remote.

There were lights in the windows of Bolton House. Jim stopped and gazed at the yellow squares, something big and powerful rising within him. Then, yielding to a sudden impulse, he approached and looked in. In a great armchair before the blazing hearth sat, or rather crouched, Andrew Bolton. He was wearing a smoking-jacket of crimson velvet and a pipe hung from his nerveless fingers. Only the man's eyes appeared alive; they were fixed upon Lydia at the piano. She was playing some light tuneful melody, with a superabundance of trills and runs. Jim did not know Lydia played; and the knowledge of this trivial accomplishment seemed to put her still further beyond his reach. He did not know, either, that she had acquired her somewhat indifferent skill after long years of dull practice, and for the single purpose of diverting the man, who sat watching her with bright, furtive eyes.... Presently she arose from the piano and crossed the room to his side. She bent over him and kissed him on his bald forehead, her white hands clinging to his shoulders. Jim saw the man shake off those hands with a rough gesture; saw the grieved look on her face; saw the man follow her slight figure with his eyes, as she stooped under pretext of mending the fire. But he could not hear the words which passed between them.

"You pretend to love me," Bolton was saying. "Why don't you do what I want you to?"

"If you'd like to go away from Brookville, father, I will go with you. You need me!"

"That's where you're dead wrong, my girl: I don't need you. What I do need is freedom! You stifle me with your fussy attentions. Give me some money; I'll go away and not bother you again."

Whereat Lydia had cried out—a little hurt cry, which reached the ears of the watcher outside.

"Don't leave me, father! I have no one but you in all the world—no one."

"And you've never even told me how much money you have," the man went on in a whining voice. "There's daughterly affection for you! By rights it all ought to be mine. I've suffered enough, God knows, to deserve a little comfort now."

"All that I have is yours, father. I want nothing for myself."

"Then hand it over—the control of it, I mean. I'll make you a handsome allowance; and I'll give you this place, too. I don't want to rot here.... Marry that good-looking parson and settle down, if you like. I don't want to settle down: been settled in one cursed place long enough, by gad! I should think you could see that."

"But you wanted to come home to Brookville, father. Don't you remember you said—"

"That was when I was back there in that hell-hole, and didn't know what I wanted. How could I? I only wanted to get out. That's what I want now—to get out and away! If you weren't so damned selfish, you'd let me go. I hate a selfish woman!"

Then it was that Jim Dodge, pressing closer to the long window, heard her say quite distinctly:

"Very well, father; we will go. Only I must go with you.... You are not strong enough to go alone. We will go anywhere you like."

Andrew Bolton got nimbly out of his chair and stood glowering at her across its back. Then he burst into a prolonged fit of laughter mixed with coughing.

"Oh, so you'll go with father, will you?" he spluttered. "You insist—eh?"

And, still coughing and laughing mirthlessly, he went out of the room.

Left to herself, the girl sat down quietly enough before the fire. Her serene face told no story of inward sorrow to the watchful eyes of the man who loved her. Over long she had concealed her feelings, even from herself. She seemed lost in revery, at once sad and profound. Had she foreseen this dire disappointment of all her hopes, he wondered.

He stole away at last, half ashamed of spying upon her lonely vigil, yet withal curiously heartened. Wesley Elliot was right: Lydia Orr needed a friend. He resolved that he would be that friend.

In the room overhead the light had leapt to full brilliancy. An uncertain hand pulled the shade down crookedly. As the young man turned for a last look at the house he perceived a shadow hurriedly passing and repassing the lighted window. Then all at once the shadow, curiously huddled, stooped and was gone. There was something sinister in the sudden disappearance of that active shadow. Jim Dodge watched the vacant window for a long minute; then with a muttered exclamation walked on toward the village.

Chapter XXVI

In the barroom of the Brookville House the flaring kerosene lamp lit up a group of men and half-grown boys, who had strayed in out of the chill darkness to warm themselves around the great stove in the middle of the floor. The wooden armchairs, which in summer made a forum of the tavern's side piazza, had been brought in and ranged in a wide semicircle about the stove, marking the formal opening of the winter session. In the central chair sat the large figure of Judge Fulsom, puffing clouds of smoke from a calabash pipe; his twinkling eyes looking forth over his fat, creased cheeks roved impartially about the circle of excited faces.

"I can understand all right about Andrew Bolton's turning up," one man was saying. "He was bound to turn up sooner or later. I seen him myself, day before yesterday, going down street. Thinks I, 'Who can that be?' There was something kind of queer about the way he dragged his feet. What you going to do about it, Judge? Have we got to put up with having a jailbird, as crazy as a loon into the bargain, living right here in our midst?"

"In luxury and idleness, like he was a captain of industry," drawled another man who was eating hot dog and sipping beer. "That's what strikes me kind of hard, Judge, in luxury and idleness, while the rest of us has to work."

Judge Fulsom gave an inarticulate grunt and smoked on imperturbably.

"Set down, boys; set down," ordered a small man in a red sweater under a corduroy coat. "Give the Jedge a chance! He ain't going to deliver no opinion whilst you boys are rammaging around. Set down and let the Jedge take th' floor."

A general scraping of chair legs and a shuffling of uneasy feet followed this exhortation; still no word from the huge, impassive figure in the central chair. The oily-faced young man behind the bar improved the opportunity by washing a dozen or so glasses, setting them down showily on a tin tray in view of the company.

"Quit that noise, Cholley!" exhorted the small man in the red sweater; "we want order in the court room—eh, Jedge?"

"What I'd like to know is where she got all that money of hers," piped an old man, with a mottled complexion and bleary eyes.

"Sure enough; where'd she get it?" chimed in half a dozen voices at once.

"She's Andrew Bolton's daughter," said the first speaker. "And she's been setting up for a fine lady, doing stunts for charity. How about our town hall an' our lov-elly library, an' our be-utiful drinking fountain, and the new shingles on our church roof? You don't want to ask too many questions, Lute."

"Don't I?" cried the man, who was eating hot dog. "You all know *me!* I ain't a-going to stand for no grab-game. If she's got money, it's more than likely the old fox salted it down before they ketched him. It's our money; that's whose money 'tis, if you want to know!"

And he swallowed his mouthful with a slow, menacing glance which swept the entire circle.

"Now, Lucius," began Judge Fulsom, removing the pipe from his mouth, "go slow! No use in talk without proof."

"But what have you got to say, Jedge? Where'd she get all that money she's been flamming about with, and that grand house, better than new, with all the latest improvements. Wa'n't we some jays to be took in like we was by a little, white-faced chit like her? Couldn't see through a grindstone with a hole in it! Bolton House.... And an automobile to fetch the old jailbird home in. Wa'n't it love-ly?"

A low growl ran around the circle.

"Durn you, Lute! Don't you see the Jedge has something to say?" demanded the man behind the bar.

Judge Fulsom slowly tapped his pipe on the arm of his chair. "If you all will keep still a second and let me speak," he began.

"I want my rights," interrupted a man with a hoarse crow.

"Your rights!" shouted the Judge. "You've got no right to a damned thing but a good horsewhipping!"

"I've got my rights to the money other folks are keeping, I'll let you know!"

Then the Judge fairly bellowed, as he got slowly to his feet:

"I tell you once for all, the whole damned lot of you," he shouted, "that every man, woman and child in Brookville has been paid, compensated, remunerated and requited in full for every cent he, she or it lost in the Andrew Bolton bank failure."

There was a snarl of dissent.

"You all better go slow, and hold your tongues, and mind your own business. Remember what I say; that girl does not owe a red cent in this town, neither does her father. She's paid in full, and you've spent a lot of it in here, too!" The Judge wiped his red face.

"Oh, come on, Jedge; you don't want to be hard on the house," protested the man in the red sweater, waving his arms as frantically as a freight brakeman. "Say, you boys! don't ye git excited! The Jedge didn't mean that; you got him kind of het up with argufying.... Down in front, boys! You, Lute—"

But it was too late: half a dozen voices were shouting at once. There was a simultaneous descent upon the bar, with loud demands for liquor of the sort Lute Parsons filled up on. Then the raucous voice of the ringleader pierced the tumult.

"Come on, boys! Let's go out to the old place and get our rights off that gal of Bolton's!"

"That's th' stuff, Lute!" yelled the others, clashing their glasses wildly. "Come on! Come on, everybody!"

In vain Judge Fulsom hammered on the bar and called for order in the court room. The majesty of the law, as embodied in his great bulk, appeared to have lost its power. Even his faithful henchman in the red sweater had joined the rioters and was yelling wildly for his rights. Somebody flung wide the door, and the barroom emptied itself into the night, leaving the oily young man at his post of duty gazing fearfully at the purple face of Judge Fulsom, who stood staring, as if stupefied, at the overturned chairs, the broken glasses and the empty darkness outside.

"Say, Jedge, them boys was sure some excited," ventured the bartender timidly. "You don't s'pose—"

The big man put himself slowly into motion.

"I'll get th' constable," he growled. "I—I'll run 'em in; and I'll give Lute Parsons the full extent of the law, if it's the last thing I do on earth. I—I'll teach them!—I'll give them all they're lookin' for."

And he, too, went out, leaving the door swinging in the cold wind.

At the corner, still meditating vengeance for this affront to his dignity, Judge Fulsom almost collided with the hurrying figure of a man approaching in the opposite direction.

"Hello!" he challenged sharply. "Where you goin' so fast, my friend?"

"Evening, Judge," responded the man, giving the other a wide margin.

"Oh, it's Jim Dodge—eh? Say, Jim, did you meet any of the boys on the road?"

"What boys?"

"Why, we got into a little discussion over to the Brookville House about this Andrew Bolton business—his coming back unexpected, you know; and some of the boys seemed to think they hadn't got all that was coming to them by rights. Lute Parsons he gets kind of worked up after about three or four glasses, and he sicked the boys onto going out there, and—"

"Going out—where? In the name of Heaven, what do you mean, Judge?"

"I told 'em to keep cool and— Say, don't be in a hurry, Jim. I had an awful good mind to call out Hank Simonson to run a few of 'em in. But I dunno as the boys'll do any real harm. They wouldn't dare. They know me, and they know—"

"Do you mean that drunken mob was headed for Bolton House? Why, Good Lord, man, she's there practically alone!"

"Well, perhaps you'd better see if you can get some help," began the Judge, whose easy-going disposition was already balking at effort.

But Jim Dodge, shouting back a few trenchant directions, had already disappeared, running at top speed.

There was a short cut to Bolton House, across plowed fields and through a patch of woodland. Jim Dodge ran all the way, wading a brook, swollen with the recent rains, tearing his way through thickets of brush and bramble, the twinkling lights in the top story of the distant house leading him on. Once he paused for an instant, thinking he heard the clamor of rude voices borne on the wind; then plunged forward again, his flying feet seemingly weighted with lead; and all the while an agonizing picture of Lydia, white and helpless, facing the crowd of drunken men flitted before his eyes.

Now he had reached the wall at the rear of the gardens; had clambered over it, dropping to his feet in the midst of a climbing rose which clutched at him with its thorny branches; had run across an acre of kitchen garden and leaped the low-growing hedge which divided it from the sunken flower garden he had made for

Lydia. Here were more rosebushes and an interminable space broken by walks and a sundial, masked by shrubs, with which he collided violently. There was no mistaking the clamor from the front of the house; the rioters had reached their quarry first! Not stopping to consider what one man, single-handed and unarmed, could do against a score of drunken opponents, the young man rounded the corner of the big house just as the door was flung wide and the slim figure of Lydia stood outlined against the bright interior.

"What do you want, men?" she called out, in her clear, fearless voice. "What has happened?"

There was a confused murmur of voices in reply. Most of the men were decent enough fellows, when sober. Some one was heard to suggest a retreat: "No need to scare the young lady. 'Tain't her fault!"

"Aw! shut up, you coward!" shouted another. "We want our money!"

"Where did you get yer money?" demanded a third. "You tell us that, young woman. That's what we're after!"

"Where's the old thief? ...We want Andrew Bolton!"

Then from somewhere in the darkness a pebble flung by a reckless hand shattered a pane of glass. At sound of the crash all pretense of decency and order seemed abandoned. The spirit of the pack broke loose!

Just what happened from the moment when he leaped upon the portico, wrenching loose a piece of iron pipe which formed the support of a giant wistaria, Jim Dodge could never afterward recall in precise detail. A sort of wild rage seized him; he struck right and left among the dark figures swarming up the steps. There were cries, shouts, curses, flying stones; then he had dragged Lydia inside and bolted the heavy door between them and the ugly clamor without.

She faced him where he stood, breathing hard, his back against the barred door.

"They were saying—" she whispered, her face still and white. "My God! What do they think I've done?"

"They're drunk," he explained. "It was only a miserable rabble from the barroom in the village. But if you'd been here alone—!"

She shook her head.

"I recognized the man who spoke first; his name is Parsons. There were others, too, who worked on the place here in the summer.... They have heard?"

He nodded, unable to speak because of something which rose in his throat choking him. Then he saw a thin trickle of red oozing from under the fair hair above her temple, and the blood hammered in his ears.

"You are hurt!" he said thickly. "The devils struck you!"

"It's nothing—a stone, perhaps."

Something in the sorrowful look she gave him broke down the flimsy barrier between them.

"Lydia—Lydia!" he cried, holding out his arms.

She clung to him like a child. They stood so for a moment, listening to the sounds from without. There were still occasional shouts and the altercation of loud, angry voices; but this was momently growing fainter; presently it died away altogether.

She stirred in his arms and he stooped to look into her face.

"I—Father will be frightened," she murmured, drawing away from him with a quick decided movement. "You must let me go."

"Not until I have told you, Lydia! I am poor, rough—not worthy to touch you—but I love you with my whole heart and soul, Lydia. You must let me take care of you. You need me, dear."

Tears overflowed her eyes, quiet, patient tears; but she answered steadily.

"Can't you see that I—I am different from other women? I have only one thing to live for. I must go to him.... You had forgotten—him."

In vain he protested, arguing his case with all lover's skill and ingenuity. She shook her head.

"Sometime you will forgive me that one moment of weakness," she said sadly. "I was frightened and—tired."

He followed her upstairs in gloomy silence. The old man, she was telling him hurriedly, would be terrified. She must reassure him; and tomorrow they would go away together for a long journey. She could see now that she had made a cruel mistake in bringing him to Brookville.

But there was no answer in response to her repeated tapping at his door; and suddenly the remembrance of that stooping shadow came back to him.

"Let me go in," he said, pushing her gently aside.

The lights, turned high in the quiet room, revealed only emptiness and disorder; drawers and wardrobes pulled wide, scattered garments apparently dropped at random on chairs and tables. The carpet, drawn aside in one corner, disclosed a shallow aperture in the floor, from which the boards had been lifted.

"Why— What?" stammered the girl, all the high courage gone from her face. "What has happened?"

He picked up a box—a common cigar box—from amid the litter of abandoned clothing. It was quite empty save for a solitary slip of greenish paper which had somehow adhered to the bottom.

Lydia clutched the box in both trembling hands, staring with piteous eyes at the damning evidence of that bit of paper.

"Money!" she whispered. "He must have hidden it before—before— Oh, father, father!"

Chapter XXVII

History is said to repeat itself, as if indeed the world were a vast pendulum, swinging between events now inconceivably remote, and again menacing and near. And if in things great and heroic, so also in the less significant aspects of life.

Mrs. Henry Daggett stood, weary but triumphant, amid the nearly completed preparations for a reception in the new church parlors, her broad, rosy face wearing a smile of satisfaction.

"Don't it look nice?" she said, by way of expressing her overflowing contentment.

Mrs. Maria Dodge, evergreen wreaths looped over one arm, nodded.

"It certainly does look fine, Abby," said she. "And I guess nobody but you would have thought of having it."

Mrs. Daggett beamed. "I thought of it the minute I heard about that city church that done it. I call it a real tasty way to treat a minister as nice as ours."

"So 'tis," agreed Mrs. Dodge with the air of complacent satisfaction she had acquired since Fanny's marriage to the minister. "And I think Wesley'll appreciate it."

Mrs. Daggett's face grew serious. Then her soft bosom heaved with mirth.

"'Tain't everybody that's lucky enough to have a minister right in the family," said she briskly. "Mebbe if I was to hear a sermon preached every day in the week I'd get some piouser myself. I've been comparing this with the fair we had last summer. It ain't so grand, but it's newer. A fair's like a work of nature, Maria; sun and rain and dew, and the scrapings from the henyard, all mixed with garden ground to fetch out cabbages, potatoes or roses. God gives the increase."

Mrs. Dodge stared at her friend in amazement.

"That sounds real beautiful, Abby," she said. "You must have thought it all out."

"That's just what I done," confirmed Mrs. Daggett happily. "I'm always meditating about something, whilst I'm working 'round th' house. And it's amazing what thoughts'll come to a body from somewheres.... What you going to do with them wreaths, Maria?"

"Why, I was thinking of putting 'em right up here," said Mrs. Dodge, pointing.

"A good place," said Mrs. Daggett. "Remember Fanny peeking through them wreaths last summer? Pretty as a pink! An' now she's Mis' Reveren' Elliot. I seen him looking at her that night.... My! My! What lots of things have took place in our midst since then."

Mrs. Dodge, from the lofty elevation of a stepladder, looked across the room.

"Here comes Ann Whittle with two baskets," she said, "and Mrs. Solomon Black carrying a big cake, and a whole crowd of ladies just behind 'em."

"Glad they ain't going to be late like they was last year," said Mrs. Daggett. "My sakes! I hadn't thought so much about that fair till today; the scent of the evergreens brings it all back. We was wondering who'd buy the things; remember, Maria?"

"I should say I did," assented Mrs. Dodge, hopping nimbly down from the ladder. "There, that looks even nicer than it did at the fair; don't you think so, Abby?"

"It looks perfectly lovely, Maria."

"Well, here we are at last," announced Mrs. Whittle as she entered. "I had to wait till the frosting stiffened up on my cake."

She bustled over to a table and began to take the things out of her baskets. Mrs. Daggett hurried forward to meet Mrs. Solomon Black, who was advancing with slow majesty, bearing a huge disk covered with tissue paper.

Mrs. Black was not the only woman in the town of Brookville who could now boast sleeves made in the latest Parisian style. Her quick black eyes had already observed the crisp blue taffeta, in which Mrs. Whittle was attired, and the fresh muslin gowns decked with uncreased ribbons worn by Mrs. Daggett and her friend, Maria

Dodge. Mrs. Solomon Black's water-waves were crisp and precise, as of yore, and her hard red cheeks glowed like apples above the elaborate embroidery of her dress.

"Here, Mis' Black, let me take your cake!" offered Abby Daggett. "I sh'd think your arm would be most broke carryin' it all the way from your house."

"Thank you, Abby; but I wouldn't das' t' resk changin' it; I'll set it right down where it's t' go."

The brisk chatter and laughter, which by now had prevaded the big place, ceased as by a preconcerted signal, and a dozen women gathered about the table toward which Mrs. Solomon Black was moving like the central figure in some stately pageant.

"Fer pity sake!" whispered Mrs. Mixter, "what d' you s'pose she's got under all that tissue paper?"

Mrs. Solomon Black set the great cake, still veiled, in the middle of the table; then she straightened herself and looked from one to the other of the eager, curious faces gathered around.

"There!" she said. "I feel now 's 'o' I could dror m' breath once more. I ain't joggled it once, so's t' hurt, since I started from home."

Then slowly she withdrew the shrouding tissue paper from the creation she had thus triumphantly borne to its place of honor, and stood off, a little to one side, her face one broad smile of satisfaction.

"Fer goodness' sake!"

"Did you ev—er!"

"Why, Mis' Black!"

"Ain't that just—"

"You never done that all yourself?"

Mrs. Black nodded slowly, almost solemnly. The huge cake which was built up in successive steps, like a pyramid, was crowned on its topmost disk by a bridal scene, a tiny man holding his tiny veiled bride by the hand in the midst of an expanse of pink frosting. About the side of the great cake, in brightly colored "mites," was inscribed "Greetings to our Pastor and his Bride."

"I thought 'twould be kind of nice, seeing our minister was just married, and so, in a way, this is a wedding reception. I don't know what the rest of you ladies'll think."

Abby Daggett stood with clasped hands, her big soft bosom rising and falling in a sort of ecstasy.

"Why, Phoebe," she said, "it's a real poem! It couldn't be no han'somer if it had been done right up in heaven!"

She put her arms about Mrs. Solomon Black and kissed her.

"And this ain't all," said Mrs. Black. "Lois Daggett is going to fetch over a chocolate cake and a batch of crullers for me when she comes."

Applause greeted this statement.

"Time was," went on Mrs. Black, "and not so long ago, neither, when I was afraid to spend a cent, for fear of a rainy day that's been long coming. 'Tain't got here yet; but I can tell you ladies, I got a lesson from *her* in generosity I don't mean to forget. 'Spend and be spent' is my motto from now on; so I didn't grudge the new-laid eggs I put in that cake, nor yet the sugar, spice nor raisins. There's three cakes in one—in token of the trinity (I do hope th' won't nobody think it's wicked t' mention r'ligion in connection with a cake); the bottom cake was baked in a milk-pan, an' it's a bride's cake, being made with the whites of fourteen perfec'ly fresh eggs; the next layer is fruit and spice, as rich as wedding cake ought to be; the top cake is best of all; and can be lifted right off and given to Rever'nd an' Mrs. Wesley Elliot.... I guess they'll like to keep the wedding couple for a souvenir."

A vigorous clapping of hands burst forth. Mrs. Solomon Black waited modestly till this gratifying demonstration had subsided, then she went on:

"I guess most of you ladies'll r'member how one short year ago Miss Lyddy Orr Bolton came a'walkin' int' our midst, lookin' sweet an' modest, like she was; and how down-in-th'-mouth we was all a-feelin', 'count o' havin' no money t' buy th' things we'd worked s' hard t' make. Some of us hadn't no more grit an' gumption 'n Ananias an' S'phira, t' say nothin' o' Jonah an' others I c'd name. In she came, an' ev'rythin' was changed from that minute! ...Now, I want we sh'd cut up that cake—after everybody's had a chance t' see it good—all but th' top layer, same's I said—an' all of us have a piece, out o' compl'ment t' our paster an' his wife, an' in memory o' her, who's gone from us."

"But Lyddy Orr ain't dead, Mis' Black," protested Mrs. Daggett warmly.

"She might 's well be, 's fur 's our seein' her 's concerned," replied Mrs. Black. "She's gone t' Boston t' stay f'r good, b'cause she couldn't stan' it no-how here in Brookville, after her pa was found dead. The' was plenty o'

91

hard talk, b'fore an' after; an' when it come t' breakin' her windows with stones an' hittin' her in th' head, so she was 'bleeged t' have three stitches took, all I c'n say is I don't wonder she went t' Boston.... Anyway, that's my wish an' d'sire 'bout that cake."

The arrival of Mr. and Mrs. Wesley Elliot offered a welcome interruption to a scene which was becoming uncomfortably tense. Whatever prickings of conscience there might have been under the gay muslin and silks of her little audience, each woman privately resented the superior attitude assumed by Mrs. Solomon Black.

"Easy f'r *her* t' talk," murmured Mrs. Fulsom, from between puckered lips; "*she* didn't lose no money off Andrew Bolton."

"An' she didn't get none, neither, when it come t' dividin' up," Mrs. Mixter reminded her.

"That's so," assented Mrs. Fulsom, as she followed in pretty Mrs. Mixter's wake to greet the newly-married pair.

"My! ain't you proud o' her," whispered Abby Daggett to Maria Dodge. "She's a perfec' pictur' o' joy, if ever I laid my eyes on one!"

Fanny stood beside her tall husband, her pretty face irradiating happiness. She felt a sincere pity welling up in her heart for Ellen Dix and Joyce Fulsom and the other girls. Compared with her own transcendent experiences, their lives seemed cold and bleak to Fanny. And all the while she was talking to the women who crowded about her.

"Yes; we are getting nicely settled, thank you, Mrs. Fulsom—all but the attic. Oh, how'd you do, Judge Fulsom?"

The big man wiped the perspiration from his bald forehead.

"Just been fetchin' in th' ice cream freezers," he said, with his booming chuckle. "I guess I'm 's well 's c'n be expected, under th' circumstances, ma'am.... An' that r'minds me, parson, a little matter was s'ggested t' me. In fact, I'd thought of it, some time ago. No more 'n right, in view o' th' facts. If you don't mind, I'll outline th' idee t' you, parson, an' see if you approve."

Fanny, striving to focus attention on the pointed remarks Miss Lois Daggett was making, caught occasional snatches of their conversation. Fanny had never liked Lois Daggett; but in her new rôle of minister's wife, it was her foreordained duty to love everybody and to condole and sympathize with the parish at large. One could easily sympathize with Lois Daggett, she was thinking; what would it be like to be obliged daily to face the reflection of that mottled complexion, that long, pointed nose, with its rasped tip, that drab lifeless hair with its sharp hairpin crimp, and those small greenish eyes with no perceptible fringe of lashes? Fanny looked down from her lovely height into Miss Daggett's upturned face and pitied her from the bottom of her heart.

"I hear your brother Jim has gone t' Boston," Miss Daggett was saying with a simper.

From the rear Fanny heard Judge Fulsom's rumbling monotone, earnestly addressed to her husband:

"Not that Boston ain't a nice town t' live in; but we'll have t' enter a demurrer against her staying there f'r good. Y' see—"

"Yes," said Fanny, smiling at Miss Daggett. "He went several days ago."

"H'm-m," murmured Miss Daggett. "*She's* livin' there, ain't she?"

"You mean Miss Orr?"

"I mean Miss Lyddy Bolton. I guess Bolton's a good 'nough name for *her*."

From the Judge, in a somewhat louder tone:

"That's th' way it looks t' me, dominie; an' if all th' leadin' citizens of Brookville'll put their name to it—an' I'm of th' opinion they will, when I make my charge t' th' jury—"

"Certainly," murmured Fanny absently, as she gazed at her husband and the judge.

She couldn't help wondering why her Wesley was speaking so earnestly to the Judge, yet in such a provokingly low tone of voice.

"I had become so accustomed to thinking of her as Lydia Orr," she finished hastily.

"Well, I don't b'lieve in givin' out a name 'at ain't yourn," said Lois Daggett, sharply. "She'd ought t' 'a' told right out who she was, an' what she come t' Brookville *for*."

Judge Fulsom and the minister had moved still further away. Fanny, with some alarm, felt herself alone.

"I don't think Miss Orr meant to be deceitful," she said nervously.

"Well, o' course, if she's a-goin' t' be in th' family, it's natural you sh'd think so," said Lois Daggett, sniffing loudly.

Fanny did not answer.

"I sh'd *hope* she an' Jim was engaged," proclaimed Miss Daggett. "If they ain't, they'd ought t' be."

"Why should you say that, Miss Lois?" asked Fanny hurriedly. "They are very good friends."

Miss Daggett bent forward, lowering her voice.

"The's one thing I'd like t' know f'r certain," she said: "Did Jim Dodge find that body?"

Fanny stared at her inquisitor resentfully.

"There were a good many persons searching," she said coldly.

Miss Daggett wagged her head in an irritated fashion.

"Of course I know *that*," she snapped. "What I want t' know is whether Jim Dodge—"

"I never asked my brother," interrupted Fanny. "It all happened so long ago, why not—"

"Not s' terrible long," disagreed Miss Daggett. "It was th' first o' November. N' I've got a mighty good reason f'r askin'."

"You have?" murmured Fanny, flashing a glance of entreaty at her husband.

"Some of us ladies was talkin' it over," pursued the spinster relentlessly, "an' I says t' Mis' Deacon Whittle: 'Who counted th' money 'at was found on Andrew Bolton's body?' I says. 'W'y,' s' she, 'th' ones 'at found him out in th' woods where he got lost, I s'pose.' But come t' sift it right down t' facts, not one o' them ladies c'd tell f'r certain who 't was 'at found that body. The' was such an' excitement 'n' hullaballoo, nobody 'd thought t' ask. It wa'n't Deacon Whittle; n'r it wa'n't th' party from th' Brookville House; ner Hank Simonson, ner any o' the boys. *It was Jim Dodge, an' she was with him!*"

"Well," said Fanny faintly.

She looked up to meet the minister's eyes, with a sense of strong relief. Wesley was so wise and good. Wesley would know just what to say to this prying woman.

"What are you and Miss Daggett talking about so earnestly?" asked the minister.

When informed of the question under discussion, he frowned thoughtfully.

"My dear Miss Daggett," he said, "if you will fetch me the dinner bell from Mrs. Whittle's kitchen, I shall be happy to answer your question and others like it which have reached me from time to time concerning this unhappy affair."

"Mis' Deacon Whittle's dinner bell?" gasped Lois Daggett. "What's that got t' do with—"

"Bring it to me, and you'll see," smiled the minister imperturbably.

"What are you going to do, Wesley?" whispered Fanny.

He gazed gravely down into her lovely eyes.

"Dearest," he whispered back, "trust me! It is time we laid this uneasy ghost; don't you think so?"

By now the large room was well filled with men, women and children. The ice cream was being passed around when suddenly the clanging sound of a dinner bell, vigorously operated by Joe Whittle, arrested attention.

"The minister's got something to say! The minister's got something to say!" shouted the boy.

Wesley Elliot, standing apart, lifted his hand in token of silence, then he spoke:

"I have taken this somewhat unusual method of asking your attention to a matter which has for many years past enlisted your sympathies," he began: "I refer to the Bolton affair."

The sound of breath sharply indrawn and the stir of many feet died into profound silence as the minister went on, slowly and with frequent pauses:

"Most of you are already familiar with the sordid details. It is not necessary for me to go back to the day, now nearly nineteen years ago, when many of you found yourselves unexpectedly impoverished because the man you trusted had defaulted.... There was much suffering in Brookville that winter, and since.... When I came to this parish I found it—sick. Because of the crime of Andrew Bolton? No. I repeat the word with emphasis: *No!* Brookville was sick, despondent, dull, gloomy and impoverished—not because of Andrew Bolton's crime; but because Brookville had never forgiven Andrew Bolton.... Hate is the one destructive element in the universe; did you know that, friends? It is impossible for a man or woman who hates another to prosper.... And I'll tell you why this is—why it must be true: God is love—the opposite of hate. Hence All Power is enlisted on the side of *love*.... Think this over, and you'll know it is true.... Now the Bolton mystery: A year ago we were holding a fair in this village, which was sick and impoverished because it had never forgiven the man who stole its money.... You all remember that occasion. There were things to sell; but nobody had money to buy them. It wasn't a pleasant occasion. Nobody was enjoying it, least of all your minister. But a miracle took place— There are miracles in the world today, as there always have been, thank God! There came into Brookville that day a

93

person who was moved by love. Every impulse of her heart; everything she did was inspired by that mightiest force of the universe. She called herself Lydia Orr.... She had been called Lydia Orr, as far back as she could remember; so she did no wrong to anyone by retaining that name. But she had another name, which she quickly found was a byword and a hissing in Brookville. Was it strange that she shrank from telling it? She believed in the forgiveness of sins; and she had come to right a great wrong.... She did what she could, as it is written of another woman, who poured out a fragrant offering of love unappreciated save by One.... There quickly followed the last chapter in the tragedy—for it was all a tragedy, friends, as I look at it: the theft; the pitiful attempt to restore fourfold all that had been taken; the return of that ruined man, Andrew Bolton, after his heavy punishment; and his tragic death.... Some of you may not know all that happened that night. You do know of the cowardly attack made upon the helpless girl. You know of the flight of the terrified man, of how he was found dead two days later three miles from the village, in a lonely spot where he had perished from hunger and exposure.... The body was discovered by James Dodge, with the aid of his dog. With him on that occasion was a detective from Boston, employed by Miss Bolton, and myself. There was a sum of money found on the body amounting to something over five thousand dollars. It had been secreted beneath the floor of Andrew Bolton's chamber, before his arrest and imprisonment. It is probable that he intended to make good his escape, but failed, owing to the illness of his wife.... This is a terrible story, friends, and it has a sad ending. Brookville had never learned to forgive. It had long ago formed the terrible habits of hate: suspicion, envy, sharp-tongued censure and the rest. Lydia Bolton could not remain here, though it was her birthplace and her home.... She longed for friendship! She asked for bread and you gave her—a stone!"

The profound silence was broken by a sob from a distant corner. The strained listeners turned with a sharp movement of relief.

"Fer pity sake!" faltered Abby Daggett, her beautiful, rosy face all quivering with grief. "Can't nobody do nothing?"

"Yes, ma'am!" shouted the big voice of Judge Fulsom. "We can all do something.... I ain't going to sum up the case against Brookville; the parson's done it already; if there's any rebuttal coming from the defendant, now's the time to bring it before the court.... Nothing to say—eh? Well, I thought so! We're guilty of the charges preferred, and I'm going to pass sentence.... But before I do that, there's one thing the parson didn't mention, that in my opinion should be told, to wit: Miss Lydia Bolton's money—all that she had—came to her from her uncle, an honest hardworkin' citizen of Boston. He made every penny of it as a soap-boiler. So you see 'twas *clean* money; and he left it to his niece, Lydia Bolton. What did she do with it? You know! She poured it out, right here in Brookville—pretty nigh all there was of it. She's got her place here; but mighty little besides. I'm her trustee, and I know. The five thousand dollars found on the dead body of Andrew Bolton, has been made a trust fund for the poor and discouraged of this community, under conditions anybody that'll take the trouble to step in to my office can find out...."

The Judge paused to clear his throat, while he produced from his pocket, with a vast deal of ceremony, a legal looking document dangling lengths of red ribbon and sealing wax.

"This Bond of Indemnity, which I'm going to ask every man, woman and child of fifteen years and up'ards, of the village of Brookville, hereinafter known as the Party of the First Part, to sign, reads as follows: Know all men by these presents that we, citizens of the village of Brookville, hereinafter known as the Party of the First Part, are held and firmly bound unto Miss Lydia Orr Bolton, hereinafter known as the Party of the Second Part.... Whereas; the above-named Party of the Second Part (don't f'rget that means Miss Lydia Bolton) did in behalf of her father—one Andrew Bolton, deceased—pay, compensate, satisfy, restore, remunerate, recompense *and re-quite* all legal indebtedness incurred by said Andrew Bolton to, for, and in behalf of the aforesaid Party of the First Part....

"You git me? If you don't, just come to my office and I'll explain in detail any of the legal terms not understood, comprehended and known by the feeble-minded of Brookville. Form in line at nine o'clock. First come, first served:

"We, the Party of the First Part, bind ourselves, and each of our heirs, executors, administrators and assigns, jointly and severally, firmly by these presents, and at all times hereafter to save, defend, keep harmless and indemnify the aforesaid Party of the Second Part (Miss Lydia Bolton) of, from and against all further costs, damages, expense, disparagements (that means spiteful gossip, ladies!) molestations, slander, vituperations, etc. (I could say more, *but* we've got something to do that'll take time.) And whereas, the said Party of the Second Part has been actually drove to Boston to live by the aforesaid slander, calumniations, aspersions and libels— which we, the said Party of the First Part do hereby acknowledge to be false and untrue (yes, and doggone mean, as I look at it)—we, the said Party of the First part do firmly bind ourselves, our heirs, executors, administrators an' assigns to quit all such illegalities from this day forth, and forever more." ...

"You want to get out of the habit of talking mean about Andrew Bolton, for one thing. It's been as catching as measles in this town since I can remember. Andrew Bolton's dead and buried in our cemetery, beside his wife. We'll be there ourselves, some day; in the meanwhile we want to reform our tongues. You get me? All right!

"And whereas, we, the Party of the First Part, otherwise known as the village of Brookville, do ask, beg, entreat, supplicate and plead the f'rgiveness of the Party of the Second Part, otherwise known as Miss Lydia Orr Bolton. And we also hereby request, petition, implore *an'* importune Miss Lydia Orr Bolton, otherwise known as the Party of the Second Part, to return to Brookville and make it her permanent place of residence, promising on our part, at all times hereafter, to save, defend, keep harmless and indemnify her against all unfriendliness, of whatever sort; and pledging ourselves to be good neighbors and loving friends from the date of this document, which, when signed by th' Party of the First Part, shall be of full force and virtue. Sealed with our seals. Dated this seventh day of June, in the year of our Lord, nineteen hundred—"

A loud uproar of applause broke loose in the pause that followed; then the minister's clear voice called for silence once more.

"The Judge has his big fountain pen filled to its capacity," he said. "Come forward and sign this—the most remarkable document on record, I am not afraid to say. Its signing will mean the wiping out of an old bitterness and the dawning of a new and better day for Brookville!"

The Reverend Wesley Elliot had mixed his metaphors sadly; but no one minded that, least of all the minister himself, as he signed his name in bold black characters to the wondrous screed, over which Judge Fulsom had literally as well as metaphorically burned the midnight oil. Deacon and Mrs. Whittle signed; Postmaster and Mrs. Daggett signed, the latter with copious tears flowing over her smooth rosy cheeks. Miss Lois Daggett was next:

"I guess I ought to be written down near the front," said she, "seeing I'm full as much to blame, and like that, as most anybody."

"Come on you, Lute Parsons!" roared the Judge, while a group of matrons meekly subscribed their signatures. "We want some live men-folks on this document.... Aw, never mind, if you did! We all know you wa'n't yourself that night, Lucius.... That's right; come right forward! We want the signature of every man that went out there that night, full of cussedness and bad whiskey.... That's the ticket! Come on, everybody! Get busy!"

Nobody had attended the door for the last hour, Joe Whittle being a spellbound witness of the proceedings; and so it chanced that nobody saw two persons, a man and a woman who entered quietly—one might almost have said timidly, as if doubtful of a welcome in the crowded place. It was Abby Daggett who caught sight of the girl's face, shining against the soft dark of the summer night like a pale star.

"Why, my sakes alive!" she cried, "if there ain't Lyddy Bolton and Jim Dodge, now! Did you ever!"

As she folded the girl's slight figure to her capacious breast, Mrs. Daggett summed up in a single pithy sentence all the legal phraseology of the Document, which by now had been signed by everybody old enough to write their names:

"Well! we certainly are glad you've come home, Lyddy; an' we hope you'll never leave us no more!"

Chapter XXVIII

"Fanny," said Ellen suddenly; "I want to tell you something."

Mrs. Wesley Elliot turned a complacently abstracted gaze upon her friend who sat beside her on the vine-shaded piazza of the parsonage. She felt the sweetest sympathy for Ellen, whenever she thought of her at all:

"Yes, dear."

"Do you remember my speaking to you about Jim— Oh, a long time ago, and how he—? It was perfectly ridiculous, you know."

Fanny's blue eyes became suddenly alert.

"You mean the time Jim kissed you," she murmured. "Oh, Ellen, I've always been so sorry for—"

"Well; you needn't be," interrupted Ellen; "I never cared a snap for Jim Dodge; so there!"

The youthful matron sighed gently: she felt that she understood poor dear Ellen perfectly, and in token thereof she patted poor dear Ellen's hand.

"I know exactly how you feel," she warbled.

Ellen burst into a gleeful laugh:

"You think you do; but you don't," she informed her friend, with a spice of malice. "Your case was entirely different from mine, my dear: You were perfectly crazy over Wesley Elliot; I was only in love with being in love."

Fanny looked sweetly mystified and a trifle piqued withal.

"I wanted to have a romance—to be madly in love," Ellen explained. "Oh, you know! Jim was merely a peg to hang it on."

The wife of the minister smiled a lofty compassion.

"Everything seems so different after one is married," she stated.

"Is that really so?" cried Ellen. "Well, I shall soon know, Fan, for I'm to be married in the fall."

"Married? Why, Ellen Dix!"

"Uh—huh," confirmed Ellen, quite satisfied with the success of her *coup*. "You don't know him, Fan; but he's perfectly elegant—and *handsome!* Just wait till you see him."

Ellen rocked herself to and fro excitedly.

"I met him in Grenoble last winter, and we're going to live there in the *sweetest* house. He fell in love with me the first minute he saw me. You never knew anyone to be so awfully in love ... m'm!"

Without in the least comprehending the reason for the phenomenon, Mrs. Wesley Elliot experienced a singular depression of spirit. Of course she was glad poor dear Ellen was to be happy. She strove to infuse a sprightly satisfaction into her tone and manner as she said:

"What wonderful news, dear. But isn't it rather—sudden? I mean, oughtn't you to have known him longer! ...You didn't tell me his name."

Ellen's piquant dark face sparkled with mischief and happiness.

"His name is Harvey Wade," she replied; "you know Wade and Hampton, where you bought your wedding things, Fan? Everybody knows the Wades, and I've known Harvey long enough to—"

She grew suddenly wistful as she eyed her friend:

"You *have* changed a lot since you were married, Fan; all the girls think so. Sometimes I feel almost afraid of you. Is it—do you—?"

Fanny's unaccountable resentment melted before a sudden rush of sympathy and understanding. She drew Ellen's blushing face close to her own in the sweetness of caresses:

"I'm *so* glad for you, dear, so *glad!*"

"And you'll tell Jim?" begged Ellen, after a silence full of thrills. "I should hate to have him suppose—"

"He doesn't, Ellen," Jim's sister assured her, out of a secret fund of knowledge to which she would never have confessed. "Jim always understood you far better than I did. And he likes you, too, better than any girl in Brookville."

"Except Lydia," amended Ellen.

"Oh, of course, except Lydia."

Chapter XXIX

There was a warm, flower-scented breeze stirring the heavy foliage drenched with the silver rain of moonlight, and the shrilling of innumerable small voices of the night. It all belonged; yet neither the man nor the woman noticed anything except each other; nor heard anything save the words the other uttered.

"To think that you love me, Lydia!" he said, triumph and humility curiously mingled in his voice.

"How could I help it, Jim? I could never have borne it all, if you—"

"Really, Lydia?"

He looked down into her face which the moonlight had spiritualized to the likeness of an angel.

She smiled and slipped her hand into his.

They were alone in the universe, so he stooped and kissed her, murmuring inarticulate words of rapture.

After uncounted minutes they walked slowly on, she within the circle of his arm, her blond head against the shoulder of his rough tweed coat.

"When shall it be, Lydia?" he asked.

She blushed—even in the moonlight he could see the adorable flutter of color in her face.

"I am all alone in the world, Jim," she said, rather sadly. "I have no one but you."

"I'll love you enough to make up for forty relations!" he declared. "And, anyway, as soon as we're married you'll have mother and Fan and—er—"

He made a wry face, as it occurred to him for the first time that the Reverend Wesley Elliot was about to become Lydia's brother-in-law.

The girl laughed.

"Haven't you learned to like him yet?" she inquired teasingly.

"I can stand him for a whole hour at a time now, without experiencing a desire to kick him," he told her. "But why should we waste time talking about Wesley Elliot?"

Lydia appeared to be considering his question with some seriousness.

"Why, Jim," she said, looking straight up into his eyes with the innocent candor he had loved in her from the beginning, "Mr. Elliot will expect to marry us."

"That's so!" conceded Jim; "Fan will expect it, too."

He looked at her eagerly:

"Aren't you in a hurry for that wonderful brother-in-law, Lydia? Don't you think—?"

The smile on her face was wonderful now; he felt curiously abashed by it, like one who has inadvertently jested in a holy place.

"Forgive me, dearest," he murmured.

"If you would like—if it is not too soon—my birthday is next Saturday. Mother used to make me a little party on my birthday, so I thought—it seemed to me—and the roses are all in bloom."

There was only one way to thank her for this halting little speech: he took her in his arms and whispered words which no one, not even the crickets in the hedge could hear, if crickets ever were listeners, and not the sole chorus on their tiny stage of life.